Five Dates With The Billionaire

Alyssa J. Montgomery

16pt

Copyright Page from the Original Book

Title: FIVE DATES WITH THE BILLIONAIRE

Published by
Escape
An imprint of Harlequin Enterprises (Australia) Pty Limited (ABN 47 001 180 918), a subsidiary of HarperCollins Publishers Australia Pty Limited (ABN 36 009 913 517)
Level 13, 201 Elizabeth St
SYDNEY NSW 2000
AUSTRALIA

www.romance.com.au

TABLE OF CONTENTS

Five Dates with the Billionaire
Alyssa J. Montgomery

'I'm insisting you date her. Five dates together, then I'll have this surgery.'

Billionaire CEO Connor Stewart is being blackmailed. By his own grandmother, no less, who is refusing to have life-saving surgery unless Connor dates Mia Simms, his dull and dowdy marketing employee.

For Violet's sake, Connor agrees to the crazy scheme. There's no risk of breaking his 'short-term only' rule with Mia Simms; she's not the kind of woman Connor is interested in ... and he's sure she's hiding something. He just doesn't expect it to be delicious curves and a firecracker personality.

Mia Simms is hiding something, and it's much more dangerous than her looks. All she wants to do is live life in the safety of the shadows and avoid discovery. But perhaps a short-term fling is exactly what she needs to remind her to live.

But what if Violet is right to push them together? Can Mia trust Connor enough to let him see the real person behind the facade she's built? Or is Violet's little scheme about to put both their lives in danger?

About the author

Alyssa lives with her husband and three children on a five-acre property nestled into a mountain range south of Sydney, Australia, and enjoys having the space for gardens, a dog, horses, goats and chickens. Visits from the native wildlife (echidnas, wallabies and a variety of native birds) are particularly welcome ... although visits from native wildlife with scales and fangs aren't met with quite as much enthusiasm!

She continues to work in her private practice as a Speech-Language Pathologist. Previously she's done a stint with Qantas Airways as an international flight attendant, completed her Master of Science degree, and has also been a professional pianist.

If you'd like to know more about Alyssa, her books, or to connect with her online, you can visit her webpage alyssajmontgomery.com

Follow her on Twitter: @Alyssaromance or like her Facebook page *AlyssaJMontgomery*.

Acknowledgements

A huge thank you to Johanna Baker, publishing executive at HarperCollins, and acquiring editor at Escape Publishing.

I've loved working with Johanna, who has taken so much time to give me some valuable feedback to strengthen my storyline and refine my writing. Sometimes she has to make the same reminders to me from one manuscript to the next, but she doesn't give up. Johanna, the tips will hopefully become second nature over time. Thank you for your patience and fabulous advice!

I also want to thank Christine Armstrong for producing such a lovely cover for this title. I especially love the vivid colours and the glimpse of the Grand Canal in Venice in the background.

Thanks to all the team at Escape Publishing for continuing to make my publication dream a reality.

As this book goes to press, three very special ladies in my life are being treated for breast cancer. Elaine, Carmel and Helen, this one is especially for you. I'm thinking of you and sending you love. Helen always says 'Have Fun'. I'm wishing you all strength, happiness and a lot of fun times to come.

Chapter One

Connor's attention jumped to the heart monitor the second his grandmother's eyes fluttered closed.

The regular sinus rhythm on the screen assured him all was well and he released a breath; she was simply resting.

It'd been a long night at London Bridge Hospital with a lot of medical staff buzzing in and out of the room and countless tests being conducted.

'You look rumpled, dear.'

Shifting his attention away from the screen he saw a weary half-smile on Gran's face. 'I thought you were dozing off.'

She shook her head. 'You're definitely in need of a shave.'

'You don't look so hot yourself,' he teased, but she did look unnaturally pale.

She reached out her hand and Connor held it. Swallowing down on the constriction in his throat he realised that this woman, who'd always been a powerhouse of strength and vitality, was as vulnerable as everyone else to the problems of ageing.

'Make certain you don't work too hard, Connor.'

'I don't need to work as hard as you did. The company's in a great position.' His grandparents had taken the Stewart family's small import company and expanded it into the world-renowned Stewart Luxe Hotels and Cruise Liners. After his grandfather, Archibald, had a major stroke, his grandmother had taken over as CEO. Under her guidance, the UK-based business expanded into the USA. She'd made it a Fortune 500 company, but she'd also worked damned long days in the process.

Five years ago she'd handed the reins to Connor, but hadn't retired completely. At eighty years old, she was still a very sharp and energetic member of the Board of Directors.

Obviously, she needed to slow down.

'Good morning.' The cardiac specialist, Dr Forrester, entered the private room.

'Good morning, doctor. Please don't beat around the bush.' Violet's tone was stoic, but Connor felt a slight tremble of her fingers. 'Tell me the news.'

The specialist took the chart at the end of the bed and scanned it. 'All the test results are back.'

Connor squeezed his grandmother's hand and tried to read the doctor's face.

Let it be good news.

'You've had angina, not a heart attack. However, this is a fortunate warning and gives us the chance to act.'

Connor felt his world tilt with uncertainty. 'What needs to be done?'

'One of the arteries is almost completely blocked. It'll require a surgical procedure to insert a stent to open it up.'

'I see,' Violet ventured a little shakily after the doctor finished detailing the procedure.

'How soon does this need to happen?' Connor asked.

'As soon as possible. If left untreated, this condition can lead to either a heart attack or stroke.'

Hell. A heart attack was bad enough but remembering what his grandfather had been through, the prospect of a stroke was worse. 'How soon can you perform the procedure?'

'Tomorrow. I'll have you added to my list, Mrs Stewart.'

Violet's eyes widened. 'So quickly?'

'Thank you, doctor.' Tomorrow was great as far as Connor was concerned.

Violet drew herself up against the pillows. 'No. Not tomorrow.'

'Gran!' *What the devil...?* 'Why not?'

'There's something I need to arrange first.'

'Nothing that's as important as this,' Connor declared.

A light appeared in his grandmother's blue eyes—one Connor recognised as sheer stubborn determination. Her pallid cheeks became tinged with colour. 'That's my decision to make.'

Connor had inherited the same stubborn determination and wielded it with ruthless efficiency in his position as CEO at Stewart Corporation. When armed with facts and convinced his points were sound, there'd never been an argument he couldn't win in the boardroom—no deal he couldn't negotiate to everyone's satisfaction.

That was the boardroom.

This was his grandmother.

'Whatever it is, I can take care of it for you,' he insisted with growing concern.

'That's my intention, but it can't be done in one day.'

What the hell is so important?

'You need to understand that this condition is like a ticking bomb,' the doctor emphasised firmly. 'It's a race against the inevitable.'

'I understand, doctor, and I promise I'll have the procedure as soon as I can.'

Damn it all! She'll have it tomorrow.

'Doctor, would you give us a few moments, please?' Connor asked.

'Certainly.' After a nod to Connor, Dr Forrester replaced the clipboard at the end of the bed. 'If you have any questions let me know, but I want to see your name on my list tomorrow, Mrs Stewart.'

The second the door closed behind the cardiologist, Connor turned to his grandmother. 'Tell me what it is you need and I'll get right on it. Don't stall on this, Gran.'

She sent him a tremulous smile. 'This trip to the hospital has made me aware of my mortality.'

'You're not dying on me yet.'

He refused to contemplate that Gran's life might be drawing to an end. It was decades ago, but it seemed like yesterday that his grandparents had saved him from living within the conflict of his parents' marriage.

The afternoon he'd locked himself in his room and phoned Violet and Archibald in tears was still firmly etched in his mind. He'd been scared witless listening to his parents' screaming match punctuated with smashing crockery. His grandparents had arrived soon after his call and announced they were taking him to live with them until his parents sorted themselves out.

He'd never moved back home.

'Connor, whatever time I have left, there's one thing I want more than anything.'

The gravity of her tone made a great weight press on his chest. 'Tell me, Gran.'

'I want to see you settled.' Her words dropped into the air between them like a boulder dropping into a still pond. Shock waves rippled out from the forceful impact and caught him off-balance.

Shit. Of all the things she could've requested of him ... 'I'm hardly *unsettled.*'

'*Married,* Connor. I want to see you happily *married.*'

Tension speared through him. 'Be reasonable. You know that's not going to happen. Ask anything else of me, Gran.'

'There's nothing else. It's my dearest wish.'

Damn it. She knew this was a no-go zone for him. How could she even think of putting him in such a position? 'One trip down the aisle with disastrous consequences was quite enough.'

'I always knew Rachel was all wrong for you.'

Yes. Gran had warned him, but he hadn't listened. He'd thought he'd found his soul mate. He'd thought Rachel had loved him and that they would build a happy life together, as his grandparents had in their marriage.

'What you and Grandad had was rare. Once, I wanted the same kind of love. Now, I'm happy without it.'

'But Connor—'

'No Gran. I'm happily divorced and not about to fall into the matrimonial trap again.' He failed to suppress a shudder. 'I should've learned from my parents.'

She squeezed on his arm. 'I know you want to avoid more pain, but you're missing out on so much happiness.'

Gran was wrong. 'I'm perfectly happy as I am.'

'Archie and I were soul mates,' his grandmother continued. 'I'm certain there's a soul mate for you.'

'Right, she's just around the corner,' he intoned with heavy sarcasm.

Violet smiled. 'You have no idea how right you are.'

'Oh hell, Gran,' he tried to make light of the serious topic. 'Have you been sizing up all the single females you've met at the hospital?'

This time, she laughed before she grew serious again. 'There's a young lady I want you to date.'

His jaw slackened as he registered the resolve in her gaze. 'You're kidding.'

'I'm not. I have a young friend I'd like you to get to know.'

His eyebrows shot up and he didn't bother trying to hide his horror. 'You're trying to play matchmaker?'

'I'm not trying, I'm insisting you date her. Five dates together, then I'll have this procedure.'

He couldn't have understood her. She couldn't really be saying...

'Mia's twenty-six. She's smart, honest, caring and perfect for you.'

'Absolutely not!'

'Connor—'

'No, Gran.' Had she gone mad? 'There's hardly anything I wouldn't do for you, but I will *never* go on a blind date—let alone one arranged by my grandmother!'

'It would hardly be a blind date. You know Mia.'

He did?

Mia.

It wasn't a particularly common name.

'The only Mia I know works for us.'

'She does indeed.'

His head jerked back sharply. 'Mia from marketing? Mia *Simms?*'

'One and the same.' His grandmother wore a self-satisfied smile.

'Now I know you're joking, but it's not remotely funny.'

'I'm deadly serious.'

Shit.

He jumped up from the chair. 'Absolutely not!'

Gran had to have lost her mind. What type of drugs had they been pumping into her?

'She's wonderful, Connor.'

Summoning up a mental image of the young woman from the marketing department, he cringed. Sure, he'd noticed the attractive slant of her high cheekbones and the fullness of her lips, but it wouldn't have mattered if she'd been the most gorgeous woman on the planet. The clothes she wore reflected her personality: dull, shapeless and downright dowdy. 'She's awful!'

'Rubbish! She's one of the sweetest young women I've ever met.'

'I don't care if she's sweet. She's completely boring. Besides, have you seen her?'

'Frequently.' Violet raised an eyebrow at him. 'Appearance isn't everything. Have you ever spoken to her?'

'Once.' He was unlikely to forget it. 'I asked her a question during a marketing presentation and I've never been game to put her through the torture again.' He looked heavenward as he remembered the incident. 'She turned beetroot red, started stammering and I thought she was going to run from the room. Someone else ended up answering my question.'

'Really? That's interesting.' Her lips quirked. 'Mia doesn't normally stammer and as for her running from a room...' Violet put her hand to her chest and laughed. 'You certainly haven't made any attempt to get to know her if you think she's nervous. I don't think I've ever met a young woman with quite as much strength.'

He tried to grapple with the absurdity of his grandmother's words. 'Mia Simms is a timid mouse and dresses more blandly than a Norland nanny! You couldn't have picked a less interesting or less attractive woman for me to date.'

'Looks can be deceiving.'

Not in this case.

'How do you even know her?' He couldn't think of a time when Miss Simms had made a presentation to a group of board members.

'Mia comes over every Saturday afternoon for tea and mahjong.'

'She comes to your home?'

'Absolutely. She's a very down-to-earth young lady whose friendship I treasure.' Violet clicked her tongue impatiently. 'Sit down, Connor. I don't like you towering over me while I'm here in a hospital bed.'

He sat down grudgingly. 'How did you meet?'

'That's not important,' Violet insisted.

'I think it is. It's hardly normal for a twenty-something year old to be playing mahjong on a Saturday evening with a group of elderly ladies.'

There was an amused twinkle in Violet's eyes. 'She's twenty-six and we're young at heart!'

'This is serious, Gran. You and your friends are all very wealthy women. What's her motive?'

'Oh Connor. Don't be offensive.' Violet shook her head. 'You are way too cynical—especially when it comes to women and money.'

'I've learned the hard way. And don't avoid the question. What do you know about her besides the fact she works for us?'

'Quite a lot as it happens, but nothing I'm prepared to share with you. When you get to know her, you'll see I'm right. She's simply delightful.'

Bloody hell.

He barely restrained himself from standing up again to pace the room. 'Miss Simms doesn't appeal to me on any level. Did she put you up to this?'

'Of course not. She knows nothing about it.'

'She must've dropped some hint she's interested in me?'

'She's never even mentioned you.' Her eyes became steely. 'No more objections. You've said you'll do anything for me and this is what I want.'

'Name someone else. There must be a woman I've dated who you approve of?'

'Now *you're* joking. Those women were all shop-dressing and no substance.' She threw her hands up in the air. 'Agreeing to your ridiculous short-term, no-strings-attached affairs! Huh! They may as well be call-girls.'

'Gran!'

'Although I think you'd be a perfect match, I'm not asking you to marry Mia. All you have to do is have five dates.' She raised one hand and pointed her finger at him in a way she hadn't done since he was a little boy. 'Then I have this surgery.'

'I can't believe you're using emotional blackmail.'

'I've been very patient. Even with Rachel, once I said what I had to say, I accepted her and didn't try to come between you.' She shifted her pillows a little then regarded him with a troubled expression. 'I've never once interfered in your love life but you're thirty-five now. It's got to the point where I feel I have no other alternative than to force this upon you.'

Bullshit! 'I will not date Mia Simms!'

'My terms are non-negotiable.' Violet crossed her arms over her chest. 'When you were taking your business call earlier, I phoned Dawson and had him arrange for a private nurse to come to the house. As soon as Dawson lets me know she's arrived with all her state-of-the-art cardiac monitoring equipment, I'm checking myself out of here and going home until you and Mia have had your dates.'

'Gran! Be reasonable. Even if I agreed to this ridiculous demand of yours, no agency nurse is going to provide the same level of care for you as you'd receive right here.'

'My mind is made up.'

Connor's molars ground together so hard it's a wonder they didn't crack.

When Violet Stewart made her mind up about something there was absolutely no shifting her.

Damn Mia Simms to hell. She had to be pulling some type of strings for Gran to even think up this wild scheme.

Whatever the marketing employee was up to, she'd rue the day she used her apparent friendship with his grandmother to manipulate him.

Chapter Two

Thud!

Mia jumped as her office door shut heavily.

She looked up so quickly from her computer screen her heavy-framed glasses were almost dislodged.

The sight of the company's handsome-as-hell CEO striding towards her desk was enough to render her rigid with shock. Connor Stewart was the only man she'd ever known who could send her pulse rate skyrocketing merely by being in the same room. Now, his impressive height and broad-shouldered frame filled her generous office space and all the oxygen whooshed from her lungs.

Uh-oh.

The man who faced her looked nothing like she'd imagined in her private fantasies. This guy was like a dark-haired avenging angel who threatened to bring down the wrath of the heavens on her head.

His normally full, sensual lips were flattened into a thin line of displeasure and there was a small muscle tic in his cheek.

Gosh! Connor wasn't angry; he was livid.

What on earth had she done to attract his attention, let alone his wrath?

Her mind flipped frantically through all her current projects...

'I understand you know my grandmother.'

No greeting.

No preamble.

His words hung between them as an accusation and his gaze pinned hers in an aggressive challenge.

This was worse than being called to task for some error in her work. This was undeniably personal and the blatant hostility in his tone made it difficult for her to muster a coherent response.

'Well, Miss Simms?'

She summoned a polite smile. 'Good afternoon, Mr Stewart.' Amazingly, her voice was steady.

'I asked you a question.'

Completely intimidating, he was unrecognisable as the man she admired for his progressive thinking and generous philanthropy. The man she—

'Answer me!'

Mia frowned at him.

Why was he so worked up about her friendship with his grandmother?

Pushing her chair back from the desk created some much needed space between them but he still crowded her. 'Yes. Your grandmother and I are friends.'

His mesmerisingly blue eyes radiated an arctic chill cold enough to stop global warming. When he spoke, his voice dripped ice. 'How is it that a junior member of my staff becomes friends with my grandmother?'

Really?

This guy must be an imposter because the man she respected would never be so condescending.

'Is there a company by-law that states only *senior* staff members can be her friend?'

For a split second his pupils flared. 'My grandmother makes a point of getting to know all the *senior* staff by taking them out to lunch.' He crossed his arms over his broad chest. 'And then there's you; a young marketing employee, yet I find out you're at her home every Saturday evening.'

There was no missing the emphasis he made on 'employee'.

Every metaphorical hackle she possessed rose. 'Do you have any idea how elitist you sound?'

'I don't give a damn how I sound.' He bent forward, resting his hands on the edge of her desk and bringing his whole body closer. The attractive masculine scent of his cologne didn't make it easy for her to think clearly. In fact, she had to resist the temptation to inhale more deeply. 'I want to know how you met my grandmother and how long you've been spending Saturday evenings with her.'

'Did you ask her?'

If he hadn't been so close she might've missed the blink that suggested he hadn't been satisfied with the answer.

He straightened up, but was no less intimidating.

Although his athletic physique was covered by his bespoke suit, he would've been more appropriately dressed in a singlet top and boxing gloves.

No. Don't even go there. Don't even think about Connor in a singlet top with the faint sheen of sweat on his bulging biceps and...

'I'm asking you.'

Hauling her thoughts away from the sexy image, Mia knew she had to come up with a reasonable explanation or he'd ask more questions.

That definitely had to be avoided.

'We serve the homeless at a soup kitchen on Saturday mornings. I've been volunteering there for almost four years,' she hedged.

If she admitted she'd met Violet over ten years ago it would raise questions Mia wasn't prepared to answer. Those emotional scars were nobody's business but her own.

'Everybody knows the city soup kitchen is one of Gran's favourite charities. All you had to do was volunteer there to get to know her.'

'To what end?' Mia's mind whirred. What kind of hidden agenda did he think she had?

Contempt blazed from his eyes. 'Don't play games with me. I love my grandmother and I won't stand by and see anyone take advantage of her.'

'I'm not taking advantage of Violet.'

'Really?'

Despite herself, Mia's heart kicked hard against her ribs. Even in the midst of this unwarranted hostility there was no denying he was the most stunningly handsome man she'd ever seen. There was something about his sheer aura of command that appealed to every feminine cell in her body.

Connor Stewart was a man people turned to when there was a crisis.

It made no sense that he stood in her office being hostile and suspicious.

Their gazes locked before he took a step around the desk and looked her up and down.

She barely resisted raising her hand defensively to touch the dark hair she'd curled tightly into a bun.

'I am not attracted to you in any way, Miss Simms. Nor will I ever be.'

Mia's eyes widened and her mouth fell open as she gawped at him.

Had he really said that?

Under her high collared blouse, her chest prickled with mortification. Still, she jumped to her feet. 'Your arrogance is incredible. And, just for the record, you're not my type either!' He had been, but he wasn't any more. No matter how handsome he was, nothing could excuse this insulting behaviour.

'I have no interest in dating you,' he said baldly.

Dating?

Oh my God!

All she could do was deny her secret crush. 'I don't remember asking you to.'

'I've underestimated you.' He ran his fingers along his slightly stubbled jaw. 'I had no idea you'd be such a firebrand. What else are you hiding beneath your buttoned-up exterior?'

Her stomach went into freefall and she took a step backward.

He mustn't guess I'm hiding something.

'I'm not hiding anything.' Fighting against the waves of animosity and suspicion that pounded at her, she forced a tight smile. 'I don't know what your problem is, but this is workplace harassment.'

'Harassment? You befriended my grandmother in the hope of dating me.'

What? 'If you're serious, you have a far bigger ego than I'd imagined.'

'Cut the crap, Miss Simms.' Restless fingertips beat an angry tattoo against the surface of a filing cabinet. 'You're not the first woman who's gone to extraordinary lengths to get my attention.'

Oh Lord. She might've dreamt of getting his attention, but now she had it she didn't want it.

Wait a minute...

Her hands flew to her hips. 'If I wanted your attention I didn't need to be friends with Violet. I work for you, for heaven's sake!'

He didn't look any happier now she'd poked a huge hole in his theory.

'You think I've been at a soup kitchen and playing mahjong every Saturday all these years on the off-chance you'd drop by? I've never heard anything so arrogant.'

'Oh, you're original.' His lip curled. 'I've met the poor female employee who feels horribly faint when she's in the elevator with me and happens to fall my way. I've had the one whose car is parked in an executive car space that doesn't belong to her with the bonnet up and an engine that won't start—just as I am about to head home. One former staff member even approached me in the car park having conveniently locked her keys in the car.'

'It happens!'

'Her keys were in her handbag.'

Really? 'I've never tried to get your attention.'

While Mia tried to calm her breathing, he regarded her in silence.

Fire and ice raged in an epic battle.

If he stayed in her office another second she was bound to say something that would make it too difficult to remain in the job she loved. 'I suggest you leave now.'

His hand ran through the luxuriously thick pelt of his dark hair. 'I wish I could, Mia.'

Mia.

If she'd ever secretly wondered how her name would sound on his lips, the contempt he managed to inject into the two syllables didn't even come close to her imaginings. He may be a raven-haired version of Adonis who merely had to speak in his rich, chocolate-coated baritone voice to hold the majority of the female population in his thrall, but he was clearly not in the mood to waste any of his reputed charm on her and she couldn't care less.

Liar. Liar. *Liar.*

The blood pulsed through her veins establishing a rhythmic litany that challenged her denial. Her gaze flew to his angular jaw line and the strong column of his throat.

How many times had she fought to keep her gaze from straying to him when they'd been in the same room, even though she knew she was torturing herself with dreams that would never become reality?

Not any more, she assured herself.

'Sit down.' Pushing away from the filing cabinet, he turned his back on her and paced towards the door.

Mia refused to sit like an obedient dog following its master's command and she drew herself up even straighter, making the most of every inch of her six feet.

When he turned, he pinned her with his gaze and dropped a bombshell. 'My grandmother expects us to date.'

'Date?' Behind her glasses, Mia's eyes widened so much she felt her muscles strain.

'Yes, Mia. *Date*. Restaurants, theatre—the things most single twenty-six-year-old women spend their Saturday evenings doing rather than playing mahjong with elderly ladies.' He clicked his tongue against his palate.

'This has to be some sort of warped practical joke.' *A terrible joke.* Even if Violet had realised that Connor sent Mia's pulse rate haywire, for her to play matchmaker...

'This was what you've wanted all along. What you've—'

'You're crazy if you think I'd put her up to arranging a date between us.'

'Not one date, Mia. *Five dates.*'

Five dates?

Good grief.

'Well you have nothing to worry about because I'd never date such a rude, conceited individual.'

Her heart took a few enormous leaps around her chest then proceeded to atrophy in sheer, bloody horror as his brows butted together in a fierce frown.

'Be very careful, Miss Simms. I could list a few choice adjectives for a woman like you and none of them would be pretty.'

He may not have listed them, but he'd made her opinion of her very clear.

'I will not, under any circumstances go out with you and I will be quite happy to tell Violet.' She shook her head so vigorously she had to push her glasses back up the bridge of her nose.

Connor stopped mid-stride. If she'd thought he'd given her the once over before, she'd been wrong. The intensity of his concentrated blue-eyed regard bore down on her.

Seconds dragged into what seemed like minutes and Mia stood statue-still, holding her breath.

'You're either a fabulous actress or you're telling me the truth.'

'Finally!' She released the word on a hiss of air and pressed the heel of one hand to her forehead. 'Listen, Mr Stewart, this can be sorted out easily. When Violet realises it's not what either of us wants, she'll be reasonable. And anyway, just because she says she wants something doesn't mean we have to agree.'

'You agree it's a bad idea?'

'It's the worst idea I've ever heard.' She crossed her fingers behind her back. Before he'd burst into her office she would've been ecstatic to go out with him.

Then, holding her hands out in front of her she willed him to believe her. 'I can understand why you're angry, but this hasn't come from me. Surely you know Violet's not a woman who'd ever let anyone manipulate her.' Mia frowned. 'I don't understand why she'd get it into her head to do this. It's not like her to be so...'

'Unreasonable?'

'Illogical. Crazy.' They were frightening words. Mia threaded her fingers together and wondered if her elderly friend was losing her mental faculties. 'Does she seem off-colour?'

Connor's shoulders lost a little of their stiffness.

Gosh. If she wasn't mistaken, concern etched itself across his brow before he paced away from her.

Sitting on the adjacent sofa he reached out to the executive toy on the coffee table, setting the balls into motion with an almost absent-minded flick of his lean fingers.

Mia's apprehension grew. 'Could this be a sign of dementia?'

'No.' His denial was swift.

'I'm sorry, but I can't think of any other reason—'

'She was rushed to hospital last night with chest pain.'

Mia stumbled and sank back into her chair. 'A heart attack?'

'Not this time, but she needs a stent to open up a blocked artery.'

Her stomach hollowed out and she half-covered her face with her hands as she absorbed the shocking news.

Above the collar of Connor's business shirt, the notch in his throat rose and fell as he swallowed. She felt his concern reach out and curl around her like a tangible thing.

'This was a warning but the specialist described her as a "ticking bomb".'

Although Connor would never know it, his grandmother had stepped into Mia's life when she'd needed her most. It was unbearable to think of losing Violet.

'The procedure is urgent,' Connor said.

'When will she have it?'

'As soon as you and I have gone on five dates,' he said bitterly.

'She's trying to blackmail us into dating?'

'Yes.' Resentment radiated off him in waves.

No wonder he was so upset. 'I'll go and talk to her. I'll make her see that this is all wrong and convince her to have it done straight away.'

'If you know her you'll know that once her mind is set on something, there's no changing it.'

'I can try.' Violet was the most stubborn individual Mia had ever met. But, in this case, Mia would push back harder.

'The whole idea of you and I...' He waved one hand in the air as he sought for words.

'Please don't. I think we've covered your sentiments on that topic.' He'd really been the ultimate charmer. 'Believe me, I don't want to go on *one* date with you, let alone five!'

He might be one of the world's sexiest men, but that didn't make up for his rude behaviour. Besides, she didn't want to date him when he'd been coerced into it.

'I'm assuming you aren't in a relationship?' he probed.

Oh, how she wished she could tell him she was about to become engaged to a gorgeous, successful guy who cherished her more than life itself. 'No.' The word tasted like ash. 'But—'

'Then we go out for dinner and get our first date over with tonight. The sooner we start, the quicker it's over and the faster Gran gets her stent.'

'You think I want to sit through more of your insults and false accusations?'

'If you care about my grandmother as much as you say you do, you'll join me tonight.'

She scowled at him. 'Of course I care about her, but—'

'I didn't set the conditions.'

No. He hadn't. And he'd made it perfectly clear she was nothing like the glamorous women he appeared with in the social pages.

Mia was far removed from the women who accompanied him all over London and the world. The girlfriend who'd cavorted around Barbados with him last week was a model.

Ah!

'I'm sure your *current* girlfriend won't agree.'

'I don't have a current girlfriend.'

Good grief. He'd dispensed of his latest lover already?

Being a seriously good-looking billionaire meant it wouldn't be long before there was another woman at his side and in his bed. Violet complained that half the women he dated were cut-throat executives married to their careers. The other half sought the media attention they received by being with him as much as they craved him.

Media attention.

The blood drained from her extremities and she shivered.

The last thing Mia needed was media attention.

What on earth had Violet been thinking?

The media would want to know who Mia was.

They might start digging into her past.

How much would they uncover?

The chilly fingers of fear wrapped around the base of her neck and threatened to choke her. 'If I don't succeed in talking her out of it, we'll go somewhere out of the way so we don't attract attention.' Her fingernails scored into her palms. 'We can work on some marketing proposals so it's not a complete waste of time.'

He sent her a long, hard look before he shook his head. 'Gran has it all planned. First date is dinner at Raphael's.'

Oh hell. Panic slithered down her spine. Raphael's French restaurant was one of the most popular restaurants in London among the wealthy and famous. There were always members of the paparazzi at the front of the building.

'Second and third dates involve a weekend away in Venice and the last two are a weekend away in Paris. We're going to skip the weekends and make it all happen in five days straight so Gran will have this procedure quickly. I'll clear your time away with your department head.'

'Oh God, no. Don't involve Michael. I refuse to be fodder for the office gossips.' She shook her head vehemently. 'If we have to go through with this I don't want a soul at work knowing about it.'

He sent her another assessing look. 'It's inevitable we'll be photographed together in London,' Connor said slowly. 'Less likely in Paris and Venice.'

Absolutely no photos. Anywhere.

Violet had to be reminded of the danger.

As for her co-workers finding out ... 'Then tell Michael you need me to go away to help you with a project.' He arched one ebony eyebrow at her. 'Oh, come on. It's believable. Michael's not going to suspect we're personally involved.'

'We *won't* be personally involved.'

The curses running through her head weren't ones she'd normally think. 'Please. Tell Michael you need a marketing opinion for a possible purchase of a hotel in those cities.'

His lips twisted before he agreed. 'Alright.'

'Thank you.'

One less problem.

'Write down your address and I'll pick you up at seven,' he commanded.

'No. I'll meet you at Violet's and we can leave from there—if I can't get her to change her mind.'

He sent her a quizzical look. 'If you're really as much a victim in this as I am, I will apologise. But this whole situation is suspect and I don't trust you.'

'I would never have guessed.'

He tilted his head slightly. 'My instinct tells me you're hiding something to do with my grandmother. If you haven't been angling for a date with me...'

Mia gulped.

'Are you hoping to be included in her will?'

'I can't believe you said that!'

'Be warned.' His words were a deadly promise. 'If there's anything you're hiding, I'll find out and you'll be sorry.'

Dread streamed through every cell.

All she could do was pray he wouldn't dig too deeply.

Chapter Three

Connor seethed all the way back to his office.

Emotions no longer played a huge part in his life and he generally prided himself on his control. But ever since Gran's butler had called him last night with the news that she was in the back of an ambulance on her way to hospital, his feelings had see-sawed from one extreme to the other.

Even though he'd thought it was safely buried, all the damped down trauma from his childhood had bubbled back to the surface. Flashbacks of the day he'd been told his father had died in a car crash. His shocked helplessness as his mother—a passenger in the car—fought for her life. Catapulted forward in time, he recalled the anguish of finding his grandfather slumped in his wheelchair from a fatal stroke.

This morning he'd managed to cloak his anxiety from his grandmother as he'd sat by her hospital bed. He'd been able to disguise his inner panic when the specialist had outlined her medical condition and the very real threat of heart attack or stroke. But when Gran had denied treatment and made her unreasonable demand, his frustration and anger had made him want to punch something.

Now he was furious with himself because he'd taken his anger out on an employee in her office. It didn't matter if she'd been behind this scheme of Gran's; he should've pulled himself together before he'd confronted her.

He strode past Grace, his assistant, with only an abrupt, 'Hold all my calls,' before he entered his own office and closed the door firmly behind him.

Shit. He had to calm down before he tore someone else's head off.

Mia Simms.

He'd behaved like an obnoxious, overbearing bully during their explosive encounter and he needed to apologise for his behaviour. She was correct; it had been harassment. As her employer, it'd been an unequal playing field.

Even had she somehow persuaded Gran to arrange the dates, he shouldn't have confronted her in her office. He should've had the showdown with her outside work hours.

Emotions had got the better of him.

'Ticking bomb.'

The cardiologist's words had been foremost in his mind.

Still, even though he was extremely worried about Gran and furious at being emotionally blackmailed, there was no excuse for directing his frustrations at Miss Simms when he had no solid proof she was to blame.

Miss Mouse from marketing.

Bloody hell! There'd been nothing mouse-like or timid about her.

She hadn't squeaked or stammered. She'd roared like a lioness using words no one else had ever dared say to his face. And he'd given her good reason.

He shook his head at his behaviour.

God, the woman might dress blandly, but she had spirit and magnificent eyes that had showered him in outraged sparks of fury.

Something unidentifiable shifted in him now as he replayed their sparring. There'd been something incredibly stimulating about the way she'd launched at him in a blistering no-holds-barred attack. And he had to admire that she'd turned his argument on its ear when he'd suggested she was using her friendship with Gran to attract his attention. It was a valid, and very obvious, point that there had been countless professional opportunities for her to get his attention if she'd wanted to.

An unknown sensation coiled in the pit of his stomach.

Guilt.

It had to be guilt.

The demons of his conscience were berating him for letting his emotions get the better of him.

That was one of the problems with emotion—it overrode logic.

It made asses of people.

Logic compelled him to acknowledge that Mia Simms would hardly dress the way she did if she was trying to attract his attention—unless she was totally clueless about how a woman should go about attracting a man.

No woman could be so ignorant.

But even if she hadn't planted any seeds in Gran's mind about the dates, Mia's close friendship with Gran was strange. Perhaps Mia didn't have any sinister motivation. If she was the social misfit he'd always pegged her as, Miss Simms might be more comfortable with elderly people than she was with people closer to her own age.

But, hang on ... What the hell was with her usual apparent lack of confidence?

Gran had laughed when Connor had referred to Mia as being weak. Now he understood why. Today's spitfire had not been daunted by him and had been more than capable of expressing her opinions confidently and concisely.

He gritted his teeth knowing Mia was a round peg who didn't fit into the square hole he'd created for her.

Who was the real Mia Simms?

More importantly, what was her agenda?

The intercom on his desk buzzed.

'Yes, Grace?'

'Connor, I know you said to hold all calls, but I have Glen Davis on line one and he said you left a message with his secretary only ten minutes ago requesting he call you back as soon as possible.'

Ah. His HR manager. 'Thanks. I'll speak with him.'

He picked up the handset. 'Hi Glen, thanks for getting back to me.'

'Hi Connor. What can I do for you?'

'I'm interested in the personnel file for Mia Simms.'

'One moment and I'll bring it up on my screen.' Glen cleared his throat. 'Okay. Mia Simms is twenty-six, a graduate from the London School of Economics and Political Science and joined us straight after graduation. Prior to tertiary education she was schooled in the south east.'

'Where does she live now?'

'Er ... At the time of the interview she only gave a postal address as she was about to move.

It's been an oversight not to have followed up but I'll phone through to her shortly and get her current residential address.'

'Hold on that for the time being.' If she was guilty of hiding anything, Connor didn't want her to know he'd already started digging in her personnel file. 'Anything on her family background?'

'Let's see. Parents were killed in a plane crash when she was a kid. Record says she has no siblings or other living relatives. There's nobody listed as a next of kin.'

Shutting off the surge of empathy he felt for her knowing she'd been orphaned too, Connor asked, 'What about her emergency contact person?' 'There's nobody listed.'

Nobody? His empathy turned quickly back to suspicion.

'What I can tell you is that all her performance appraisals have been first-rate,' Glen continued. 'She's never missed a day of work, nobody ever has a bad word to say about her and her record is perfect.'

Connor was well aware the head of marketing sang Mia's praises, but nobody was perfect. 'Could you email the file to me?'

'Certainly.'

'Thanks, Glen.' He'd read through it as soon as possible.

Connor disconnected the call and thought more on the perfect Miss Simms.

No address.

No emergency contact person.

Gran was normally a very shrewd judge of character, but could she be missing something about Miss Simms?

He deliberated calling one of his close friends who had a private investigation and personal security business to ask him to do some digging but dismissed the idea just as quickly.

Instead of jumping to any more negative conclusions, he'd apologise to Miss Simms and give her the benefit of the doubt—for now. He'd still be on his guard, but if he could get her to relax over dinner and open up, he might be able to get a feel for her integrity.

If there was anything that didn't add up, then he'd ask Tony to launch an investigation and leave no stone unturned.

Chapter Four

'Miss Simms to see you, Ma'am.' Dawson, the distinguished butler, made the announcement with formal flourish as he showed Mia into Violet's favourite sitting room.

'Mia!' Violet put her book down. 'What a lovely surprise. Come in!'

There may have been surprise on the older woman's face, but there was also a shadow of guilt.

'You weren't expecting me?' Mia asked dryly.

'Not right now, dear.' Violet stood up so she could give Mia a hug. 'Shouldn't you be at work?'

'Shouldn't you be in hospital?' Mia looked her friend over, trying to gauge how strongly she could call her to task given the state of her heart.

'No. I'm being well looked after at home.'

Violet was tall and slender, immaculately dressed and never had a hair out of place. She wasn't exhibiting any shortness of breath, but did look tired. 'Dawson said you gave him and Nell a scare last night.'

'Connor told you first though, didn't he?'

'Of course he told me. I'm fairly certain he made a bee-line for my office the second you delivered your ultimatum.'

'Hmm.'

'How are you feeling?'

'At the moment I feel fine.'

'But you should be in hospital, Violet.'

'I have the most delightful young nurse looking after me and you know how I abhor hospitals.' She made a dismissive gesture with her hand.

'Why didn't you tell me you weren't well?'

Violet motioned to a richly upholstered settee. 'Sit down. I'm sure Nell will send Dawson in with some tea for us shortly.' As they sat, she explained, 'I didn't want you to worry unnecessarily. Last night, I had some tightness in my chest and I was breathless so Dawson called an ambulance.'

'I'm glad he did!'

'They all take care of me,' she agreed. 'Anyway, it was only late this morning I got the results back, but I'll be as right as rain once I have this surgical procedure.'

'You need to be admitted as soon as possible.'

'I promise I will be as soon as you and Connor have done as I ask.'

'Violet, you know I love you but this is crazy.' Mia ran her hands down over her face. 'Why have you insisted we go out together?'

The elderly lady closed her eyes for a moment and let out a long breath. 'This heart problem is easily fixed but none of us know how much time we have left. I should've got you and Connor together years ago.'

'Wrong. I'm nothing like the women he dates.'

'You're exactly the type of young woman he should be dating.'

'What are you hoping to achieve? Do you really think we're going to fall for each other?'

'Why wouldn't you?'

'Oh, for—'

'Look me in the eye, Mia, and tell me you don't think Connor's a handsome young man.'

'Yes, he's good looking but—'

'Don't think I haven't noticed how hard you try to look disinterested when I mention his name.'

And Mia thought she'd hidden her crush!

'I don't blame you,' Violet continued. 'You'd have to be indifferent to men not to be attracted to him—he's very like Archibald was at that age. Very debonair.'

Mia rolled her eyes. 'Perhaps, but—' 'I'm doing you both a favour,' Violet insisted.

Mia imagined the fireworks that'd taken place between grandmother and grandson earlier when they were having this same conversation. Both were equally strong-willed.

'You know very well that Connor and I have nothing in common apart from shared concern for your welfare—and you shouldn't be exploiting our love for you.'

'Rubbish! You have plenty in common. You're both bright, educated young people.'

'That—'

'You both play tennis.'

'*Really?*' It was laughable. 'I've only been taking lessons for a month. I can barely hit a serve in.'

Mia's protest fell on deaf ears.

'You both enjoy travelling, theatre, good food and wine.' Violet raised her fingers as she listed each point, but it was very telling that she ran out of points before she had to use her other hand. 'I'm sure you'll find you have a lot more in common once you get to know each other.'

'Millions of people like those things, but it doesn't mean they'd be a romantic match. And now—thanks to you—he's under the impression I've put you up to this.'

Violet scoffed. 'He said as much to me and I told him he's way off-base.'

'He doesn't believe you. He accused me of being your friend with the sole objective of getting to know him. Then, when he finally seemed to get the message that I don't want to go out with him, he accused me of trying to be named in your will!'

Violet's lips twitched. 'Yes, well, he can be rather cynical.'

'Cynical? He's not just cynical. He's incredibly arrogant.'

'People have tried to take advantage of him before and now he's wary.'

'Don't make excuses for him.' She started fuming all over again. 'He harassed me at work! Any other employee might've seriously considered making a formal complaint.'

'It's only because he's so protective of me.' She hung her head a little. 'I provoked him and he went off like Vesuvius. I was worried he might lash out at you because he feels like I've pinned him into a corner.'

'Well, thanks for the warning!' Tilting her head to one side she asked, 'Why did you do it?'

'Because I'm worried about him.' She took Mia's hands in hers and patted them. 'He's a strong, capable young man who's been incredibly hurt and is unwilling to take a chance again on love. I felt it was past time to point him in the right direction.'

'I'm the wrong direction.' Mia wondered about Connor's ex-wife. She remembered Violet had been worried about the match and had never liked the woman. Although Violet had never confided in her about the reason the marriage had ended, it'd apparently blow up in spectacular fashion after only a few months.

'He has a heart of gold and he's definitely worthy of you my dear.'

Mia made a sound of annoyance. 'You obviously don't like me as much as I thought. Besides, he told me—very scathingly—he didn't find me attractive and never would.'

'Huh!' She wore a deep scowl as she looked Mia up and down. 'He hasn't even seen the real you.'

'Which brings me to the most crucial point. You know very well why I present myself like this. I—'

'I agreed some superficial changes to disguise your appearance were absolutely necessary, but you didn't have to go to such extremes.' Violet's lips tightened in displeasure. 'You were unrecognisable enough after the orthodontic work and the nose job. We only changed your hair colour to be absolutely certain. There was never any need to wear glasses or those God-awful clothes.'

Mia cringed. 'You and Connor must've been comparing notes.'

Violet ignored her and reasoned, 'Besides, you're a woman now, not a teenager. There's no need to fade into the shadows.'

'I'm more than comfortable in the shadows.' She deliberately avoided looking at her reflection in the gilded mirror hanging above the marble fireplace.

'Mia.' Violet squeezed her hand. 'It's been ten years. I'm sure you're safe now.'

Safe.

Oh, how she wished she was safe.

'Giovanni is still alive.'

The name hung between them.

It was a stark reminder of the menacing threat Mia had lived with every day for the past decade.

Violet blanched. 'He must've given up looking for you by now,' she said quietly.

'According to the FBI, as long as he's alive, my life's in danger.'

'If he's still searching for you, he's more than likely scouring the USA, not London.'

Violet was deluding herself. 'Not necessarily. He knows my mother was British.'

'But he also knows she was disowned by her mother once she ran off to Hollywood. Besides, if he bothered checking, he'd have learned your grandmother died a few days after she learned of your mother's death. He'd know you have no living relatives and he'd even discover you weren't named as a beneficiary in your grandmother's will.' Violet shook her head adamantly. 'There's nothing to tie you to London.'

'Violet, I—'

'There's definitely nothing that can tie you to me or to Stanley either. Nothing that can lead Giovanni to Mia Simms.'

'I can't afford to take any chances.' Anxiety swirled through her. 'Giovanni's reach is like an octopus's tentacles. It's long and it knows no geographical boundaries.' She willed her friend to understand. 'Life in the shadows keeps me safe.'

'Life in the shadows is hardly life.' The older lady pressed one hand briefly to her forehead before she reasoned, 'Your young life is passing you by and it's time for you to shine.'

Restlessness and angst churned in Mia's gut. 'I'm happy with my life. I'm happy to *have* a life.'

'You have no friends your own age.'

'Because I choose not to lie to people.'

'You and I both know you wouldn't lie if there was any other choice. You have to accept your circumstances and move forward.' Violet's tongue clicked against the roof of her mouth. 'It's time you started to live a normal life. Stanley and I won't be here forever.'

Mia didn't want to dwell on the warning. Violet and her close friend, Stanley, were the two most important people in Mia's life and she couldn't bear the thought of losing either of them.

On behalf of Mia's grandmother, Stanley, former chief of MI5, had used his connections and liaised with the FBI so Mia could leave her life in the USA and be relocated to the UK. Stanley and Violet had honoured their promise to Mia's dying grandmother. They'd guided Mia and loved her like a grandchild.

'You'd be such a wonderful wife and mother. You need to give yourself a chance to fall in love and have a family, Mia.'

'I can't!' She jumped up from the comfortable couch and wrung her hands together while she paced the floor. Taking tea with Violet in the beautiful yellow and blue sitting room was normally relaxing. Now, it was like a dark cloud had settled over Mia and she was too agitated to enjoy the soothing opulence of her surroundings.

'How can I have a normal life when the threat of Giovanni is constantly hanging over my head? There's no way I'd ever become involved with a guy when I know he might end up dead because of me, so why on earth would I subject children to this threat?'

'After all this time, you still don't feel safe?'

'No. You've helped me stay safe, but can't you see that if you insist on these dates and I'm seen publicly with Connor you'll be thrusting me into the public spotlight and I might end up with *no life.*'

'You could have an army of bodyguards if you needed them.'

'No thank you. Listen, Violet, I'm as free right now as I'll ever be. But the paparazzi follow Connor and that exposure could put me in danger.'

'You're exaggerating. So what if the paparazzi take a photo of you? You're Mia Simms now, not Callie Buckley.'

Callie Buckley.

Mia closed her eyes when she heard the name.

So much had happened since she was Callie Buckley.

Life hadn't been completely happy and certainly hadn't been stress-free back then, but at least she'd lived her life honestly. She'd been able to form friendships based on who she really was—not someone she was pretending to be.

Now her life was one lie after another and there was an ever-pressing need to keep looking back over her shoulder.

A soft knock sounded on the door. 'Ma'am, your tea.'

The butler wheeled in the ornate wooden tea trolley.

'Thank you, Dawson, and pass on my thanks to Nell. We'll serve ourselves.' The butler gave a slight bow and left. No sooner had the study door closed behind him than Violet patted the couch beside her.

Mia declined the unspoken invitation. She was way too wired right now to sit still.

'Giovanni would never look at you and see the teenager you were,' Violet launched as she poured the tea from the fine bone china teapot.

'Think, Violet. Every woman Connor dates is a beautiful *somebody*. If he's seen out with a plain, unknown woman, the media is going to be all the keener to discover who I am and how I came to be dating him.'

'And they'll learn you're Mia Simms, an employee in his company.' She added some cream to each tea cup then picked up a spoon to stir. 'They'll assume you met at work.'

'I work hard at my job. I don't want to be viewed as the CEO's latest fling. And apart from that, the press would wonder where I'm from.'

'The background created for you will stick. The FBI have been doing this sort of thing for decades and Stanley used all his MI5 connections to liaise with them. He's perfectly satisfied there are no holes left unplugged or he'd have ensured you had a personal bodyguard right from the beginning.' She handed Mia a cup of tea. 'He wouldn't be able to sleep at night if he thought your life was in danger. Neither would I.'

'But Mia Simms is employed by Stewart Corporation. She works at the same soup kitchen with Violet Stewart who happened to be the closest friend of Callie Buckley's grandmother. How long would it take Giovanni to work it out? How long before he realises that Stanley was Archibald's cousin and all three of you were good friends with my grandparents?'

'I refuse to believe he'd trace you.' She made a dismissive gesture with one of her hands and the diamonds from her rings flashed as they caught the light. 'You don't even sound American now.'

'Violet, please forget your demands and go back to hospital.' Mia sat back down on the edge of the settee, a seething mass of angst. 'You've already forced Connor into noticing me and he's not interested. Accept it.'

'He hasn't had a chance to see the real you. He thinks you have no spine!'

Gee, thanks for sharing that with me!

'I doubt he thinks so any more,' Mia said with a grimace. 'When he came storming into my office to confront me, I lashed right back at him.'

'Perfect! That's just what he needs!'

Mia groaned.

'Dear, isn't there a single ounce of feminine pride in you that makes you want to show him how beautiful you truly are?'

It was her own need more than pride that wanted him to reconsider her appeal as a woman, but she squashed the thought. 'I'm not Cinderella and you're not my fairy godmother.'

Violet sipped her tea then smiled. 'Oh, but you could be, Mia and I definitely have it in me to play fairy godmother. Biscuit, dear?'

'No, thank you.'

Violet sat calmly drinking tea and nibbling on a shortbread biscuit as though she'd never launched her outlandish scheme. Meanwhile, nerves ate into Mia and the last thing she felt like doing was eating a damned thing.

'Frankly, the way your grandson spoke to me today was so hurtful—so insulting—I'm not interested in dating him. I don't even respect him professionally after the way he behaved.'

'It wasn't the CEO of Stewart Corporation who confronted you today.' Violet sighed and regret bracketed her mouth. 'I believe the person you saw wasn't even the man, but the grief-stricken boy who lost his parents, lost his grandfather and now fears he's in danger of losing me.'

Knowing all about loss, Mia contemplated Violet's words.

'To anyone who doesn't know my grandson well, Connor would've appeared to take the news of my heart problem in his stride.' She poked her index finger against her own breastbone as she emphasised, 'I saw the pallor beneath his tan when the doctor told us the news. I felt the tension in him as he drove me home and I know he's worried sick about my health.'

'Then have the operation. Your demand has only made him more stressed.'

'Don't you see, Mia? I'm not immortal and the time will come when I will die. He'll lose me and you'll lose me.' Violet's heartfelt concern wrapped itself around Mia. 'I don't want either of you to be alone in the world. And when I join Archibald in heaven, I want to be able to tell him Connor is married to a wonderful woman and I've been able to bounce our great grandchildren on my knee.'

Mia's anxiety ramped up. Marriage and children?

Good Lord.

About to take Violet to task, Mia stopped when she saw the unshed tears in the older woman's eyes.

'Oh, Violet.' She put down her tea and rested her hand on Violet's shoulder. 'I've been under Connor's nose all this time and he's never noticed me.' Realising her words might've held an ounce of disappointment Mia added quickly, 'And he's not exactly the type of guy I'd date.'

Violet had just picked up her cup again, but now it clinked back onto the saucer. Her still-moist eyes were steel blue as she challenged, 'Tell me about the type of man you want to date, my dear, because as far as I'm aware, you've *never* dated.'

'I haven't.' She shifted a little on the chair as she made the admission. 'But, if I did, I wouldn't date a guy with Connor's track record.'

'I know he's had his share of relationships but—'

'Violet! Ever since his divorce, none of his liaisons have lasted long enough to be classified as serious relationships, and if he was a woman he'd be called a very unsavoury name.' She lifted her hand to forestall the defence of the doting grandmother. 'You know it's true because you've lamented about it often enough to me.'

'How could he form a relationship with any of those women? They're all shallow gold-diggers. I think he's deliberately gone out with them because he immediately sees them for what they are and they can't hurt him like that b—' Violet stopped abruptly and amended her choice of words, '—woman he was married to.'

She looked closely at Violet. With Connor's reference to the 'ticking bomb' at the forefront of her mind, Mia needed to push back against her friend's wishes without lighting the fuse.

'Connor thinks *I'm* a shallow gold-digger.'

'Ha! If he only knew how wrong he is!' Violet laughed. 'He needs a suitable woman. *You,* Mia. You're the woman.'

'You're pinning your hopes on an unrealistic dream.' Connor might have once been Mia's unrealistic dream, but today she'd had a reality check. 'Call this off. Connor already senses I'm hiding something. I don't want him having me investigated.'

'I'm only sorry he's had to be kept in the dark about you all these years.' She sent Mia a searching look.

'No, Violet. Don't even think about it. We were all sworn to secrecy.'

She sighed and gave a brief nod of agreement. 'Five dates, Mia. That's all I ask of you both.'

Mia had to grit her teeth together to stop herself from screaming out her objection. 'If anyone had suggested that you'd ever try to use emotional blackmail against me, I would've been appalled and jumped straight to your defence.'

'I may not have much time left on this earth—'

'See? Emotional blackmail!'

'—but in the time I have I want the two young people I love the most to get to know each other. If nothing else, you might at least be a comfort to each other when I'm gone.'

'Oh, please.' Mia replaced her cup on the serving trolley and raised her hands to each temple. Rubbing the areas with her fingertips, she tried to ease the build-up of tension there. Connor had been right. Violet was holding steadfast to her plan and milking her heart condition for all it was worth.

If only Stanley was in London, Mia would be calling him to come and talk some sense into Violet. He would certainly see the folly of Violet's plan and make her see how dangerous it was. Unfortunately, he wasn't due home until the end of the following week.

Even though he'd been retired for years, Stanley had been asked to chair meetings to facilitate the sharing of information between MI5 and the French equivalent, DGSE. He'd said the meetings would be intense so Mia didn't want to call him and burden him with what was unfolding at home.

There was another soft knock on the sitting room door.

'Come in,' Violet called.

'Hello, Mrs Stewart.' A petite red-headed young lady entered. 'I'm sorry to interrupt you, but it's time to take your blood pressure and give you your medication.'

'Thank you, Giselle. I'd like you to meet my very good friend, Mia.' As greetings were exchanged Violet sent Mia a pointed look and told the nurse, 'You might find my blood pressure's a little higher than it should be. Mia has been disagreeing with me. Please tell her she shouldn't disagree with me, Giselle—it's bad for my health.'

'Violet!' Mia admonished as the young nurse looked quite uncomfortable.

'It is important you keep calm and don't get too worked up about anything,' Giselle said dutifully.

Hm. Violet was being a thoroughly unrepentant manipulator.

When Giselle finished her duties and left them, Mia said, 'At least let us stay in London and go to places that aren't going to attract media attention.'

Connor's grandmother pursed her lips thoughtfully before she finally said, 'Alright. I'll compromise. You can dine at an obscure restaurant in London but you still have to go to Venice and Paris. Connor doesn't have a high profile in either of those countries, so the paparazzi there aren't likely to be bothered with him.'

Mia let out a pent-up breath of exasperation. 'Why Venice and—?'

'Uh. I haven't finished.' It was like being taken to task by a principal. 'I'll only give quarter on the restaurant in London, not the weekends away—and only on one condition.'

'Really?' Violet had never been so exasperating! 'Another condition?'

'You must have a makeover.'

'No. That's out.'

'It's my condition for not dining at Raphael's.'

Picking up a cushion, Mia raised it in front of her face and used it to smother a growl of frustration. 'Connor's going to think I'm trying to attract him.'

'Nonsense. I'll take responsibility and tell him it was my condition.'

Mia's shoulders sagged in defeat. 'You're impossible.'

'I know.' The sparkle of mischief was back in Violet's eyes. She was obviously enjoying herself immensely.

Trying to spell out a few terms of her own, Mia insisted, 'Only these five dates and then we'll never speak of this again and you promise there'll be no more plots to try to get Connor and me together.'

'Agreed.'

'But I'm not happy.'

'You might be cursing me now, but before too long you and Connor will both be thanking me.' Violet smiled. 'Now I'm going to get busy on the phone and organise your makeover. You sit and finish your tea. I'll have a team of stylists here within the hour.' She stood up and hummed all the way to the door. When she was there she turned back and gave Mia a broad smile. 'I do believe you've given me a new lease on life.'

Mia raised her eyes heavenwards and shook her head.

When she was alone, her gaze traced the intricate pattern on the Royal Doulton tea set.

She sat quietly drinking her tea until she no longer felt agitated. Now, she simply felt numb.

Chapter Five

Connor's grip tightened around the steering wheel of his Maserati Grancabrio sports car while the security gates opened at his grandmother's home in St James Park.

Dinner hadn't been cancelled, so he'd use the evening to make his apology to his employee and gain more insight into her character.

Gates open, he drove down the cobblestone driveway towards the double-storey Edwardian house he'd grown up in.

It was a massive home had a pretty, protruding porch extending around the main entrance. Instead of down-sizing when Archibald died, Gran had all her household staff live in. She could afford the upkeep and liked the central London location, but most of all she liked the memories of having lived here with her husband and making it a happy home for her son and then Connor.

When he turned off the engine, Connor got out of the car, made his way up the entry stairs two at a time and rang the bell. It didn't matter that this had been his home, Gran's butler considered it an affront if Connor walked in unannounced.

Surprisingly, it was Violet, and not Dawson, who answered the door.

'Gran.' She was six feet one, but he still had to lean down to plant a kiss on her cheek. 'Shouldn't you be in bed? Where's Dawson?'

'No, I shouldn't be in bed and I gave him the evening off. I think he and Nell went to the cinema.'

'But—'

'I have a fully qualified nurse living in now, so don't start panicking. Lucy is also staying in tonight and we're planning on watching a BBC documentary that starts in,' she looked at her watch, 'thirty minutes.'

'Good.' If anything went wrong Lucy, Gran's housekeeper, would be there as an extra pair of hands for the nurse. Lucy was a sensible, middle-aged woman who often sat with Gran in the evenings. 'I don't want you to be alone until you've had the surgery and the doctor clears you.'

'I know.' She smiled and reached up to pat him on the cheek. 'Thank you for caring, Connor.'

'I love you Gran.' He put his hands on her shoulders. 'Promise me you'll look after yourself.'

'I love you too and I promise I will.' After a quick hug, she pulled back. 'Now, for heaven's sake, come in. You need to get your skates on and go out for dinner.'

'Miss Simms asked me to meet her here.'

'Don't be stuffy, Connor. Call her Mia.' She turned on her heel as he shut the front door behind him. 'She's upstairs getting ready but will be down any minute.' Gran paused, placed her hand on his right arm and steered him towards the small drawing room. 'Thank you for agreeing to this, Connor.'

'You left me with no choice and I'm not going to pretend to be happy about it.'

'Mia said the same thing, but I think you'll both change your minds.' Instead of continuing, his grandmother stopped at the base of the grand curved staircase that swept up to the second floor. 'I insisted Mia consult with some stylists this afternoon and I've had such a lovely time watching the butterfly emerge from the cocoon.'

Connor conjured up his employee's image. She'd certainly need a team of beauticians and stylists to transform her. But, despite Mia's high cheekbones and full lips, he doubted even the experts could produce a butterfly.

Not that she was ugly; she was just ... plain. Though she hadn't looked plain when she'd been railing at him this afternoon. Her cheeks had flushed and her eyes had been quite—

'Ah, Mia. You're ready!' Violet announced.

Connor steeled himself to keep his features neutral. After having already been less than pleasant to Miss Simms he didn't want to squash her self-esteem if she saw he was unimpressed with the stylists' best efforts.

Polite, social mask in place, he looked up.

Good God!

A butterfly had indeed emerged from the cocoon. *An exquisite butterfly.*

For a split second he was disoriented. As disbelief pounded through him he forced himself to look away and marshal his thoughts. When he looked back, his attention was riveted on the woman in red making her way gracefully down the wide staircase.

Connor's jaw slackened.

If it wasn't for her hair colour and those same awful glasses, he would've sworn it couldn't be Mia.

Rendered momentarily speechless, all he could do was stare as he tried to absorb her appearance. Her figure...

Hell! What had she been thinking hiding under the shapeless clothes she wore to the office? He would never have guessed in a million years that she had such a sexy figure.

Sexy?

Hell, yeah. *Sexy.*

He barely refrained from raising his hand to the side of his head and giving himself a whack to try to dislodge the thought.

Her legs—shown off to advantage by killer heels and a dress ending mid-thigh—her legs were *amazing*.

Even when he tore his gaze away from them and tried to banish the X-rated visions filling his mind about how those legs could be wrapped around him, his rapid pulse didn't recover. He couldn't stop assessing every little detail about her. Her hips curved perfectly from her slender waist and her breasts were more than ample.

Wavy dark hair framed her face, caressed her shoulders and cascaded down her back. Connor's fingers wanted to thread through it to see if it was as silky as it looked. Who could've guessed that the tightly wound bun she always wore hid such lustrous hair?

This was Mia Simms, the frumpy member of his marketing team?

He couldn't reconcile the woman he'd seen countless times with this vision of fabulous femininity who was descending the stairs in front of him. First, she'd stunned him with their verbal sparring match this afternoon and now this...

He swallowed hard.

'Announcing Mia Simms,' Violet said smugly from where she stood looking from one of them to the other. Then in a voice so low only Connor would hear, she added in French, 'Le *papillon.*'

Butterfly indeed.

'Good evening, Mr Stewart.'

Shit. Even her voice was sexier—sultrier.

'Now, Mia. I've already given Connor a serve for being stuffy and I'll have no more of this formality,' Violet insisted. 'From now on, it's Mia and Connor.'

Whichever make-up artist Violet had hired for this 'transformation' needed a gold medal. He or she had definitely highlighted Mia's features. His attention snagged on her glasses. They needed to go. He guessed the stylists hadn't had time to replace them with contact lenses, or at least a more flattering frame.

Mia scowled as she saw him looking her up and down. 'None of this,' she swept her hands down in front of her, 'was my idea.'

'It was a very good idea.' He cursed inwardly at his hoarse words.

An enchanting blush rose from her chest, swept up her neck and stained her cheeks. Then she shifted her weight from one foot to the other, looking entirely uncertain, and reminding him of the employee he'd first encountered.

She was embarrassed because she suddenly looked like a goddess?

Connor felt like a fool as he recalled his declaration that he wasn't in the slightest bit attracted to her and never would be. Gran's team of professional stylists had wrought a miracle. The woman who stood before him was equal to the most desirable he'd ever escorted out for dinner. If they had still been going to Raphael's the photographers would definitely have assumed Mia was his latest lover.

'I'm taking full credit and don't you shoot daggers at me, Mia. I've wanted to change your style for years.' His grandmother's delight made her eyes sparkle and she looked ten years younger despite the night she'd spent in hospital. 'Now, go and enjoy your dinner, Cinderella. And, my darling Connor—do try to behave like Prince Charming.'

Chapter Six

'Why?' Connor asked, as he sat in the driver's seat and looked at Mia.

'Why what?'

'Why do you hide yourself in those shapeless clothes when you've got such an amazing figure?'

'I...'

There was such genuine surprise on her face, he knew she had no idea how stunning she now looked. 'There's no reason you couldn't model. How tall are you? Six feet?' Funny how the frumpy clothes she'd worn had always diminished her height.

It seemed to take a moment for her to process his words. 'Six feet exactly and you're being ridiculous.'

'It's the clothes you wear to work that are ridiculous.'

She thrust her chin forward. 'They're way more comfortable than this dress, and high heels are impractical at any time—let alone to wear to the office.'

But those heels brought her closer to his height—the perfect height for him to lower his head and claim her lips with his own.

Damn. He wasn't supposed to have thoughts like that about a staff member!

'Mia.' He cleared his throat and tried to remember what he'd been going to say. 'Put simply, tonight you look great.' Great was too mediocre to describe her figure, but he hardly wanted to admit the full impact she had on him.

If she lost the glasses great could be stunning. *Out-of-this-world, mouth-wateringly beautiful.*

On second thoughts, it might be safer for both of them if the glasses were kept firmly in place.

'Excuse me?' She sat straighter against the plush leather seat. 'When I want your opinion, I'll ask for it. I didn't appreciate your assessment of me this afternoon and I don't appreciate it now. Let me get one thing perfectly straight. This makeover of Violet's...' Every word screamed of her exasperation. '...This is not who I am and I'm distinctly uncomfortable being fawned over in an attempt to make me look glamorous. Next you'll be telling me I've changed my appearance to try to impress you and that this was all part of some plan I've been hatching for years to get your attention,' she huffed. 'Believe me, this was all the stylists' doing and if it hadn't been for Violet's insistence—'

'It was one of my grandmother's better ideas.'

She crossed her arms over her chest, drawing his attention to her breasts. 'If you're pleased about these dates now, you're very shallow.' She gave him no time to defend himself as she ranted, 'The stylists give my hair a blow dry, apply a bit of makeup and dress me in something that leaves little to the imagination and suddenly you're not quite so averse to taking me out for dinner? Thanks very much, but that's no compliment.'

'That's not what I said.'

'I wish I could say I felt the same way.' She obviously wasn't listening to him. 'Sadly, I don't think there's a stylist I could send you to who's quite perfected the art of personality transplants and that would be the only thing that'd make this evening any more enjoyable for me.'

Far from being insulted, Connor was amazed. Nobody had ever told him off so spectacularly and he'd never imagined in his wildest dreams that Miss Mouse from marketing would be the one to do it. 'You really didn't put Gran up to arranging these dates, did you.'

'I've been telling you that all along.' Her words were delivered with a ferocious glare but her stiff posture signalled her unease.

'If you're nervous, there's no reason to be.'

'Huh!' she scoffed. 'You can treat me with disdain and insult me all you like, but you don't *scare* me.'

Connor winced inwardly at her summary of his treatment so far. 'Mia, I didn't say these dates were a good idea. I was only talking about your makeover.'

'I don't want to be defined by the way I look. Appearances aren't everything.'

'Of course they aren't.' He knew all too well that appearances were often deceiving.

Rachel had taught him that.

However, there were obvious differences between his ex-wife and his employee.

Rachel dressed to highlight her assets and Mia downplayed her physical appeal.

Rachel had agreed with everything he said and Mia challenged him at every turn.

The two women were chalk and cheese.

'You're said to be London's most eligible bachelor, but that doesn't impress me. I don't care how good looking you are. No amount of money would ever induce me to put up with a man who's so insulting.'

'About that—'

'I've always admired your business acumen and the way you put yourself out to support worthy charities, but now I know I don't like you, so I can't think of a single reason I'd want to spend *one* evening with you, let alone five.' The quick rise of her chest said that she'd only paused because she'd run out of breath. 'I'm here under sufferance and only because I adore Violet.'

Her outburst had brought more colour to her cheeks and her blue eyes sparked with enmity just as they had this afternoon.

'Is there anything else you'd like to get off your chest?'

The look she shot him told him she suspected a double entendre, but it hadn't been his intention. She was so stressed and hostile he imagined she'd worked herself up tighter with every minute that'd passed this afternoon and every alteration the stylist or Gran had made to her appearance.

'That's it. For now,' she told him sternly.

Great. Maybe now I'll be able to get my apology in!

'You're quite a novelty. I've never met a woman who's disliked me.'

'Novelty?' Her head thumped back against the plush leather head rest. 'Thanks so much. You keep those compliments rolling and I'm certain to join your fan club by the end of the night. I might even run for club presidency.'

Oh hell. He'd voiced his thoughts without thinking and she'd found offence in them again. But as much as he was kicking himself, it was impossible to keep from chuckling. Her animosity radiated from her and it stirred something indefinable in him.

It was refreshing.

A challenge.

A challenge?

Whoa. This is not going anywhere, he reminded himself sternly.

The duck may have turned into a graceful swan, but Mia Simms was his employee. And, if that wasn't reason enough to ensure he only appreciated those killer legs from afar, he also refused to be manipulated by his grandmother. He wouldn't see Miss Simms again after the agreed upon five dates. He would not, under any circumstances, launch into an affair with his grandmother's *friend*.

Another look at the firm set of Mia's mouth told him that even if she thought he was good looking, he was probably the last person she wanted to jump into bed with.

Just as well. Her antipathy would cool his libido.

Yet ... She definitely intrigued him. Suddenly the dates didn't seem quite as onerous as he'd first expected—and not simply because she looked great. No, he found he enjoyed her verve and was looking forward to unravelling the mystery of Mia.

Clearly, she had no interest in impressing him. She wasn't falling over herself to pay him compliments or to have him flatter her which made her stand out from his other dates.

This woman had drawn battle lines in the sand and she was amazing.

'Are we going out for dinner or is take-out going to be delivered to the car?' she asked.

Connor laughed.

As interesting as it was to have her breathe fire at him, he owed her an apology and wanted to do it before they started out to the restaurant.

Girding himself against having his words thrown back in his face, he ventured, 'I'm sincerely sorry for my manner this afternoon.'

Mia turned her head so quickly he was surprised she didn't end up with whiplash.

'Did I just hear you apologise?'

'Yes.' He'd never been afraid to admit when he was wrong, but he could see she was stunned. 'I apologise for my hostility. You were quite right. I was overbearing and antagonistic.'

Her eyes narrowed with suspicion behind those owlish glasses. 'You're only apologising to me because of my makeover.'

He realised he had that coming. 'Your appearance has nothing to do with it. I'd already realised after I left your office that I needed to ask for your forgiveness.' He rested one hand against the steering wheel. The apology should be enough, yet for some inexplicable reason he found himself wanting to make her understand why he'd not been himself. 'I was worried about Gran's health and then she threw the curve ball at me. I was shocked and angry about her manipulation and I lost my cool. I jumped to the conclusion that you were to blame for her demand. I'm sorry I took everything out on you.'

'You're not the only one she's manipulating here.'

He sent her what he hoped was an apologetic look. 'You're right. I can see you've been as much a pawn in all of this as I have. Please accept my apology and let's get through this as best we can.'

She was quiet as she looked at him. In the dim light cast into the car interior by one of the stately lamps lining the driveway, he watched her bite her lower lip.

He felt a small, unwelcome, pull in his groin as her action reminded him how lush her lips were.

Damn it! He didn't need to torture himself by drinking in her appealing features—her determined chin, pert little nose and of course, her stunning cheekbones.

'Apology accepted. Although I'm tempted to make you grovel, I'm not so petty.'

Grovel? Unlikely. He didn't want continued hostility, but he wasn't about to grovel when there were questions he still wanted answered.

'Shall we declare a truce and start afresh?' he suggested smoothly.

'I suppose so.'

'Thank you.' Satisfied for now with her reluctant concession, he turned on the engine and started down the driveway.

While he waited for the gate to open, he saw her hands were tightly clenched on her lap. He could hardly blame her for being unwilling to accept their truce. He'd behaved like an ass and now he needed to let her see that his behaviour this afternoon had been an aberration.

'Where are we going?' she asked.

'A small, out of the way Italian restaurant recommended by my housekeeper.' The news earned him a small nod of her approval. 'How did you talk Gran out of dinner at Raphael's?'

'By agreeing to the makeover,' she said through gritted teeth.

'I know you were concerned about photographers, but even if photos did appear in the newspaper, nobody from work would recognise you as you are now—if you removed your glasses.'

'The glasses stay and there'd better not be any photos. I don't want to be pictured with you.'

If he'd had a fragile ego, her comment certainly would've put a dent in it. When had any woman he'd dated not wanted to be photographed with him and labelled in the papers as his latest 'love' interest?

The high-necked, button-up blouses Mia wore to work might have morphed into this stunning red dress with the vee neckline and spaghetti straps that showed off flawless creamy skin, but she still had the uptight and straight-laced aura of a Victorian spinster.

He longed to get her to loosen up.

What would her laughter sound like?

He fought a frown.

Since when had the need to hear a woman laugh ever been so acute?

A more pressing thought intruded. What would Mia sound like during passionate lovemaking? Would she cry out in the throes of her orgasm or would she stay silent as she rode it out, her nails digging into his shoulders?

Crunch.

Bloody hell! The wayward thought of Mia naked and underneath him in bed had made him jerk the gears.

Steady on, Connor.

His inner voice was right to caution him. The scene playing out in his head would never happen.

Not only was she his employee, but Mia remained a total conundrum. For the moment, he'd give her the benefit of the doubt. But his instincts warned him to be on his guard.

Chapter Seven

Prince Charming.

In a complete about-face, Connor was the gentleman Mia had always expected he'd be: opening the car door for her when they parked down the road from the restaurant and behaving with such courtesy that he'd give Prince Charming a damned good run for his money.

There was no sign of the hostile man who'd confronted her hours earlier.

Mia wanted to believe that his remorse had been genuine—that her admiration of him for all these years hadn't been misplaced. It was easy to see how his earlier rudeness and suspicion could've been a knee-jerk reaction caused by his concern for Violet. Sheer pragmatism told her to give him the benefit of the doubt so they could get through this as pleasantly as possible.

When they were seated opposite each other and had given the waiter their orders, their gazes met.

A woman could drown in the ocean-blue depths of his eyes.

'Tell me about yourself, Mia.'

Uh-oh. 'Let's talk about work instead. I think it's a safer topic.'

'Safer?'

'Wiser,' she amended hastily in response to his sharp look. She'd have to be on her guard. 'Violet and work are the only two things you and I have in common.'

'That's not what Gran told me. She insisted we have a lot of shared interests.'

'Right. Like our love of tennis.' Mia rolled her eyes. 'You don't like tennis?'

'Oh, I love tennis but I think it's safer for me to be a spectator rather than a player.'

'There's the word again—safer.'

'Safe is good.'

'You don't think life would be more fun if you lived dangerously?'

Refusing to dwell on all the reasons why her very life was a prime example of living dangerously, she gave a small laugh. 'Believe me, life is definitely dangerous when I have a tennis racquet in my hand—not for me, but for others.'

'Have you had lessons?'

'A few. I'll probably never be allowed on the court again after a particularly embarrassing incident last weekend.'

He leaned forward. 'You can't leave me guessing. What happened?'

'A ball I hit went sailing out of my court, into the one next to me. It gave a boy a huge lump on his poor little forehead.' She felt her cheeks grow hot at the memory.

'He might be rethinking his lessons, too.' Connor smiled and for a moment her breath hitched in her chest.

Lord but he was gorgeous.

'Anyway, I think we've established that Violet's trying too hard to sell these outings to us,' she rushed, trying to stop thinking about how handsome Connor was. 'From what I've heard she was an incredible CEO, but she obviously isn't aware of the first rule of marketing.'

'Which is?'

'Don't oversell your product.'

'I'll remember that,' he told her with an easy smile. 'Do you enjoy your job?'

'Immensely.' Coming up with innovative marketing plans was exciting and rewarding.

'What do you love about it?'

'Looking at a product with fresh eyes.' Satisfaction welled in her chest. 'The product is like a clump of rock. In marketing, I hold it up at all different angles until I find the precious seam of gold. Then I have to work out the best vantage point so that when I hold it aloft, everyone else can see the gold too. I want them to be able to focus on the gold to the point where they're not even aware of any surrounding rock.'

He sat back in his chair and a little thrill shot through her veins as she saw the respect in his eyes. 'That's quite an analogy.'

She shrugged. Passionate about what she did, it was hard to stop talking about it once she started. 'When I was at university I had some stand-up arguments with some of my lecturers about the ethics of marketing. It can be an unscrupulous field and I'm glad I'm working for your company.

'I know any product we're selling from the Stewart Corporation is good, but I still need to tap into consumers so the gold is precious to them. I don't want them to take one look at it, dismiss it as fool's gold and walk away. They need to see it and believe it's the genuine thing—the thing they want. The thing they *need* to have.'

As the waiter arrived at their table and poured their wine, Connor said, 'I've never heard anyone speak so passionately about marketing. If you didn't work for me I'd headhunt you.'

Pleasant warmth spread through her chest. It was so nice to be appreciated—especially by this dynamic man.

'This promises to be a very enlightening evening,' he held out his glass to hers when they were alone again and Mia accepted the toast.

She enjoyed the taste of the wine on her tongue and the slide of it down her throat. Maybe she was bolder on one sip of the alcohol or simply heady from his compliment because she couldn't resist teasing, 'Maybe I'll have you so sold on the work we do, everyone in marketing will get a raise.'

'Ah. Now I know your aim, I'm forewarned.'

'Seriously, though, I do love my job.'

He twirled his wine glass around on the table, but his focus was on her face. 'I know it's crucial to our business, but I've never spent much time thinking about it.'

'You don't need to. You have a department working on it while you oversee the big picture—the development of the product. You steer the entire corporation.'

It wasn't the first time she'd thought about how Connor needed to keep on top of the many interests under the Stewart Corporation conglomerate. He was a very powerful man and had even been on the cover of Time magazine.

Connor had expanded the Stewart business empire and was committed to innovation and making all aspects of the business as environmentally sustainable as possible. In his time as CEO, the corporation had gone from being listed as a Fortune 500 company to a

Fortune 100 company and share prices had skyrocketed.

'You have to keep your finger on all the interests of Stewart Corporation. You can't get lost in the detail.'

'The success of the company is only as good as all its key parts,' he recognized.

'And the soldiers are deployed on the orders of the general who has the overall battle plan.'

'Do I hear a note of grudging respect?' he teased.

Oh no. There could be no more teasing tonight. He was way too attractive wearing that expression on his face.

'I admire the way you do your job, Connor.'

Of course, the way he did his job wasn't the only thing she admired about him.

Her gaze was drawn to the strong column of this throat as he swallowed his wine then lowered to the exposed, tanned flesh at the vee of his white business shirt where he hadn't bothered to wear a tie.

Please give me the strength to look away and don't let me turn radish red right now.

Desperate to divert her thoughts, she blurted, 'What's your favourite position?'

Connor choked on his wine and she realised what she'd said.

'Oh hell.' Her face became as hot as a furnace as she conjured up all kinds of lurid images. 'That came out so wrong. I mean what's your favourite part about your position—you know, the thing you like most about being CEO?'

Oh, stop rambling, Mia!

Once he'd recovered from his coughing, he still failed to suppress his laughter. 'I've been asked a lot of questions, but I don't think I've ever been asked that one.'

'Oh, stop it!' she said staunchly. But it was either see the funny side or slide under the table so she laughed too. 'I really didn't—'

'It's okay.' He put his hand up to stop her protest. 'I know you didn't.' He laughed again. 'I've done a lot of interviews, but no journalist has ever asked what I like best about what I do.'

Mia was genuinely interested in his response but was also employing a strategy she'd developed. She knew if she could get people talking about themselves then she didn't have to talk about herself.

Connor proceeded to tell her about the many facets of his role and how he loved trouble-shooting and ensuring a satisfactory outcome for all parties. She was even more impressed when he outlined a few of the recent issues he'd handled.

Every second that whizzed by, her fascination with him grew. She was going to have to guard against going all moon-eyed.

Placing her cutlery on her empty plate, Mia couldn't believe how many times she and Connor had laughed together and how easily the conversation had flowed. It was a dream date, although if she thought about how she'd like the evening to end, she was likely to blush vivid scarlet.

'Do your family live in London?' he asked.

Oops. The evening *had* been going well.

Why did he have to ask something personal? *Damn.*

But wasn't this normal conversation?

He wasn't to know that any personal question would put her on the defensive because it would force her to lie. God knows she'd had to lie to everyone in her life who'd asked her anything about her past. It'd never become any easier for her to perpetuate the lies. Somehow, the thought of lying to Connor was even worse than it had been when she'd trotted out her FBI-invented background to anyone else.

'My parents died when I was young. I have no siblings.'

There. Done.

'I'm sorry to hear that.' He leaned a little closer as he rested his arms on the table. 'How old were you?'

'Er ... almost sixteen.' The lingering taste of the lovely Italian food turned pasty in her mouth and her tongue felt heavy and unwilling to articulate any more speech.

'How did they die?'

'Plane crash.'

His voice softened. 'There's no good age to lose your parents. I was six when my parents died. Were your parents travelling for work?'

'No. They were going to holiday in Australia and the plane crashed over India. I would've gone with them, but it was school term so I stayed with a friend.'

This was why she avoided forming relationships.

How could she ever have a proper friendship, let alone a relationship, when the person she was with would never know who she really was and what she'd been through?

How could she ever hope to build a happy future on a past built on secrets and lies?

If she ever had a serious relationship, her partner would surely feel betrayed, disillusioned and maybe even embittered if he ever discovered Mia wasn't the person she claimed to be.

'It must've been tough on you. Who took care of you when they died?'

'A family friend.' At least that was the truth.

As part of the witness protection program, the FBI had been planning to relocate her to another part of the US. But her grandmother had intervened right before she'd died and asked Stanley to use his MI5 connections to bring Mia to London.

Stanley had met her at Heathrow, taken her to a safe house and it was there she'd met Violet. It'd all been top secret and they'd supported her tirelessly as she'd worked to rid herself of her American accent, had facial surgery and orthodontic work to alter her appearance, and tutored her endlessly about her false background.

Connor could never know.

Nobody could ever know.

If anyone found out it could put both them and Mia in terrible danger.

'It was a traumatic time for me,' she said. 'I still don't like to talk about it.'

His gaze searched her face for a moment before he said, 'Of course. I understand. Even though I thought I'd buried my grief, I remembered today how agonized I was to learn of my father's death and how helpless I'd felt as a kid that I could do nothing to help my mother as she fought for her life in intensive care after the crash.'

He'd been battling more emotions than his concern over Violet, then.

'Violet has mentioned your parents' accident.' Their personal tragedies created a connection between them—even though Mia hadn't been able to share the true heart-wrenching details of her past.

A connection based on a lie is no connection at all, Mia.

The voice of her conscience felt like a stone dropping into the pit of her stomach.

Don't get caught up in your own fantasy.

This is not a date.

The truth was hard to swallow but had to be faced. Connor was only here because of Violet's emotional blackmail and she needed to remember it.

Chapter Eight

When their dinner plates were cleared away, Connor took a long sip of his wine. 'One more course and we're through our first date. I'll be the first to admit it's been an enjoyable evening.'

His attention was drawn to Mia's cheeks dimpling as she teased, 'As long as you're the first to admit it, I don't mind being the second.'

God but she really was gorgeous.

Even when she'd appeared and descended the staircase as a vision in red, he'd had no idea how enjoyable the evening would be—how much they'd connect on an intellectual level and how easily they'd converse.

It would suit him right now if the night didn't end. If she wasn't his employee he wouldn't be leaving when he drove her back to her place—well, not until morning.

Dragging his thoughts away from sharing a bed with Mia, he said, 'My assistant has rescheduled my most crucial meetings to tomorrow morning, and postponed the rest until Thursday next week. I should be finished by 3pm.' *The morning would drag.* 'Whether or not you go into the office tomorrow morning is up to you. As you suggested, I've told Mike we're doing a trip to the cities on a fact-finding mission about purchasing hotels in each place.'

'Thank you.'

Again, it struck him how different she was from other women he'd dated. She genuinely didn't want to be linked with him and had looked around the restaurant nervously when they'd entered, only seeming to relax when their host had shown them to a very secluded corner.

'We're booked on a commercial flight departing at five o'clock from London City Airport.'

'Venice for the weekend. It seems surreal.' She reached for her napkin and dabbed at her mouth. 'What's the plan exactly?'

'Two full days in Venice, fly to Paris Sunday evening, back to London Tuesday evening and then Gran will have the surgery on Wednesday.'

'I'm worried about her but there's no getting her to go to hospital any earlier. She's the most stubborn person I've ever met.'

Mia was right. He wasn't a bit happy leaving London while Gran's condition 'ticked' away. 'I've told Dawson I expect the nurse and another member of her household staff to be within earshot of her the entire time.'

'She'd hate knowing she was being monitored, but I'm glad there are people close in case she needs help.'

'Dawson and Nell are very protective of her.' They'd worked for his grandparents since before he'd moved in and he had fond memories of sitting in the kitchen while Nell cooked up a storm. Lucy had joined the team after his grandfather's first stroke—almost twenty years ago. It was a very harmonious household. 'Nell came close to boxing my ears a few times when I snuck into the kitchen and stole one of her famous chocolate biscuits right before dinner.'

Mia's laugh was a melodious sound. 'I can't imagine you as a child. Oh, I've seen photos of you on Violet's mantelpiece, but it threw me to see you without your trademark stubble. It's so much a part of you I wouldn't have been surprised if you'd been born with it.'

Her comment took him by surprise.

Was she flirting with him or was this simply Mia—a woman who called things as she saw them?

'Born with a silver spoon in your mouth and a silver razor on the bath stand,' she laughed.

The musical lilt was infectious.

'Oh dear.' She stifled another laugh. 'I probably shouldn't have said that!'

Connor smiled. He enjoyed her poking fun at him. Had any woman—apart from his grandmother—ever done that?

Even his very capable assistant never cracked jokes with him.

Was he too serious?

Mia sobered. 'Back to Venice, Violet told me she's busy planning our itinerary.'

Oh, yes. 'She'll email us tomorrow and expects each place or experience on her list to be ticked off before we return.' His lips twisted. 'She also said she wants photographic proof.'

'That's so Violet.' Mia shook her head. 'I asked her to let us see each other here in London but she wouldn't budge.'

'She's hell-bent on Venice and Paris.'

'Why those two cities?'

Connor shifted uncomfortably in his chair. 'Venice is where she and my grandfather met and fell in love.' He expelled an audible breath. 'Paris is where they spent their honeymoon.'

The skin across Mia's chest became blotchy. 'Nothing subtle about our Violet, is there?'

His fingers twirled his wine glass around very slowly on the pristine white linen tablecloth as he tried to untangle his feelings and put them into words. 'Mia, when I drove to pick you up I still resented this whole scheme.'

Her focus was on her hands, clasped tightly together on the edge of the table. 'I wasn't any happier about it.'

'But it's turned out well. We've both admitted we've enjoyed ourselves tonight.'

Mia looked up quickly and her eyes scanned his face before she replied. 'We have.'

What had she expected to see in his expression? Was she still questioning his sincerity? 'Tonight's been really surprising. Although I wouldn't admit it to Gran, I've really enjoyed your company, and I'm looking forward to the next few days.'

'Really?'

'Honestly. I'm only concerned about leaving Gran.'

'Oh.' Her fingertips plucked at the tablecloth and colour swept up her neck and into her cheeks. 'Er ... Have you been to either place before?'

'Many times, but it's always been for business and there's never been any time for sightseeing.'

'I've visited Paris, but not Venice.'

Her words were stilted and he wanted to restore the easy atmosphere between them. 'Shall we make the most of it and enjoy playing tourist together?' She didn't answer immediately and he grimaced. 'You have to think so long and hard about it?'

She shook her head, but answered tentatively, 'Our truce has held over dinner.'

'Easily.' Then he teased, 'Surely you don't think I'm quite as conceited, arrogant and egotistical as you did earlier today?'

'I wouldn't go *quite* that far now.'

Connor laughed. He could see she was trying to keep a straight face, but her dimples were peeking at him. 'What if I admit I no longer think you put Gran up to this?'

She quirked an eyebrow at him. 'You mean you no longer think I'm some deranged Connor Stewart groupie?'

'You've convinced me I was wrong.'

'Good, because that was pretty conceited.'

'I'm—'

'But you insulted me far more with your insinuation that I'm out to fleece Violet and the mahjong ladies.'

'I'm sorry.' Connor had few regrets, but he wished he could go back in time and change the way he'd behaved in her office. 'I let my cynical nature get the better of me and jumped to conclusions. I have to eat a lot of my words from this afternoon.' He paused, looked at his wine glass for a second before he looked back at Mia and confessed, 'I said I'd never be attracted to you, but I was wrong.'

Mia gulped. 'Anyone can have a makeover. This isn't me.'

'Mia. Please.' He didn't want her to think this was only about her appearance.

Clamping her lips together, she looked as though she braced herself for whatever was coming next.

Damn!

'I'm not as shallow as you seem to think.' He shook his head as he tried to explain. 'Yes, I was attracted to you the second I saw you coming down the stairs—any heterosexual male would've been—but that was purely a physical reaction.'

He heard her breath catch.

'You're also attractive to me because you're an intelligent and articulate woman. I admire the passion you have for your work and I've enjoyed all our conversation.' Her lips had parted and she frowned as though she couldn't quite believe what he told her. 'I like your straight shooting and I've laughed more with you tonight than I can ever recall laughing on a date. In fact, I can't remember when I've enjoyed a dinner date more.'

Her head snapped back. 'Violet was right. You've definitely been dating the wrong women.'

This time he didn't laugh. 'Gran was right thinking we'd get along well together—that I'd be attracted to the spirit you have—but you can relax. I have no intention of acting on my attraction. This can't go any further than friendship.'

'It can't?' She sounded disappointed and gave herself a small shake. 'I mean, of course it can't.'

It hadn't been necessary for him to admit his attraction but, for some pressing reason, it was important to him that she knew she was attractive. He wanted her to have the confidence to show everyone who she really was and not revert to being Miss Mouse who hugged the wall of the meeting room and studied her feet rather than the presentation slides.

He knew it would be impossible now to sit through one of her presentations without wanting to talk to her, but he was her boss and he had to curb his desire.

'I don't enter into relationships with any type of long-term plan in mind, Mia,' he warned. 'And when it comes to my employees, I keep it strictly professional.'

***

'I'm glad to hear it.'

Well, Mia was glad he wasn't looking for something serious, anyway. Had he been prepared to date employees she would've signed the dotted line on a contract offering a casual relationship.

Her heart beat faster at the thought of having any sort of relationship with Connor. Without meaning to, her gaze zeroed in on his mouth.

It would be so good to be kissed by him.

'You spoke earlier about how important it is to find the seam of gold.' For a moment, his lean fingers ran up and down the stem of his wineglass. 'Gran has found your gold and brought it to the surface. Now it's up to you to hold it up for all to see. You're the real deal, aren't you Mia Simms?'

Oh, no.

His words were a stark, painful reminder that so much about her was fake.

'What you see is fool's gold, Connor.' Her voice was wooden. 'The way I look tonight isn't me.' She drew a breath to ease the constriction in her chest.

None of what you see before you is really who I am.

None of what I tell you about my past is the truth.

I'm so sorry I have to lie to you.

He surprised her by saying, 'Cinderella's clothes may have turned back to rags as the clock struck midnight, but she still had the same soul.'

'I'm no Cinderella and it would be dangerous for you to think otherwise.' She couldn't let him buy into Violet's fairytale.

'Dangerous? I don't think so.' He frowned. 'You've mentioned safety a couple of times. What are you afraid of?'

Discovery.

Death.

She looked across at Connor and saw he was waiting for her response as though he cared. Digging deep, she reminded herself that no matter what Violet had planned, there could be no relationship in her future.

Not with Connor.

Not with anyone.

No relationship built on lies could endure.

'Everyone has fears.' She shrugged. 'But I'm no longer worried about spending time with you.'

'You've given up on the idea of me having a personality transplant?'

She couldn't help but grin. 'Yes.'

'I'm glad to hear it.' His tone was casual, but his eyes still held questions.

Avoiding those questions, her gaze dropped to his mouth. Instantly her pulse accelerated and fluttered at the base of her neck and inside her wrists.

'If you weren't my employee, Mia, and if you were the sort of woman who might accept a short-term relationship, I'd be tempted...'

She was tempted too.

'I have no intention of resigning from my job any time soon.'

The note of regret in her voice was obvious and he looked sharply at her but Mia signalled to the waiter that she was ready for dessert.

It was good Connor wasn't intent on trying to turn their four days into a fling because it would be impossible for her to resist the man she'd had dinner with this evening. When Connor Stewart turned on the charm, the only hope any woman had to resist him would be to invest in a chastity belt and throw away the key.

But who in their right mind would want to resist him?

Chapter Nine

Mia's steps were light as she walked through the sumptuous Aman Canal Grande Hotel to meet Connor. During the flight over—when he hadn't been busy on his laptop—the mood between them had been relaxed and she couldn't wait to explore Venice with him.

Violet and the stylist had overridden all Mia's arguments and packed stylish new outfits which made the most of her figure. Today's three-quarter length navy pants and off-the-shoulder white shirt with a gold, red and blue insignia were very classy and looked so good, Mia had given into a wave of recklessness.

Slipping off the manacles of her self-restraint, she'd swept her hair into a loose ponytail instead of confining it into a bun. She'd even decided to shove her spectacles into her tote bag and opted to hide behind her more fashionable sunglasses. A fizz of satisfaction had burst through her veins as she'd regarded herself in the mirror. A little flame flickered with the hope that Connor would find her too attractive to resist.

But, as she reached the foyer, she realised that making the most of her looks had been a mistake. She was drawing too much attention. Too many admiring male glances.

Head down, she continued out onto the covered jetty at the front of the hotel.

I'm in Venice and I'm safe. Nobody is going to recognise me here.

'Buongiorno bellissima signorina.' The doorman greeted her with a flirtatious wink. 'Would you like me to arrange a gondola or water taxi for you?'

Her hands were clammy and she wished to hell she'd remembered how much comfort there was in blending into the shadows.

'Buongiorno,' she replied automatically. 'Not yet, thanks. I'm waiting for my ... friend.'

With an almost wolfish smile, the man said, 'He is very lucky.'

'I didn't say it was a man.'

He smiled broadly. 'You didn't have to signorina.'

'Oh.' Feeling horribly out of her depth she moved further down the jetty.

Dressing like this had been a mistake. A terrible mistake.

She could always use the hair elastic and wind her hair into a bun again rather than a ponytail, and once her lipstick had worn off, she wouldn't re-apply it.

Would that be enough to stop attracting attention? Mia kept her gaze firmly focused on the canal. She watched a vaporetto passing by and saw that the public waterbus was filled with tourists, many of whom had cameras pointed in the direction of the famous hotel.

Sully!

Mia's eyes widened and her hand flew to cover her mouth as she gasped.

Surely not?

Her gaze zeroed in on a man whose attention was on the facade of the hotel.

No!

Resisting the urge to run back inside, she turned quickly and put her head down, pretending to look for something in her bag.

Perspiration beaded her upper lip and her heart punched against her rib cage.

It'd been over ten years since she'd seen Giovani's henchman and she couldn't be certain it was him, but she didn't dare risk taking another look.

Breathe, Mia.

I must be wrong.

Sully couldn't be in Venice. He rarely strayed from Giovanni's side and Giovanni never left New York.

She must be mistaken. It couldn't have been Sully.

Taking a deep breath, she tried to banish her fears. All she'd had was a fleeting look at the man. It was just her overactive imagination.

She'd projected her dread of being recognised, and linked the man in the vaporetto with her past.

A past you left behind years ago.

A past that lies thousands of miles away.

Steeling herself, she turned to look back at the man. The vaporetto had moved further down the canal and she could only see his back, but tension drained from her shoulders and she gave a small laugh in relief.

The man's hair was plaited in a long ponytail.

Sully had always kept his hair short. Besides, hadn't Sully been taller and not quite as thick set?

She leaned on the railing for support as she put her paranoia firmly from her mind.

Today was going to be a good day.

She had nothing to worry about.

'Good morning, Mia. You look stunning.'

Looking up at Connor, her cares were forgotten. Dressed casually in denim jeans and a blue polo top, Connor embodied the definition of stunning. 'Good morning.' 'Did you sleep well?'

'Yes, thanks. It's quiet here without cars.'

'The vaporettos aren't exactly silent.'

'No, but they're nowhere near as noisy as London traffic.'

He sent her a bemused frown. 'You were very vague about where you lived when you wouldn't allow me to drop you home the other night. Which part of London do you call home?'

She couldn't tell him she lived around the corner from Violet or it would raise questions she wasn't prepared to answer. 'I'm not really sure I do call London home,' she prevaricated. 'I think I'm more of a country than a city girl.'

'Where did you grow up?'

Damn. Damn.

Guilt pressed hard on her shoulders and a familiar heaviness settled in her chest. She had to tell Connor a bald-faced lie and stick with the background Mia Simms had been given. She would always be a prisoner to this deceit. 'Southern England.'

'That makes sense. You speak with the received pronunciation one would expect from the south. Did you go to a private school?'

For a second her memory files went blank and she almost blurted out the name of the high school she'd attended in the States. 'For a time.'

When he arched an eyebrow, she expanded, 'I went to public school initially, then finished in private school once my parents passed away.'

Another half-truth.

What she'd said about school was right because Stanley and Violet had enrolled her in a posh private girls' school when it'd come time for her to re-enter the world and complete her last years of school in the UK.

What she'd said about her 'parents' was an out and out lie because she'd never known her father. She didn't know whether he was alive or dead. She didn't even know his name.

'So, first stop this morning is the Doge's Palace, then we explore the other sites around St Mark's Square?' she asked, before he could delve any deeper into her fabricated background.

'That's right. After we've toured through the palace we can enjoy a coffee on the Square. Unless you've changed your mind and want to have breakfast first rather than brunch?'

'No. The concierge insisted it was important to get to the palace early or the queues would be horrendous.'

The doorman who'd greeted Mia earlier signalled to them that a gondola had arrived. They'd used the hotel's water taxi from the airport, so this would be Mia's first authentic experience on the canal.

'*Buongiorno*,' the gondolier greeted. 'I am Vincento. I take you to Piazza San Marco, *si?*'

'Here, take my hand to steady yourself,' Connor told Mia as she went to hop into the beautiful black boat.

Holding Connor's hand may have been meant to steady her, but it had quite the opposite effect. The second her hand was encased in the warm, masculine strength of his, she was bombarded with sensory signals telling her how good it felt. Her legs felt weak and uncoordinated as every other thought process was obliterated for a few micro seconds. Just enough time for her to completely lose her balance.

If it hadn't been for Connor's firm hold, and Vincento grabbing her flailing left arm, she would've ended up in the aqua waters of the canal.

'Oh my gosh!' She sucked in a huge breath as the men guided her onto the plush red velvet seat.

'Are you alright, *signorina?*' Vincento asked.

'Yes, thank you. Just a bit breathless.'

The cause of her breathlessness stepped into the gondola and sat beside her. 'The idea is to see the Grand Canal from the gondola,' Connor said with a smile. 'The hotel has a pool if you really want to go for a swim.'

Feeling all sorts of foolish, Mia laughed along. 'I'm sorry. I should warn you that I'm a bit accident prone.'

'Hm. As one young tennis player can confirm, right?'

'Yes,' she responded sheepishly. 'I should never have told you that story. You're going to tease me unmercifully about it, aren't you?'

'Guaranteed!'

Oh dear. Connor's smile made her heart flip every time.

She turned her head to look up at the gondolier. 'Venice has turned on spectacular weather for us, Vincento.'

'But of course, *signorina*. Venice has always the beautiful weather.'

'Of course it does,' she agreed with a broad smile.

'Sit back and stop flirting with Vincento,' Connor said lightly. 'You're supposed to enjoy the scenery.'

Flirting? Hardly. Mia was quite certain she didn't know how to flirt. But she sat back anyway, wanting to enjoy the postcard perfect shots of life on the Grand Canal.

But ... oh! When she reclined, Connor's body was hard up against hers and she was acutely aware of his muscular thigh and the strength and heat radiating from it.

As her mouth dried, she wished she'd brought a bottle of water with her from the hotel.

'You are from England, no?' Vincento asked as he powered them along with smooth strokes.

'Yes,' Connor answered.

'Your first time to Venice?'

'I've been here before, but it's Mia's first visit.'

'Then I play tour guide for you, *signorina*.'

It was fantastic to ride down the Grand Canal and have the native Venetian speak proudly of his heritage. He pointed out various buildings and the Moroccan influence on the architecture of some of them. Once or twice she even managed to stop focusing on the feel of Connor's body next to hers—for all of about ten seconds.

'Why are all the gondolas black, Vincento?' Her question was as much out of needing to distract herself from her awareness of Connor as it was from genuine curiosity.

'Not all are black but all working boats must be black. Years ago, Venetian families spent very much money to have the most beautiful gondolas. Too much was spent and the Venice Senate passed a law in 1562 forcing all gondolas to be painted black. Today...'

Mia didn't take in the rest of his explanation because Connor shifted and put one arm around her shoulders before he leaned to whisper in her ear, 'I hope you don't mind. I wouldn't tell a Venetian, but it's a bit cramped in these things.'

Most Venetians weren't built with shoulders so broad they'd pass for rugby players. Was it a convenient way of avoiding cramp? Mia kind of hoped Connor was looking for an excuse to sit closer.

No. He'd made it clear he wasn't going to pursue an affair with her.

Even if he doesn't mean anything by it, why not enjoy it? Why not relax and pretend I'm in Venice with my lover?

Another gondolier in his trademark striped top, red sash and white straw hat overtook them. As he passed he made a comment to Vincento in rapid-fire Italian and both men laughed heartily.

'This is fantastic,' she told Connor. 'There's so much atmosphere and elegance in this city. I've got to admit I'm glad Violet insisted we come.'

Vincento said, 'Venice is very romantic city, *si?*

'*Si,*' Mia agreed.

'My friend who go past, he tell me I should sing for you.'

She was surprised. 'I thought the gondoliers didn't sing—that we'd need to hire a singer and accordionist for that.'

'You are in luck! I am one of few who sing.' He proceeded to burst into song.

When he finished the tune, Mia applauded. 'Well done, Vincento!'

He paused mid-stroke and took a slight bow. 'Ah, but I should have explained. There is a fee for my singing.'

Mia and Connor both chuckled in wry amusement.

'Of course there is,' Connor agreed.

'That was traditional Venetian love song and the fee is my passengers must kiss as we pass under next bridge.'

Mia had thought he meant an extra monetary fee. Her amusement ended at the mention of a kiss and she looked at Connor uncertainly.

Holding one hand up, he sent her a cheeky grin and said, 'I promise I didn't pay him earlier to say that.'

It's all a joke.

We're not really expected to kiss and, anyway, Connor would never kiss me.

Relief should've had her smiling, yet she couldn't deny that disappointment made her pulse sluggish. 'Obviously a Venetian sense of humour.'

'You think?' Connor sent her a doubtful look.

'Get ready, lovers,' Vincento urged. 'Bridge coming up.'

'Are you ready, Mia?'

'No...' Connor couldn't be serious.

He moved his head so his words husked in her ear. 'We can't be bad sports about this.'

'We can't kiss!' Sluggishness turned into panic. 'We'll tell him we're cousins, or I've got a throat infection!'

'Come on, Mia.' The smile hovering around his lips told her he was enjoying watching her squirm. 'One little kiss won't hurt us as payment for Vincento's talented singing.'

'Stop it,' she hissed in a vehement undertone as he slid her sunglasses off her nose and placed them on her lap. 'You're making fun of me. I know you have absolutely no intention of kissing me.'

'I would never make fun of you.' The wink Connor sent her made her heart flip. 'When in Venice, do as the Venetians do!'

Her heart went into overdrive when he focused on her mouth with unmistakably single-minded intent. One hand lifted and slid around her neck and under her ponytail while the other cupped her chin. His thumb brushed down her cheek and grazed the corner of her mouth.

The contact was electric.

Everywhere he touched left her skin tingling and the current arced through her and earthed right at the juncture of her thighs.

Oh, dear Lord. He really was going to kiss her.

Her heart hammered.

Her breaths were rapid and shallow.

Tension knotted inside her and every word of protest jammed in her dry throat.

He's playing with me. There's no need to panic. He'll just deliver a peck and be done with it. I mustn't let him see I'm rattled ... or how much I'd like it to be a real kiss.

As his dark head angled down towards hers, she willed herself to relax; to pretend she was sophisticated and could take all this in her stride. But even anticipating the kiss would be over before it had begun, acute—almost torturous—expectation zapped across every nerve synapse.

His gaze caught and held hers as his head drew closer.

Closing her eyes was supposed to provide her with a screen so he couldn't see her emotions and guess at her inner turmoil. All it did was make matters worse. It sharpened her senses to the subtle citrus scent of his cologne, the possessive, confident touch of his hands on her skin and the warmth of his breath on the corner of her mouth before it fanned across her lips.

All rational thought was driven from her mind as she found herself leaning towards the warmth, wanting his kiss more than she wanted to draw her next breath, knowing innately that he could unleash his full sensual expertise to make her senses swim.

Oh.

Her lips parted on an exclamation of delight as his mouth settled over hers and began an unhurried, tantalising and feather-light exploration. The pressure may have been gentle, but the heat melding their mouths together seared through her as though he branded her. And, when he increased the pressure of his kisses, she responded to his expert persuasion without any thought of resistance.

Oh wow.

The sweep of his tongue against her lower lip detonated desire deep within her; in a place she'd never recognised as being so achingly hollow. The sensations bombarding her were so amazing she could hardly register them all. Unable to tread water in this deep sea of sensuality, she was pulled along in his tow and swept away from all she'd ever known and towards all she'd hoped to discover.

The world dissolved around her and she became lost to everything but him and the incredibly intimate hint of mint on his tongue as it glided slowly against hers and engaged her in an erotic, evocative dance that was as entrancing as a sorcerer's spell. Flames danced high around them, whipped up into a passionate tango the likes of which she'd never known.

Mia was a willing captive to the riotous sensations pervading every cell. Her arms reached up of their own volition and thrilled at the tactile delight of having her fingers spear through his thick hair.

As he transferred his attention to nibbling gently on her lower lip, her breasts tingled. They seemed to swell, protesting at being confined and begging for the intimacy of his touch.

It would be heaven if she could simply rid herself of her clothing and offer her pouting breasts to Connor so his mouth could wreak the same havoc on each tip the way he was doing to her lips and tongue.

A soft moan of protest escaped as he ended the kiss.

Mia's eyelids snapped open, her gaze was ensnared by his and she was powerless to mask her need. She had neither the will, nor the sophistication, to do so. What had happened was completely outside her experience.

'Bravo!' Vincento exclaimed. 'Now you have no need to visit the tragic Bridge of Sighs, *signore*. You have made this the romantic bridge of your *signorina's* sighs and one she will always remember!'

Oh hell!

Mia came back to earth with a thump and felt the heat of a blush on her chest sweeping up her neck and all the way to her cheeks. Damn her inability to control her blushes.

She'd forgotten the gondolier stood behind them; forgotten they were in the very public space of the canal. Everything but Connor and his bone-meltingly expert kisses had faded from her mind.

She wasn't dreaming.

Connor had kissed her.

Thoroughly.

And Mia had responded.

Enthusiastically.

What had she been thinking?

What had *he* been thinking?

Completely unaware that Connor's kisses had rocked Mia's world more effectively than the wash of a passing vaporetto against the gondola, Vincento continued the tour. 'On your left...'

Mia was unable to focus on a single thing the gondolier said. Sliding her sunglasses firmly back into place, she stared straight ahead of her. She wasn't taking in any of the sights, she was merely trying to avoid eye contact with Connor and come to grips with what had happened and how she felt about it.

How on earth did they proceed from here?

Mortified by her ready and willing response to him, she decided the only way to continue was to pretend it had never happened.

When they pulled into the jetty near the famous palace, Mia was quick to alight the gondola and was surprised when a teenage boy ran towards them calling out a greeting.

'This is Peppi,' Vincento said proudly. 'He is my son and excellent photographer. He has souvenir for you, *si*?'

'Oh!'

Peppi must have been in prime position on the bridge because he'd captured several polaroid photos of Connor and Mia immediately before, during and after their lips had locked together.

'You like?' Peppi asked eagerly.

No. Mia didn't like them. Not one little bit.

They exposed way too much of what she'd been feeling.

Way too much starry-eyed satisfaction.

Way too much dreamy desire for more when the kisses had come to an end.

If Mia had possessed the ability to become invisible, she would have. She couldn't think of a suitable response. If only she'd still had her sunglasses in place, the photos would be less damning.

'I think you've done an excellent job capturing the moment, Peppi.' Connor pulled some Euro notes out of his wallet, handing them to Peppi. 'We'll purchase all the photos from you. *Grazi* Peppi. *Grazi* Vincento.'

At least the incriminating evidence wouldn't fall into anyone else's hands. How horrifying if the press got hold of these images!

'Enjoy your time in our beautiful city,' Vincento said with a bow.

After their farewells, Connor handed Mia the photos. 'You blush beautifully, Mia, but why are you so embarrassed by our kiss?'

'It should never have happened.' She thrust the photos into her open tote bag and kept walking.

'We couldn't ignore Vincento's request and we made Peppi's day. He has quite a nice little sideline going there and I like to reward entrepreneurs.'

Never mind making Peppi's day. The delicious kiss had been the highlight of Mia's life, but she wasn't going to let Connor know it. 'If you wanted to humour Vincento, you could've kept it to a chaste peck.' If he had kept it brief, she wouldn't have embarrassed herself by responding to him so unreservedly when he obviously hadn't been affected at all.

'Where would be the fun in that?'

'It wasn't fun. It was...'

'A fabulously good first kiss.'

She stopped dead and turned towards him aghast. 'How did you know?'

Had she kissed so badly?

'Know what?'

'That it was my first...' Trailing off, she frowned.

He jerked his head back and his eyes widened. 'You've never been kissed before?'

The pulse of the awkward silence throbbed through her.

'But you knew.' Confusion clouded her mind. 'You called it a first kiss.'

Connor gave a small sound of disbelief. 'I meant it was *our* first kiss.'

Mia groaned. Was it possible for her to blush any more before someone picked her up and threw her in the canal to cool off?

'I had no idea,' Connor told her. 'How is it that you're twenty-six...?' He rolled his eyes heavenward and grimaced.

The obvious went unsaid. Nobody had kissed her because she generally looked so unappealing. Her disguise had been so effective, she hadn't even been asked out on a date by the most boring, introverted and desperate staff member of the accounting department.

And that's the way it has to be.

'Forget I asked,' he groaned.

'Better still, forget it happened!' she fired back.

'That might be a problem.' Connor placed his hands on her shoulders and gave her an intense look. 'I thought it was a great kiss. Maybe the wisest course of action would be for both of us to forget it happened, but I don't want to.' His hand moved quickly to fish the top photo from where she'd thrown them carelessly into her tote bag. Holding it up so they could both see it, he said, 'If it's true that a picture paints a thousand words, I doubt you'll be able to forget about it either.'

Connor was completely focused on her response and his intensity made her weak at the knees.

She snatched the photo from his hand and shoved it back in the bag before transferring her bag to the opposite shoulder away from him. 'I can and I will.' 'Liar,' he said softly.

'What would be the point in remembering it?'

He reached out and perched her sunglasses on top of her head. 'This is the point.' Then his lips descended again.

Mia's lips parted on a gasp a split second before his brushed over the contours of hers.

This kiss was a leisurely, teasing exploration that was so pleasurably erotic, she couldn't contemplate resisting him. As his tongue tip flicked over her lower lip, then probed the interior of her mouth to tangle with hers, it no longer mattered why Connor was kissing her. The only thing of importance was for him to keep kissing her and not stop.

Held in the thrall of wonderment of each new, intimate sensation, Mia heard the mewl of pleasure emerging from deep in the back of her throat as her hands crept to his chest and spread over the fabric of his polo shirt.

This was exquisite.

Divine.

The only way it could possibly be better was if she could bunch up the fabric in her hands and haul the shirt up over his head so she could feel the heat of his naked flesh, learn the contours of his body and feel his strong heartbeat without the barrier between them.

The wolf whistle from a passing local would've gone unheeded by Mia, but Connor drew his head back and broke their kiss.

No! That's not what she wanted. She wanted him to go on kissing her all day. Kissing her until everything else was forgotten.

His voice was husky as he said, 'Not only is it worth remembering. It also bears repeating.'

Then let's do it again and again.

Kiss me over and over and don't ever stop.

It was only when Connor dropped her sunglasses into her tote bag that she realised they'd come off her head at some point and he'd held them in his hand.

Common sense told her she needed to fight for some small measure of composure, especially when they were in full view of all passers-by. 'Connor?'

'A good first kiss deserves a second, and a second definitely deserves a third...'

Yes, please.

The gentle introduction was over and as fabulous as it had been, she welcomed the difference.

This time, when he cupped her face with his hands, her mouth was ready for his. At least she thought it was. What she hadn't been ready for was the passion being dialled up to scorching hot. This searing kiss made flames lick along each fibre of her being and threatened to send her into complete meltdown. It made her lean into his body to draw from his strength and to stay upright.

Unlike his other kisses, this time his mouth was a passionate furnace burning with possession, stopping the breath in her throat and making her heartbeat reverberate through her skull.

The increased pressure of his mouth made each kiss more urgent. The slick invasion of his tongue into the warm cavity of her mouth made each kiss more intimate.

The flames licked higher.

Unadulterated excitement pounded through her.

The blood in her veins beat a rapid tattoo of need at the base of her throat and in her ears.

Oh more.

She wanted so much more as she trembled against his powerfully broad frame with unfulfilled need. Even though she didn't understand what she craved, she knew intuitively that Connor did—and that he could deliver it.

Then the kiss was over.

An unfamiliar throaty sound of protest pushed past her vocal cords when he lifted his mouth away from hers. Although her lips still tingled and the slightly minty taste of him lingered in her mouth, it wasn't enough.

'Amazing!' He shook his head as he looked at her in confusion. 'That was madness, but I don't regret it.' His hands still cradled her head. 'It wasn't supposed to happen, Mia. I promised myself it wouldn't happen and that I'd keep myself in check. Hell! I gave you assurances. But somehow when I'm around you, I don't act the way I should.'

'It's mutual.' She lowered her eyes and heard him let out a long breath.

'You're my employee.'

'Yes.' But did it really matter?

'You told me you're not resigning any time soon.'

'I'm not.'

'I vowed I wouldn't give into this. I barely know you.' 'Do you really need to?'

A furrow appeared between his brows. 'You're not exactly open to discussing your life, are you?'

'No.' A sliver of unease shot through her. 'But neither of us wants a long-term relationship.'

He sent her a considering look. 'Our chemistry is undeniable and it's growing stronger every second I'm with you.'

Chemistry.

It was amazing he felt it too, but even as he acknowledged it, a thousand nagging doubts flitted through her mind.

She shook her head to discourage a vendor who caught her eye and held out a stick full of Harlequin puppets. Then she faced Connor again. 'You would never have kissed me if I hadn't had a makeover.'

His mouth compressed. 'You're possibly right.'

She wasn't sure whether to be crushed when he didn't bother denying it or whether she should respect his honesty. 'There's no *possibly* about it. I'm definitely right.'

His frown was thoughtful—as though he was reaching deep inside himself and analysing his own actions. 'You're a very attractive woman now. But, even before your makeover, there was a definite spark between us the afternoon I came to your office.'

'That's an understatement!' she said with a wry smile. 'I would've classified it as more of an explosion.'

'You impressed me the way you held your ground. I found it sassy. Sexy.'

Sexy? 'You seemed more ticked off than attracted.'

'Mm. Well, I was already in a mood and having holes blown into my theories about you didn't help.'

'I've been part of the marketing team for years and have made countless presentations to you. You've never been attracted to me.' She was shooting herself in the foot here, but she had to hold on to reality before this chemistry tipped her over the edge and made her believe her fantasies could come true.

'But I'm only beginning to see the real you, aren't I?' he countered. 'The woman who's made all those presentations to me wasn't really who you are. You've been hiding her away all this time—cloaking your body, subduing your spirit and leashing your innate sensuality.'

Innate sensuality?

Oh hell. His words made her world spin. They were so flattering, but they also reminded her of why she'd hidden away.

How could she have forgotten how imperative it was to continue with her masquerade?

'It doesn't matter that your grandmother put me in fancy clothes, I'm still the woman who works in your marketing department and when we return from this trip I'll be that woman again.'

'Are you seriously telling me you'd rather continue to be mousy Mia than the sexy woman I'm with now who has every male head turning her way?'

She had to work hard to concentrate on his question because he'd called her sexy. Again. 'I'll have no use for these clothes when I return to London.'

'You didn't look at your reflection this morning and get a kick of pleasure?'

How did he know?

She closed her eyes for a second, trying desperately to work out how she could express herself so he'd leave the topic alone. 'I ... I'm not feeling at all like myself right now. Looking like this ... Being here in Venice with you ... It's all very surreal and confusing.'

His hands fell away and he took a step backwards. 'It would be wrong of me to take advantage of your confusion.'

No! He was giving up way too easily. Despite her protest—and knowing it was too dangerous to keep playing this role—the second he let her go she felt gutted.

Why did this have to be so complicated when it was so simple?

Connor wanted to kiss her and she wanted to kiss him.

Damn that there were so many things that stood in the way of it happening again.

'I had no idea you were so inexperienced.' Was he talking to her or to himself? 'To take this to its natural conclusion would be unthinkable on so many levels.'

The pragmatic part of her brain told her she should be thankful he seemed to be talking himself out of it. If Connor decided to turn on the charm and pursue her, she wouldn't be safe. She'd be powerless to resist the pull of her own desire.

Safe.

There was the word that had dominated her life ever since she'd been a little girl.

Safe meant staying alive, yet Violet had questioned whether Mia was truly living.

Searching Connor's profile as he turned away from her, Mia considered her options. For her, relationships couldn't be completely honest so they had to be avoided. But Connor didn't have relationships. He'd avoided true relationships since his divorce. Now, he only had affairs.

Wouldn't it be better to have a passionate affair than to remain a virgin for the rest of her life?

And, as well as an almost iron-clad guarantee of fabulous sex, any affair she had with Connor wouldn't involve hurt feelings. He would be the one to break it off which would mean that she didn't have to worry about hurting him.

Chemistry, he'd said.

If he was truly attracted to her, how dangerous could it be to indulge in a little flirtation with him as they spent the next four days together in two of the most beautiful cities in the world? No one would end up heartbroken, and she'd enjoy a hot, sexy, once-in-a-lifetime fling.

A little imp in Mia's ear said she needn't feel guilty about deceiving Connor about her past. The future couldn't be built on lies of the past, but if Connor was never going to be interested in offering her a future, the imp told her should consider seizing the present.

To hell with it. She was more than open to it. If Connor's kisses could blow her away so much, his lovemaking would surely be as incredible as she'd always imagined it would be.

But maybe he didn't want to make love to a virgin. Or maybe he wouldn't want to complicate matters between them when he was her boss and his grandmother was her friend.

Courage, Mia, she told herself. *You've been playing safe most of your life.*

Live for the moment.

Live a little dangerously, but LIVE.

'Connor?'

He turned back to face her.

'I'm not actually here as your employee, am I?' she asked boldly. 'Despite what you told Mike, this trip has nothing to do with work.'

He stared at her for a moment. 'Don't tempt me, Mia.'

He turned away from her and looked out at the canal, but not before she saw his inner struggle. The indecision in his eyes was both thrilling and disappointing. That he was fighting against his attraction confirmed he wasn't a selfish cad. He was considering how it would play out for her, too, if they indulged in an affair. On the other hand, it was bitterly disappointing. She'd played her hand and lost.

Where to from here?

Keep calm and drink tea.

The very British adage was good advice. As soon as they'd toured the Doge's Palace, she'd sit back on the square and order a cup of Earl Grey even if she'd rather have a stiff shot of vodka.

No, screamed the part of her who'd spent the first sixteen years of her life as an American. *Don't give into the stiff upper lip attitude when this is something you want so much; something that's in your reach if you're brave enough to grab it.*

Perhaps the American in her had been suppressed for too long because now she was breaking free with vengeance. For once in her life she was going to push the safety barriers away and embrace a little danger.

Chapter Ten

Irrational.

Insensitive.

Selfish.

Connor berated himself and wondered what it was about Mia that made him lose control and behave so *badly* out of character.

First, he'd launched a scathing, unwarranted attack on her in her office and now he'd abandoned his principles about employer-employee relations and kissed her.

Kissed her when she'd never damned well been kissed before!

What was wrong with him?

Yes, their dinner in London had been the most enjoyable and memorable he'd had. Yes, he admired Mia's fiery spirit and respected the passion she had for her work. And yes, both her personality and her made-over appearance had turned her into one of the sexiest women he'd ever met, but *none of that mattered.*

It was imperative he control his physical attraction to her. He should never have given into the moment of impulsive insanity and kissed her.

Stifling the groan that threatened to rumble from his throat when he recalled those kisses, he was frustrated he'd let instinct overtake logic. Their kisses had turned his mind to mush and his body into a raging mass of sexual desire the like of which he hadn't known since he was a hormone-driven teenager. Damn it all! A powerful spike of lust had made him want to carry her to the nearest bed and drive into her until she came apart in his arms and called out his name in rapture.

Her voice broke into his thoughts. 'According to my map, the entrance to the palace is over there.'

The palace.

Trying to pull himself together, he looked back out onto the water traffic on the busy Grand Canal before he turned back to her.

They were here to see the palace.

They needed to go and join the line.

As much as he tried to put what had happened behind him, it was impossible. He gave her a brief nod and fell into step beside her.

She'd never been kissed before.

Of course she'd looked all passion-glazed in Peppi's photos. It was her first kiss for God's sake. She probably would've responded like that to any man who'd kissed her. Even if she had felt the explosion he'd felt, she wouldn't know how high voltage the kisses were because she had nothing to compare them to.

Connor knew.

Of all the women he'd kissed, none of them had made him completely lose control, drawing him like a magnet the way Mia had. Oh, he'd told himself he was merely playing along with Vincento's suggestion—that it would be churlish to refuse—but it'd been an excuse.

Deep down, he'd been wondering what it would be like to kiss Mia ever since she'd walked down Gran's staircase; maybe even earlier when she'd stood up to him in her office. And, when he'd seen her on the jetty this morning, all he could think about was having her in his arms.

On the gondola, he'd cupped her face and told himself he'd only have a small taste. Just enough to satisfy his curiosity.

Nothing in his significant experience had prepared him for how sweet the taste would be. The intended relatively chaste kiss had turned into something else entirely and, from the second their lips had met, sensation had taken over and demanded the kiss be deepened. Sipping at her lips hadn't been enough. Connor had wanted—needed—to explore the delights of her mouth. The way she'd returned his kisses with unfettered abandon had encouraged him, lighting the fuse to a powder keg of pleasure bordering on sheer delirium.

Mia Simms was a naturally sensual woman.

Mia Simms was also out of bounds.

If she'd never been kissed before, she had to be a virgin and Connor did not take virgins to bed.

Besides, given her age, Mia must surely be holding out for her Mr Right to come along, fall madly in love with her and put a ring on her finger. Connor knew he was Mr Wrong. His lovers were experienced women who weren't looking for a wedding ring.

'I thought there'd be more pigeons.'

Pigeons?

She was looking up at the tops of the buildings.

He was castigating his behaviour and agonising over how he was going to keep his hands off her for the next four days and she was thinking about bloody pigeons?

'In all the photos I've seen of St Mark's Square there've been more pigeons,' she elaborated.

Was she really able to go from those explosive kisses to thinking about crapping bloody pigeons in less than a hundred paces? Obviously, she hadn't been as affected by their kisses as he had. How could she hint they have an affair in one breath and then accept so easily when he'd told her it wasn't going to happen?

Fine. He'd follow her lead.

'The officials banned people from feeding the birds over a decade ago,' he said. 'If we sit on the square at Caffè Florian I'm certain we'll be pestered by them.'

'I'm glad Violet included the cafe on our itinerary. I did a quick look at "must-do" lists for Venice and Paris and she certainly seems to have picked the most popular tourist destinations for us.'

Good on Gran. He imagined the next conversation he was going to have with her. *Well, Gran. So much for you playing cupid. No love, but take better aim next time because your arrow of lust hit me but not Mia.*

A few nights of cold showers were going to be his short-term reality.

Fan-bloody-tastic.

Shoving what he'd really like to say to Mia right to the back of his mind he replied, 'After the Doge's Palace, we visit Florian's. From there we look through St Mark's Basilica, go to the top of the Campanile for a view of the lagoon and city, then we head to Harry's Bar so you can try a Bellini cocktail.' He'd started out the day looking forward to playing tourist with her at his side. Now, traipsing around Venice to all the popular destinations held zero appeal.

Flat.

Frustrated.

They were the best two words to describe his current state.

'I know the itinerary off by heart,' she prattled as they walked along. 'Violet mentioned we should try to organise a special visit to the cell in Prigioni prison where Casanova was held and made his daring escape through a hole in the ceiling.'

'Do you have a fascination with Casanova?' he baited.

Even as her cheeks flushed, she squared her shoulders. 'There was a good deal more to his life than he's remembered for.'

They walked into the shade of the building and she replaced her sunglasses with those awful glasses she wore. Pity. She really had beautiful eyes when they weren't hidden behind frames.

'All most people know is that Casanova was a sybarite who revelled in casual, short-term liaisons,' she continued. 'It was commonplace with the nobles of the time; not much different from the way some wealthy men lead their lives today.'

It was a not very subtle dig at his short-term affairs and he wondered whether she'd been more affected by his rejection than he'd thought. He should let her comment go...

'I think that's the end of the line for the palace,' she said. 'Not too many people ahead of us.'

The line could wait.

He stopped and reached out so she faced him. 'When we spoke at dinner about making this trip more interesting, there were two reasons I decided we couldn't. You told me you weren't planning on leaving your job any time soon, but you made no comment about how you'd feel about a short-term affair. Just now you seemed open to it.'

Her throat worked up and down as she swallowed. Then she looked him directly in the eye. 'A short-term relationship would suit me. I'm not interested in a long-term commitment. Ever.'

That couldn't be true. From what he could tell she was an old-fashioned girl. 'Are you a virgin, Mia?'

Her cheeks went tomato red. 'Why does it matter?'

'I think you are. I also think you're starting to live dangerously and wading into water that's way out of your depth.'

'Violet told me I should.'

'Lose your virginity?' Shock rolled through him.

'No. Of course not. She told me I should start living more dangerously.' She waved one hand around in front of her. 'Take chances.' Her shoulders rose as she inhaled. 'You said more or less the same thing when we were having dinner.'

'There's loosening up and there's living dangerously.' He had to make her see she was playing with fire. 'You strike me as a woman who'd want a serious commitment.'

'How on earth do you figure that?'

'You've never had a lover. You must be waiting for the right man.'

'Ha!' Somehow, she managed to look half-amused and half-cynical. 'You've never re-married, so does that mean you're waiting for the right woman?'

'Absolutely not!'

'Well, don't make assumptions about me! I've never had a relationship because I've never wanted to be bogged down in a long-term commitment.'

The absolute certainty in her voice completely floored him. Again, he was left wondering what made this woman tick. 'Why are you so averse to commitment?'

'I...' He watched as she swallowed hard. 'I like my independence. I don't want to be answerable to anybody for what I do and when I do it. I don't want to share all of myself with any man. Maybe it makes me sound selfish, but it's who I am.'

His eyes narrowed. Somehow, her words didn't ring true. 'Is that why you've dressed and acted as you do—to avoid romantic entanglements?'

She seemed to be choosing her words carefully as she told him, 'You're well known to avoid romantic entanglements. You obviously enjoy the physical satisfaction of affairs without the emotional elements. Why should I be any different?'

The question of her clothing had been completely avoided and Connor's suspicions kicked in again. She seemed to have gone to great lengths to hide her physical appeal. He was no psychologist, but every instinct told him there was something more she was hiding from the world.

It might be the reason she didn't want a relationship.

It might be the reason she was still a virgin.

Oh God, Connor. What are you thinking? You're not seriously becoming involved with a virgin?

'Scusi.' A photographer claimed their attention.

A woman on stilts, dressed in some sort of historical outfit with a hooped skirt, accompanied him. 'Photo *signore?*'

'No thank you.'

Damn. This was a conversation he and Mia should be having in private.

The photographer gave a gracious bow and the couple moved off to find other tourists.

'We should join the queue,' Mia said.

Connor couldn't care less about seeing the palace. 'You and I are completely different. If you wanted an affair based on slaking physical desire, you'd have dressed differently before now, gone to some club and picked up a guy at a bar.'

'You're assuming I haven't. Maybe I've tried. Maybe I need someone who stimulates me intellectually as well as physically and that person doesn't hang out in the bars I've been to.'

That threw him.

The muscles across his shoulders and up the back of his neck tightened. Every vertebra felt as if it'd been pulled rigid. 'Have you?'

'No.' She gave the answer grudgingly, then her tone was almost pleading. 'I don't want a relationship, Connor, but that doesn't mean I want to die a virgin, either.' He watched her chest rise and fall as she took a breath. 'What I want is great sex with someone who wants the same thing—no strings attached and very short term.'

Shit. The thought of Mia flaunting herself at a bar to pick up a random guy to experiment in casual sex did crazy, stupid things to his blood pressure and winded him like a kick to the groin. He needed to look away from her for a moment while he tried to shield himself from the bombardment of unfamiliar emotions.

Let it go. It's got nothing to do with you.

But what if it did have something to do with him? What if those kisses they'd shared had stirred her reckless line of thinking to life?

Mia was Gran's friend and his employee and he felt protective of her.

'Please don't go out looking for some stranger to initiate you into sex.'

The tilt of her chin was a clear challenge. 'Why?'

Hell. How had he ever got into this conversation?

'Because you're a woman.'

She started to splutter in outrage. 'What an incredibly sexist—'

'No. Hear me out. Despite the push for absolute equality, there are some fundamental differences between men and women.' He steamrolled over her predictable reaction and tried to make her see sense. 'For starters, picking up a total stranger from a bar puts you at physical risk: you have no way of knowing he's not some serial killer and unless you have some qualification in martial arts you haven't mentioned, there's a good chance he could overpower you if he wanted to.'

'Oh, for goodness sake!'

He didn't care if it was farfetched. One way or another he had to make her see sense. 'Secondly, it's apparently not ... a comfortable physical experience for a woman the first time around. If you choose the wrong lover—an inconsiderate one who's more out for his own pleasure than yours—it could be a bad experience for you.'

'Fine.' It looked as though it was costing her to stand there and face him without shifting awkwardly from one foot to the other. Her voice was shaky as she asked, 'Can you recommend anyone?'

For a good ten seconds, it was impossible for Connor to draw breath.

If anyone had told him he'd be having this conversation with any woman—let alone Mia Simms—he would've ridiculed them. She kept wrong-footing him. He would think he pretty much had her pegged and then she'd say or do something to throw the picture he formed out the window.

Oh hell. He didn't know what to think of her anymore. But if she was inexperienced and he took her to bed, it could cause a mountain of problems. He didn't want to break her heart.

Hell! If Mia became emotionally attached to him, Gran would probably insist they get married!

You wouldn't be taking advantage of her. She's issuing you with an invitation and at least you'd make the experience good for her.

Bloody hell. He was going crazy here.

Never mind protecting Mia. More and more it felt as though he was the one who was way out of his depth and in danger of drowning.

'You're on your own there, Mia,' he told her abruptly. 'Let's join the queue.'

Gritting his teeth, he made for the end of the line.

If she kept these conversations up, it was going to be a hell of a long four days. And a guy could only be expected to take so much temptation...

Chapter Eleven

Tension simmered between Connor and Mia as they toured the Doge's Palace.

Damn Connor and the mixed messages he kept sending her.

He'd been the one to suggest—more than once—that this trip could've been more interesting. He'd been the one to kiss her. Then he'd done some spectacular backpedalling when she'd thrown caution to the wind and let him know she'd be open to a short-term affair.

Men!

If he didn't want an affair, why did he keep looking at her when everyone else was marvelling at the murals on the palace ceiling?

Why had he kissed her more than once?

She suspected Connor was more tempted than he was letting on and by the time they reached Caffè Florian, she decided to test his limits. After enjoying a delicious Insalata Florian, which was so much more exquisite than any other shrimp salad she'd ever had, she decided to order the triple chocolate crispy mousse. Making a great show of spooning the creamy dessert into her mouth and lingering over each mouthful, she made appreciative noises from the back of her throat.

There was suspicion in his expression and he shifted in his chair. 'You're being deliberately provocative.'

After swallowing another mouthful very slowly and letting her tongue dart out to lick her upper lip, she raised her eyebrows. 'Maybe.'

'Tease.'

'I'm a tease? You're the one who kissed me. Thoroughly. I was minding my own business, enjoying the gondola ride and you crossed the line.'

'Which I've already apologised for.'

'You don't get to play with me like that then not expect to get payback, Connor.' She dropped her spoon and it clattered on the table top. 'If I'm a tease, what does that make you?'

'Frustrated.'

The admission rocked her against the back of her chair and she stared at him. 'Then you don't have to be Einstein to figure out a solution.'

'This isn't a matter of what I want I take, Mia.' She was pleased to hear he grated the words out. He sounded as frustrated as she felt. 'Even if you think you're okay with the thought of us having sex, I'm not sure you know what you want. Earlier you said you were confused. Only a few days ago you proclaimed you didn't want to go on one date with me, let alone five.'

'And you were telling me you had absolutely no interest in me and never would have!' she huffed.

He looked disgruntled and she was satisfied she'd scored a win with her comeback.

'Gran has a lot to answer for.'

'So do you,' she insisted. 'Correct me if I'm wrong, but I get the impression that when you're out and about and you see a woman you're attracted to it's very much a matter of what you want you take.'

'Only if it's mutual.'

'Trust me, *it's mutual.*'

He shook his head. 'It's not the same. You're a virgin.'

'And, if we have sex together, I won't be.'

'Shit, Mia. I—'

'We still have the best part of four days together. In my books, that counts as a short-term fling.' The women at the table closest to them had stopped their conversation and were now looking over at them with interest. Great. Mia leaned forward and lowered her voice. 'Why is my lack of experience such a turn off? I'd never been kissed before and you seemed to enjoy our kisses enough for repeat performances.'

He groaned. 'You have no idea what you're getting into. A lot of women can't separate the physical from the emotional. Those I take to bed can.' He looked like he gritted his teeth together for a moment before he continued. 'They've had plenty of practice and I know they'll accept the end of the affair without getting clingy.'

'You're saying I need practice at walking away from an affair? How many lovers do I need to have had? One, two...?'

'For God's sake, Mia. Why are you suddenly in such a rush to have sex?'

'Because—as you pointed out—I'm twenty-six. I have enjoyed your company and your kisses. I know your behaviour in my office was out of character, and I've let it go. I truly admire you as a man. But the icing on the cake is knowing you have absolutely no interest in forming any type of attachment to me.' She dug her nails into her palms as she steeled herself to continue. 'No messy end to the affair. No regrets. And last, but definitely not least, I think you'd make the experience enjoyable for me.'

Connor swore under his breath. 'You make me feel like a bloody gigolo.'

'I'm sorry. That's not my intention.' She took another spoonful of her dessert. 'Think about it. What I propose finishes when we arrive back in London.' When he didn't respond, she took a sip of her iced water and willed herself to continue. 'We go back and it will be as though nothing happened. Miss Simms and Mr Stewart, with nobody being any the wiser.'

'You really think you can do that?'

'Can't you?'

'It's too calculated, Mia. If you were experienced you'd know that even short affairs aren't so cut and dried—particularly when those involved have to see each other in the work environment on a regular basis.'

'Because I work for you, it's even *more* important that this is cut and dried.'

His inner conflict was reflected in his expression. 'I've never approached an affair with an absolute end date in mind.'

'Oh, come on, Connor. You know you're not going to marry your lovers and, from what I've heard, they last for a couple of weeks at the most.'

He shook his head. 'Because the only thing we have in common is physical attraction.'

'He came and he conquered.'

'Mock me all you like, but when I embark on an affair I don't go into it thinking the woman will be out of my bed in *x* number of days.' He drank some iced water then put his glass on the table so firmly the liquid sloshed over the rim. 'It's an organic thing. It simply runs its course.'

Oh boy. Mia's self-respect told her she shouldn't have to fight so hard to get Connor to take her to bed. How could she convince him her didn't need to be so considerate of her? She took a deep breath, then launched, 'I'm going to ask you three questions.'

'Mia—'

'Question number one. Am I the love of your life?'

'Oh, for God's sake!'

She arched an eyebrow at him. 'We both know the answer is a resounding no. Question Two. Are you going to be heartbroken at the end of four days when we return to London and go our separate ways?'

He crossed his arms over his chest. 'You know that's a no.'

'Exactly. No to both questions from both of us. But here's a question I'd answer yes to. Question Three. If we don't have sex, will you be left wondering how good it would've been?' When he remained tight-lipped, she said, 'I will be. I'll always wonder and every time I see you at the office, I'll wonder what it would've been like to have had you as my lover.'

'Damn it!' Indecision clouded his eyes. 'This attraction between us isn't going away.'

Was that resignation mixed with his irritation?

'It doesn't matter how many times I tell myself all the reasons we shouldn't take this further,' he continued, 'the more time I spend with you, the more I want to make love to you.'

'Isn't it better to get it out of our systems now than have it continue when we have to see each other at work?'

His lips firmed and he sent her a searching look. 'Are you absolutely certain this won't follow us back to work?'

'Yes.' A fling was all she could have.

In an ideal world—or the world of her dreams—Mia would have a romance of mutual love where she and her lover could lay firm plans for the future. In Mia's reality, the brief affair she wanted to embark on with Connor was tailor-made.

'Because I'll have moved on, Mia,' he warned her harshly.

'You don't pull any punches, do you?'

'I don't want you getting hurt. This isn't a game you're used to playing.'

'I'm a big girl, Connor. I'm more than capable of taking care of myself and moving on too.'

'To another lover?'

It was doubtful, but she forced herself to say, 'To another *temporary* lover if, and when, the opportunity presents itself.'

The penetrating look he sent peeled back the very layers of her soul and Mia steeled herself not to betray any indecision.

'I don't understand you, Mia. You say the right things but it feels like you're trying to convince yourself as hard as you're trying to convince me ... that marketing oversell you mentioned.'

She pressed her lips together and simply shook her head.

Every instinct told her he was caving.

She was absolutely ready for this.

A sexy-as-hell man whom she liked and respected was about to make love to her with no expectation from either of them that this would lead to anything more.

For the first time, her past didn't matter.

It was only the present that counted.

Connor signalled to the waiter for the bill and told Mia, 'The Basilica can wait.'

Chapter Twelve

It'd never been a problem for Connor to admit when he was wrong. As he made his way across the square with Mia to catch a water taxi back to the hotel, he knew he'd been all kinds of wrong about Mia. They walked with their arms around each other's waists and it was good to have her at his side.

He still had questions about her, but his instinct told him she had difficulties trusting others—not that she was someone who couldn't be trusted. If he could win her trust, he believed she'd open up. He wanted to know her, but right now he was ruled by his desire.

He burned for Mia.

'It's such a perfect day.' There was a sigh in her voice.

He brushed his lips against her temple, enjoying the fragrance of her hair and the silky feel of it against his cheek. 'I promise you it will be.'

'I believe you.'

Being her first lover added an extra edge to his anticipation and a need to make this perfect for her. Becoming lovers had a certain inevitability to it and even a sense of rightness. It blew him away how strongly connected he felt to her after the brief period of time they'd shared in each other's company; especially given his initial suspicion and resentment.

Mia's untutored lips were the sweetest temptation and left him wanting far more. Their first kiss ... Well, his own reactions had been captured in Peppi's prints and he'd felt completely exposed until he'd seen Mia's expression echoing his own.

From that moment, Connor had wanted to forget the day of sightseeing and take her back to the hotel. The exquisite Alcova Tiepolo Suite, with its magnificent eighteenth-century frescoes on the ceiling, was his idea of perfect sightseeing if viewed from the bed with Mia. Now they were heading back there.

'Mia, I'm not taking you to bed lightly.'

A little tinkle of laughter escaped from her lips. 'You're telling me you'll still respect me in the morning?'

'Yes.'

'Good, because your respect is important to me.'

He promised himself he'd employ every bit of erotic expertise he possessed to deliver her a slow, sweet seduction that would saturate her senses with sheer bliss. He would awaken her untried body to its mysteries until every one of her nerve synapses was singing with pleasure, and every cell, fibre and muscle screamed for release before hurtling towards heaven. And afterwards, when she was languorous and sated, he'd hold her until she fell asleep in his arms.

His blood surged south as he played out the scenario in his mind.

Good lord! Was his hand trembling as he lifted it to knead the muscles of one of her shoulders?

Mia shifted against him in the water taxi, turned back to him and planted a kiss on his stubbled jaw line. 'Nearly there.'

The longing in her voice made his chest tighten. It wasn't the only part of him that was uncomfortably tight.

'Your suite or mine?' she asked breathlessly a few minutes later when they docked at the hotel jetty.

'Mine.'

When the suite door closed behind them, Mia dropped her bag on the floor and turned to him with a shy smile.

His heart hammered and his shaft throbbed as she walked to him. Her slender arms reached up around his neck and she initiated a slow kiss. It was a feathering of her lips against his, working up to the foray of her tongue tip along his lower lip before venturing in to play with his tongue.

Each stroke of their tongues was electric.

The heat of her palms scalded him through his shirt and he couldn't wait to be rid of it and come into skin to skin contact with his innocent seductress.

'Too many clothes,' she husked, as though she could read his mind.

Connor took a half step away from her to lift her top over her head. The vision of her full breasts cupped demurely in white lace reminded him of her purity. Her flat stomach, hand-span waist and perfectly curved hips were all unexplored territory; his territory to awaken.

'You're temptation personified,' he said on a hoarse whisper. 'So desirable.'

'Show me how desirable I am, Connor. For these few days, make me feel like I'm the most desirable woman in your world.'

You are. He let one hand cup the nape of her neck as the other eased her hair from its ponytail so it fell like a dark silky curtain around her gorgeous face. Then he captured one of her hands in his and turned it so he could place a kiss on her palm and let his teeth scrape across the fleshy pad beneath her thumb.

He wasn't the one who was untried here but he was in unchartered territory. He'd never made love to a virgin.

He kissed the inside of her wrist then allowed the tip of his tongue to flick up before he drew her index finger into his mouth and sucked on it.

Mia's eyes widened and her pupils dilated with pleasure. 'You ... That's amazing.'

'I'm going to introduce you to erogenous zones you never knew you possessed,' he promised. 'We'll both learn what you enjoy most.'

Placing his hands at her waist he let them move over her taut skin, exploring the outline of her body, splaying across her firm stomach before travelling along the valley of her spine. He released the hooks of her bra and eased the straps off her shoulders and down her arms. There was no suppressing his groan as he admired the beauty of her unfettered breasts as they rose and fell with each shallow breath of excitement.

'Touch me,' she urged, as the bra dropped to the floor between them.

'I think *I'm* the one who's being seduced,' he said, as he cupped her breasts in his hands and rejoiced in the feel of them.

'Oh!' Her head fell back a little, exposing the creamy flesh of her neck.

Connor seized the opportunity to taste the skin in the hollow at the base of her neck and to lick a little along her slender collarbones. Briefly, he shifted his attention to nibble at the sensitive shell of her ear before he zeroed in on the delightfully rosy areola of her breast. He drew the nipple, that pouted proudly and invitingly, deep into his mouth and revelled in her responsiveness as she rasped his name and made little sounds that drove him crazy with fervent need.

He fell to his knees before her, kissed down her body as his fingers worked to unbutton and unzip her pants and send them dropping to the floor.

One hand cupped her mound and found the silk and lace of her knickers damp with her arousal. 'You're so ready.'

'Yes,' she whispered as she placed each hand at the side of his head and urged him to stand back up. 'But let me discover you.'

The second he stood, her hands bunched the material of his polo shirt to reef it up over his head. Then her fingers, completely lacking any finesse, grappled with the fastening of his trousers, her knuckles brushing against his turgid erection through the material and making him clench his teeth together to keep himself from bursting at her touch.

'No,' he grated out. 'You'll send me crazy and this'll all be over before it's begun.'

Sweeping her protest aside and her body up into his arms, he carried her further into the suite so he could set her down on his bed. She was delectable. So God-damned desirable, the need to possess her warred with the need to savour every second as the passion ramped up between them.

'Let me see all of you.' In response to his request she raised her hips and began easing her knickers down. He did a double-take. 'You're blond.'

'Yes.'

Amazing. He'd heard of brunettes turning themselves into blonds but never the other way around. It seemed a strange choice. Still, her dark hair and blue eyes were a potent combination.

His mouth dried as she bent her legs, removed the lacy garment completely then let it drop over the side of the bed. It was a seductive move. He would've called it a practised move if it weren't for the colour that blotched across her chest and the deep muscle tremor in her calves.

'I feel rather exposed,' she admitted. 'I think you should even things up.'

Loving that she could express her needs, he removed his wallet from his trousers and took out several foil packets to put them on the bedside table.

'Oh!' She blushed a deeper red. 'Good thinking!'

Connor didn't waste time replying. Instead he got on with removing his pants. The awed appreciation in her eyes as she gazed upon his nakedness made him feel omnipotent and painfully aware of the hard need between his legs, impatient for release.

Sinking to the mattress on his knees he bent over to kiss her tenderly. 'Better?'

One of her hands caressed the valley of his spine while the other reached between them.

He sucked in a breath.

Shy and tentative initially, Mia's fingers traced delicately along the rigidity of his penis and the sensitive sac beneath. Feather-like strokes. Teasing touches around the head, making him ache. He fought to stay still to grant her this exploration.

Connor groaned. 'Firmer.'

Gaining confidence, her strokes became bolder before her warm fingers closed around his length, and squeezed.

Oh God. Heat sizzled through him and he felt light-headed—dizzy—as exquisite sensation streaked through his entire body, all the way down to his toes.

He pulled back, pulse thundering. 'Too much,' he panted as he shook his head in sheer bloody wonderment that her inexperienced touch could have such a powerful effect on his body.

He needed to focus on her—on arousing her and bringing her to fulfilment.

Harnessing every bit of self-control he possessed, he bent over her and used the tip of his tongue and his fingertips to trail a lazy path down her gorgeous body. The evocative scent of her arousal teased his nostrils and called to him like a siren to come and taste.

'Your skin is delicious, but I want to feast on all of you.'

As his tongue trailed erotic circles around her navel, his fingertips moved across to the firm ridge of her hip bone before moving lower and nudging her thighs further apart. He met with some resistance. 'Are you okay?' he asked.

She nodded.

'Open your legs for me, Mia.'

She bit down on her lower lip before she swallowed.

'You still want this?' *God, please don't let her deny me now.*

'Yes. I ... I'm sorry. I didn't realise I'd be so ... nervous. But I haven't changed my mind.'

He drew in a deep breath. 'You're in control here, Mia. Just because you agreed doesn't mean you can't change your mind.'

'I want it to be you.'

Thank God. 'Then relax and enjoy.'

Her fingers threaded through his hair, holding him back from his intended destination. 'I don't know what to do.'

'But I do. Trust me to make it good for you.'

She nodded then released her hold on him. They held each other's gaze as he blew gently on the feminine curls that covered her entrance.

Her chest rose and fell more rapidly and he could see the uncertainty in her eyes. 'Relax,' he said softly.

Holding one hand on her hip, he parted her feminine folds with the other. With exquisite care, he stroked her there.

She moaned.

He kissed the soft silky skin of her inner thigh. 'Put your head back. Close your eyes and enjoy every sensation.'

Slowly, he felt her body melt into the mattress as he explored her flesh again with his fingertips, stroking and teasing her nub of sensitive nerve endings. He alternated with firmer pressure until she was incoherent with need.

Her body jack-knifed as he put his mouth to her, but his hands held her firm as he used his tongue in an intimate dance dedicated to her pleasure. Actually, it wasn't all her pleasure. The exquisite honeyed taste of her inflamed him. Her cry of shocked pleasure as he eased his fingers into the sweet, drenching heat of her was an intoxicating mixture of innocence and lust. His own throbbing ache wound tighter as her body tensed.

He could feel her stretching for the pinnacle, and she began to whimper and beg for completion. When he drew the taut nub of her desire into his mouth and began to suck on it, she bucked, cried out, then sobbed with her pleasure.

Revelling in her responsiveness, Connor was deeply satisfied he'd given her this climax. He moved up beside her and gathered her in his arms, wiping away the tears trailing down her cheeks. 'You're crying?'

'They're happy tears.' She sniffled, then laughed, her wonder etched into every feature. 'I never dreamed it could be so good.'

He kissed her forehead. 'That was just the beginning.'

'My body feels so good. My limbs are heavy but there's still a part of me, deep inside, that's aching—clenching—with emptiness. I can feel these little contractions that I've never felt before. Is that normal?'

Connor's erection surged at her innocent wonderment and his heart flipped around his chest at her honesty and her trust. 'I'd say so. I'm aching to fill that emptiness.'

She lifted her head to kiss him then sent him a small smile as she screwed her nose up. 'Less talk and more action, then?'

He laughed. 'That'd be good.'

But all traces of their humour vanished and laughter was replaced by Mia's small mewls of neediness as Connor kissed her passionately and used his hands and mouth to stoke her again to an inferno of need.

Certain she was absolutely ready for their joining, he reached for the foil packet, tore it open with his teeth and sheathed himself. He prided himself on being a generous lover, but he'd never known such an acute need to have his lover caught up in a maelstrom of perfect bliss.

'Lift your hands above your head,' he instructed.

Mia didn't hesitate and Connor took one of her hands in his and entwined his fingers with hers, wanting to connect with her in every way possible; to have as much of their flesh touching as their bodies joined.

With his other hand, he guided his rigid length to rub against her clitoris while he watched her face, tuning in to her body to assess her readiness. Gently, he probed against the entrance then paused to commit this transcendent moment to his memory, even though his entire body was raging with primitive need to make her his. Holding her gaze, his heart swelled at the trust in her eyes.

'Mia.'

She sent him an inviting, needy smile. 'Connor.'

Knowing she was still with him, he gritted his teeth together and exerted supreme effort to slow down; to suppress his own passion and rein back from plunging swiftly inside her. Gently. Slowly. He began to inch into her and paused each time her body stiffened even a little as she stretched to accommodate him.

'More.'

Stopping as he felt the fragile barrier of her resistance, he felt the sweat beading on his brow. 'A little pain, Mia, then it'll be over.' At least he hoped to hell that was what would happen.

That was what was supposed to happen, wasn't it?

While he steeled himself to deliver the sharp sting of pain, Mia took matters into her own hands. She thrust upwards at the same time as she put her hands firmly on his hipbones and pulled him down into her.

One pained cry from Mia while he thought he would die from sheer pleasure hardly seemed fair. 'Oh God, Mia.'

She shook her head. 'I'm good.'

A surge of emotion unlike any he'd ever known flared through him at the way this beautiful woman so honestly expressed her needs. Answering those needs, he began to withdraw before thrusting slowly back in to the sweet welcome of her tight body. Her muscles stretched to accommodate him in a perfect fit and were like quick sand, pulling him back so he could sink into her. Deep in. So deep it was impossible to tell where he ended and she began.

His name was rent from her lips on a sob as her hips moved inexpertly, trying to find the rhythm and filling him with a primitive satisfaction that he'd be the one to teach her body how to fly in ecstasy.

Before long, Mia learnt the age-old primal rhythm and her pelvis rose to meet his body thrust for thrust as her inner muscles learnt to clench around his sensitive shaft, squeezing him tight as he thrust deep, drawing a tortured groan from his throat, then releasing him as he withdrew.

Nirvana.

Utopia.

Divine Ecstasy like none he'd ever known beckoned him.

Desperation gathered in Mia's face like storm clouds.

Urgent need pounded through Connor's body and the pressure built to the brink of eruption. It was rapturous torture and he felt the muscles of his body, the sinews of his arms and the tendons of his neck strain as he thrust harder and deeper to bring her over the edge.

At the point when he thought he could bear it no more, her eyes widened in wild abandon and she cried out as she shattered and tumbled over the edge, her climax ripping through her. The potent contractions pummelling through her body spasmed around him and he gave into his own release, throwing his head back and calling out her name as his whole frame shuddered and his desire pumped out.

Blown away by the force of his orgasm, Connor dropped his forehead against Mia's but continued to support the weight of his upper body so he didn't crush her. Looking down at her in awe, he was overcome with a joy he'd never experienced.

Their breaths mingled on each exhalation, their bodies seeming to be in complete harmony. Even the pulse he could see at the base of her neck was keeping time with the one he could feel at his temple. Their bodies still joined, there was a completeness about their intimate union that was entirely surreal and he didn't want to end this connection.

Mia might have been a virgin but her body had drawn out the most explosive orgasm of his life. It was hard to credit. In fact, it was hard to process anything because his brain had been fried by the pure pleasure of being sheathed tightly inside her moist heat. Aftershocks of her passion still caused little intermittent convulsions around him. The whole experience had been richer than he'd ever known, and now he was replete, thoroughly sated and yet wanting to make love to her again to know whether it would be equally as sensational the second time.

Reluctantly, he eased out of her, needing to dispose of their protection. 'I'll be back with you in a second,' he told her, as he got up and went through to the bathroom.

When he came back, his heart catapulted around his chest at the vision of her lying naked against the white linen sheets. Her lips were still slightly swollen from their kisses. Her dark hair, usually repressed into that stifling bun, was free and tangling wildly around her flushed face and across his pillows. The picture was accurate. Mia was a woman who'd been made love to thoroughly—by him. It was a picture he wanted to freeze-frame.

A miniscule part of him wanted to run from this need and sense of oneness he felt when he was with her—scared by the perfection of what he felt. The other part craved more.

He lay beside her and she was unresisting as he drew her back into his arms. Actually, she snuggled closer to him, pillowed her head over his heart and let out a long, contented sigh.

'Tired?' he asked.

'Tired. Exhilarated. Amazed,' she said. 'It's funny how I'm feeling so many different things at once. I can tell you one thing I'm *not* feeling...'

'What's that?'

She shifted so her chin was against his breastbone and she was looking up at him. 'Disappointed.'

He used his hand to smooth her hair over her head and sent her a smile.

'Thank you for being my first lover. I realise it's probably not quite etiquette to do a post-coital review, but God, Connor. That was sensational.'

Miss Mouse from marketing couldn't be further away. Had she ever even existed?

He tried to pinpoint exactly how he felt. The rich experience of making love to Mia would stay with him for a very long time. Maybe forever. 'Sensational sounds about right.'

God, would he ever get enough of her?

It was ironic that she'd been the one to set the limit on their time together; a far shorter time frame than his average affair. All she was giving him was a few days.

He stroked a wisp of hair away from her flushed cheek and knew if they stayed here much longer, they'd never leave the suite. 'Venice awaits. Do you want to go and see all the things that are still on Gran's agenda?'

Pulling a little away from him, she leaned on her elbow and propped her head up with her hand. 'I'm doing all the sightseeing I want to do right now...' She shot him a mischievous look as she looked over his naked body.

'You really are a tease.'

With a laugh, she flipped back to nestle her head against the pillows and stare up at the ceiling with an impish smile playing around her mouth. 'I mean the magnificent fresco on the ceiling. Only in Venice would I be able to lie in bed and stare up at a magnificent fresco by Giovanni Battista Tiepolo.' She sighed. 'I get that the little angels are in the clouds with the doves, but is that seriously a pig's head behind that one?'

Connor pulled himself up so he could look down at her better. 'You're long-sighted then, not short-sighted?'

He felt her tense next to him and he frowned as he remembered she'd taken off her sunglasses as they'd entered the hotel but hadn't bothered to put her normal glasses back on.

'Er ... Yes.'

But she always wore her glasses—whether she was reading or presenting. 'Do you wear multifocal lenses?'

She reached out to trace the contours of his chest with her other hand. 'Do we really need to be talking about my eyesight when there are so many other things we could be doing?'

'You have beautiful eyes, Mia. You shouldn't hide them.'

Instead of answering him, she shifted so she could place her mouth where her fingers had been. 'Do you think Violet knew this would happen between us?' She asked between kisses. 'Do you think it's why she demanded photographic evidence that we'd visited everything on her itinerary?'

'Lord, I hope not!' He grimaced. 'It was probably to make certain we didn't dump each other the second we arrived and do our own sightseeing.'

Her smile broadened and he was captured again by her dimples. 'Maybe we could stay here all day tomorrow and simply photoshop ourselves into the photos?'

'Miss Simms, you have the best ideas. I really like your creativity.'

'Hold on to that thought, because I'm about to get really creative.'

It was beyond Connor to hold on to any thought in the hours that followed. Mia made it clear she was on a mission to discover everything there was to know about making love and he was all too happy to teach her.

Chapter Thirteen

'Even though I'm looking forward to Paris, I'll be sad to leave Venice,' Mia confessed the following evening as she and Connor strolled through St Mark's Square hand in hand. They were on their way to have dinner at Club del Doge before their evening flight to the French capital.

'Are you disappointed we didn't get to see the glass blowing at Murano?'

'No.' They'd spent the afternoon back in bed today and she didn't regret it for a second. Her time as Connor's lover was going to come to a screeching halt when they returned to London and she'd already decided that being in his arms was her favourite place in the world. 'I'll see it next time.'

'At least we managed to see everything else on Gran's list—even if only to get the mandatory photo.'

'I hope she's okay,' Mia said. 'She said she wouldn't take any calls from me while we're away.'

'She said the same thing to me, but I've been calling Dawson twice a day. He says Gran's following doctor's orders and doing really well.'

'Good.' Mia shifted closer to Connor to avoid a group of tourists who weren't watching where they were going. Tourists and locals alike were out in force, enjoying the balmy night.

'Of all my trips to Venice, this has definitely been the most enjoyable,' Connor said.

'I can't believe you've been here and never played tourist.'

'I'm glad I didn't,' he said. 'It's been fun seeing the city with you. Though, if Gran hadn't insisted on photographic proof, I know where I would've liked to have spent the day.' His thumb traced the back of her hand.

Oh yes, she was going to miss being with Connor.

He lifted her hand so his lips could brush the sensitive skin at the base of her wrist. 'Every time I think of Venice, I will think of our first kiss in Vincento's gondola.'

'Really?'

He nodded. 'It was that kiss. The small taste I intended to have was so seductive it burnt itself into my memory. The build up from our first kiss to making love was sweet agony and made it all the more explosive.'

Her womb clenched with need.

Visions played out in her head making her cheeks heat and she turned her head away from Connor so he wouldn't see her blush. But, in avoiding Connor's gaze, her attention snagged on a familiar face.

Shit!

She froze mid-stride.

Her happiness shattered.

Every heart beat jack-hammered against her rib cage.

Two men walked their way, deep in conversation and this time she knew she wasn't mistaken. Even with his long hair, she would recognise his crooked nose and deeply pock-marked skin anywhere. One of the men was definitely Sully.

Her panic was accompanied by a rush of anger.

She should have trusted her instincts yesterday morning when she thought she saw him.

She should have found a way to get out of Venice without being recognised.

But no. She'd been too caught up in the fantasy that she could actually seize a couple of days of bliss and live without the fear that haunted her.

'Mia?'

Connor's voice was the key that unlocked her body from its paralysis. Looking around desperately, she searched for an alleyway she could duck into, but found nothing.

No! She couldn't be seen.

She couldn't take the chance Sully might recognise her.

Mia spun around and stepped in front of Connor. On her tiptoes, she raised her arms around his neck and buried her hands in his hair to draw his head towards hers. 'Kiss me, Connor.'

There was no time to wait for him to respond. Every passing second was one more step Sully took towards them. Her lips found his and she kissed him as though her life depended on it.

It possibly did.

A low sound of longing emerged from the back of his throat and he deepened the intensity of the kiss, his mouth hard and hungry as his tongue laced with hers. Mia moulded herself against him and gave into the mounting passion between them. It swamped her senses and almost made her forget why she'd started kissing him in the first place.

Drowning in the sensuous enchantment, it was easy to focus on Connor and the need he aroused. The kiss went on and on, his hands firm and urgent against the small of her back, pulling her closer. She was in no doubt of the physical effect she had on him.

When he eventually pulled away, they were both breathing raggedly and Mia's head was spinning while her body ached for more.

For a few seconds, all she could do was look into Connor's eyes. Then, her gaze flicked behind him and she was relieved to see the men had walked straight past them, still deep in discussion.

What was Sully doing in Venice?

A chill shot through her.

If he was here, did that mean Giovanni was here too?

'That was spontaneous,' Connor said against her ear. 'I think I could grow accustomed to spontaneity.'

'Let's go back to the hotel and order room service.' She needed to be off the streets of Venice and safely out of sight.

'You're a shameless hussy,' he teased, 'but tonight I'm not giving in to you—not until we're in Paris, anyway.'

Thank God we'll be in Paris tonight!

'Why don't we go straight to the airport and try for an earlier flight?'

Connor brushed his lips over hers again. 'As much as I'm tempted, you haven't been to Venice until you've eaten at this restaurant. The traditional Venetian cuisine here is sumptuous and there's an excellent view of the Grand Canal.'

'There's an excellent view of the canal from our hotel, too.' Even as she pushed the point, she told herself to calm down. There was no need to panic. Sully was heading in the opposite direction. She'd be safe enough at the restaurant, then she'd be off to the airport.

Besides, Sully wouldn't expect to see her in Venice and she looked so different from the teenager he'd known.

'Hm. I'm beginning to regret selling my private jet,' Connor said close to her ear. 'If I still owned it, we'd be making love all the way to Paris.'

'It was fabulous you deliberately reduced your carbon footprint.' She shot one last look over her shoulder to make certain Sully continued away from them. Trying to banish him from her mind, she focused on Connor. 'I was even more impressed when I heard you donated the money from the sale towards the Amazon reforestation project.'

'Careful, or I might think you've decided to join the fan club you spoke of only a few nights ago.'

'You're right. We couldn't have that, could we?'

Had it only been a few nights ago?

So much had changed over the last few days.

Her most cherished fantasy had come true, but seeing Sully had burst her bubble of happiness. Awful scenarios pounded through her head. The anxiety made acidic bile churn in her stomach and she wasn't sure how she'd manage to eat a thing.

Mia placed one foot in front of the other, trying not to give Connor any hint of how wound up she was.

'This is it,' Connor announced. 'The best food in Venice.'

Thank God.

Mia couldn't get inside fast enough and even as they were shown to their table, her gaze flew around the restaurant making certain she was safe. There'd be no relaxing now until they were on the plane to Paris.

It was a terrible twist of fate that Sully was in Venice.

Giovanni's personal bodyguard rarely left his side. And she remembered Giovanni saying once that he'd never been out of America. He'd boasted that New York was his city—his empire—and he had no desire to leave it.

Besides, in New York he was protected. It wouldn't make sense for him to leave his territory and expose himself to the possibility of a hit from another Mafia gang. If he travelled anywhere, it would hardly be to Italy where other Mafia families were in control.

Once they were seated, they looked at the menu. Stomach still roiling, Mia decided to skip the main meal and only have an entrée and dessert. Connor did the same.

Order placed, Connor reached across the table and took her hands in his. 'There's something I want to ask you.'

'Ask.' The word was a whisper. She wasn't sure she'd want to answer—particularly if she had to lie about her past again.

He cleared his throat. 'Why set a time limit? When this is so sensational between us, why not let it runs its course?'

Oh. Oh. *Oh.*

She had to be dreaming. It was so tempting and she longed to say yes. It was only an affair. It wasn't as though she'd be basing a relationship with a future on a web of lies. Judging by Connor's average track record, it would still all be over in a couple of weeks.

That could be another ten or so more nights of ecstasy.

More out-of-this-world lovemaking with the man who'd been her fantasy crush since the first time she'd set eyes on him and who'd risen to hero status as she'd learned more about him in her years at Stewart Corporation.

All her life she'd lived in fear but in Venice with Connor she'd managed to forget the danger. She'd seized the day and she'd lived. And while she'd been angry at herself for forgetting the reality of her life, seeing Sully and having the uncertainty of her life thrust back firmly in her face only made her want to grasp tighter at the happiness Connor offered. She wanted to enjoy it while she could.

She took a long sip of her wine for fortification then set the glass back on the table.

'Yes.'

'Yes?'

'Yes, I agree to letting this run its course. I know it's only temporary and I know it's about sex not emotion but, for as long as this lasts, let's enjoy it.'

Connor's lips compressed and he frowned. 'I know you don't have the experience to realise it, but this is not only about the sex, Mia.'

'It's not?'

'Not for me, it isn't.' He shook his head. 'I enjoy your company. The sex is ... It's beyond wonderful. But it's as good as it is because there's a connection between us that's more tangible than any I've experienced.' He squeezed her hand. 'We don't just make love. We talk. We laugh.'

'Isn't that normal?'

'Not in my experience.'

She couldn't imagine sharing her body and all the intimacy she'd known with Connor without the companionship as well. She was pleased to hear him say their connection was stronger than he was used to, but it also set alarm bells off in her head.

Surely Connor wasn't telling her there was the possibility of a future between them beyond a couple of weeks?

She disengaged her hand from his and looked away from him as she tried to untangle her emotions. Any normal woman would be thrilled at the prospect of having a future with Connor. But Mia was not a normal woman. She couldn't afford to be.

She was a fake.

A phoney.

A woman with a made-up past, a fake identity and a woman who could endanger anyone she became close to.

'Connor, if we continued to be lovers when we returned to London, I'd want it to be kept under wraps. I don't want to be in the papers as your latest lover and I certainly don't want anyone at the office to know.'

The muscles in his cheeks clenched before he demanded, 'What am I supposed to do when

I have to attend a high-profile charity event—leave you at home?'

'*Signorina* and *Signore*. Your entrées.'

The waiter had barely set down the plates, wished them *Bon appétit* and walked away when Mia asked, 'Do you have one to attend in the next week or two?'

'I don't know, Mia. My assistant takes care of my calendar.' He looked away from her and she sensed his discontent as he picked up his fork and jabbed at his linguini. 'And I wish you'd get this week or two deadline out of your head.'

'There hardly seems any point in talking hypothetically but, if you need to attend some high-profile event, would it kill you to go alone?' She raised her hand and ran her fingers through her hair as she tried to gather her thoughts. 'While we're together, I don't want you to be with anyone else.'

Was that too bold?

Too demanding?

'Two-timing has never been my style.' He sent her a narrow-eyed look while she let out a pent-up breath. 'You're right. Let's take this day by day.'

Mia was unsettled.

Concerned.

She began on her meal as she tried to untangle her feelings.

It was on the tip of her tongue to remind him that she wasn't interested in a long-term relationship, but this was the man who'd sworn off serious relationships—the last person she needed to caution against forming plans for the future.

Their conversation became stilted.

Mia chewed her food without tasting it and wished she could do something to make things easier again between them.

Connor said nothing as their plates were cleared and a waiter topped up their wine glasses.

Sitting back in her chair, Mia avoided making eye contact with Connor and looked around the restaurant instead.

That's when she saw *him*.

Recognition hit hard and her blood chilled.

Someone far more frightening than Sully.

Far more dangerous.

Lou Correlli.

The name punched at her solar plexus and she gasped for breath.

'Mia? Are you okay? You've gone very pale.'

She hardly heard Connor's comment as she stared beyond him.

It was definitely Lou. Giovanni's right-hand man.

Short and squat. Balding now, but still with that lecherous look in his eye as he passed by a female diner and leered at her. His walk was the same sleazy swagger and the scar that ran from the right corner of his mouth all the way up his cheek hadn't faded. It'd always made her fearful of him and she knew now that her childhood instincts were right. He was a man to be feared. A man to be avoided at all costs. A man she couldn't avoid because he was coming her way.

'Mia?' Connor repeated. 'I'm sorry. I didn't mean to upset you or try to tie you into a situation you're uncomfortable with.'

'I'm fine. I ... er ... I've dropped my napkin.' It was lame in the extreme, but it gave her a chance to bend down under the table to hide her face. Hopefully Lou would walk past their table if she stalled for long enough.

If Sully and Lou were both in Venice, surely that meant Giovanni was here too.

Breaking out in a cold sweat, she scanned the floor from underneath the tablecloth. She waited to see Lou's shoes as he passed by and prayed fervently that Giovanni wasn't here too.

Damn it! What was taking Lou so long?

Had he stopped to talk to someone or had he been seated at a table before he'd reached theirs? If so, she hoped to hell he wasn't in a position where he'd see her.

'Mia?'

'Oh ... dear!' Thinking fast, she grabbed the clasp on her handbag and let the contents fall on the carpet. 'I'm so clumsy. Everything's dropped out of my handbag.'

Connor's head appeared under the table, level with hers. He was looking at her in disbelief. 'Do you need a hand?'

'No. I'll just gather everything up.'

The movement of shiny black shoes in her peripheral vision made her freeze.

The shoes stopped right in front of a...

Dear God! Her gold lipstick tube had rolled directly into the path of the man she was trying to avoid.

Horrified, she watched silently as the tube was picked up by short, chubby fingers—one sporting a large silver onyx signet ring. They were fingers that had reputedly pulled a trigger to end the lives of many of Giovanni's enemies.

'As long as you're being clumsy and not hiding away from me.' Connor's voice caught her attention. 'I actually find your clumsiness rather cute.' His face wore an amused expression as he held her phone out to her under the table. 'I think that's everything.'

'Are you good people looking for this?' The distinctive New York accent made all the fine hairs at the nape of her neck stand on end and her heart pounded against her ribs.

Connor's face disappeared from her line of sight as he straightened up from under the table. She heard him say, 'Thank you.'

Mia stayed right where she was, taking her time pretending to organise the contents of her bag.

'No problem.'

'Mia, do you need a hand up?' Connor asked.

Her upper lip was damp with perspiration.

Shit. Shit.

She couldn't stay down here under the table or she'd draw even more attention to herself.

Lou's not going to recognise me.

I mustn't show that I recognise him.

'I'm quite alright.' Although she'd protested about all the laborious elocution lessons she'd been subjected to as a teenager to rid herself of every trace of her American accent, she was thankful for them now. Sitting back up, she spoke with the most upper-crust British accent she could muster. 'Thank you ever so much.' She reached for the lipstick Lou held out, but couldn't bring herself to look him in the eye. 'I'm so awfully glad you didn't trip on it.'

Her hand was shaking so badly she practically snatched the lipstick from him, then busied herself by putting it back into her handbag.

'Thank you again,' Connor repeated, signalling the end of the interaction.

Lou didn't take the hint. 'You look very familiar, ma'am. Have we met?'

Nausea churned in her gut.

She couldn't avoid his eye contact any longer and steeled herself to remain calm as she looked at him. 'I don't believe so. You're American or Canadian, aren't you?'

'New York born and bred.'

He may have been born and raised in New York, but she knew his heritage was Sicilian and his ties to the New York Mafia ran deep.

'I've never visited your country.' It was true. She'd been a resident, not a visitor.

Oh, please go away! Her pulse at the base of her neck must be visible. It was pounding so strongly it was reverberating through her skull.

'Strange. I never forget a face.' He scratched behind his ear. 'You definitely remind me of someone.'

Mia could do nothing to prevent her nervous swallow.

'They say everyone has a double,' Connor put in.

'Yes. That's what they say.' He smiled, but it didn't reach his cold, snake eyes.

The second Mia reached up to touch the pendant at her chest she knew she'd made a mistake. The subconscious gesture she often made when she was under stress landed her in more hot water as Lou's gaze dropped to her chest. 'That's a most exquisite pendant. An emerald I believe?'

No. No. *No.*

Her mother had worn this pendant almost constantly.

Stupid. Stupid. *Stupid.*

She should never have touched it.

She should never have worn it with this outfit.

The only thing she could do now was to try to bluff her way out of it.

'It's gorgeous, isn't it?' But her fingers covered it rather than offering him a closer look. 'When I saw it at the Hampstead Heath markets, I simply fell in love with it.'

'It's very strange.' His voice was casual as he shook his head, but his eyes narrowed. 'Even your pendant seems familiar.'

Mia forced a laugh. 'Not so strange. I'm told it's a popular replica of an antique piece.' She shrugged. 'I was so disappointed. I thought I may have stumbled across a genuine treasure but no such luck.' She continued to finger the piece as she spoke, trying to make it look as though the action was done absent-mindedly while really preventing him from getting a closer look at it. 'The jeweller I took it to for valuation said it's worthless. It's a mass-produced copy of a Georgian lover's knot—worth very little, but I still love it. Are you a collector of antique jewellery?'

'No.' There was an edge to his voice. 'Yours caught my eye and I swear I've seen it before.'

She manufactured a puzzled look and tried to breathe evenly while her heart cramped. 'There's a good chance you have. As I've said, it's quite a popular design.'

'Excuse me, *signore*.' A waitress hovered, waiting for Lou to move so she could serve the desserts.

Lou moved to let the waitress set the dishes down, but he didn't walk away.

Mia resisted wiping at the perspiration which gathered at her hairline.

'It was nice talking to you people. Lou Correlli's the name.' He extended his hand to Connor first.

No, Connor! Whatever you do, don't tell him your name.

'Connor Stewart.'

Shit.

Then it was Mia's turn. Stomach roiling, she had to accept Lou's handshake, praying he wouldn't notice the clamminess of her hands. 'I hope you enjoy your stay in Venice, Mr Comelli.'

'Correlli,' he corrected. 'I'm sorry, I didn't catch your name.'

'Mia.' Connor had already called her by her first name, but there was no way she was giving Lou her surname as well.

'Enjoy your sweets,' Lou told them before he turned back to Mia. 'It's going to bug me all night now until I remember who you remind me of.'

'Interesting to know I may have a double.'

Even as Lou turned and continued his journey towards a table at the back of the restaurant, fear bubbled up in her like a hot spring and she couldn't help but watch him move off.

Thank God. Giovanni wasn't at the table Lou sat at, but that only afforded Mia brief relief.

What if Lou realised it was her mother he was thinking of?

Shit.

What the hell would she do if he realised who she was? Change her identity again and walk away from this life as well? Walk away from Connor?

Oh, stop it! It's not like you have a future with Connor. You're going to have to walk away from him sooner or later.

But it would need to be sooner now Lou had seen her with Connor.

Clasping her hands together in her lap, Mia tried to pull herself together.

There was nothing for it. She would have to break things off with Connor tonight. She couldn't risk putting him in jeopardy.

She cursed inwardly.

So much for her changing her appearance. Even with the change in hair colour, she must still resemble her mother far more than she'd realised.

When she'd been growing up, people had often said their bone structure was similar—except for the bump on Mia's nose from a slight skirmish she'd had on the basketball court. But the bump had been repaired to make her look less recognisable as Callie. Nobody had considered that in removing the bump, she'd end up looking more like her mother.

Leave everything from your old life behind, the FBI agent had warned her.

Mia hadn't been able to. She'd buried her own identity, but had needed something to link her to her mother, so she'd smuggled her mother's treasured jewellery box and this pendant into her belongings.

'Mia!'

Belatedly, she registered that Connor was leaning forward in his seat and trying to gain her attention.

Questions danced in his eyes. Questions she couldn't answer.

Oh God, but she wished she could. More than once he'd stripped her of her clothing and she'd laid her body bare for him, but she could never bare her soul. No matter how long they were together, she'd always be holding something back from him—her true self. Her awful past.

'Would you like to tell me what the bloody hell that was all about?' Every word was quiet but held determined intensity.

Her stomach knotted up and she wanted to scream out with the fear of discovery and the agony of her deceit. 'Pardon?'

'Don't treat me like a fool,' he warned. 'You *have* met that man before, haven't you?'

Her throat worked up and down as she swallowed hard. Digging deep, she tried to come up with an Academy Award winning performance.

I have to lie for Connor's protection as much as my own.

'As far as I'm aware,' she said, carefully, 'we've never been introduced.' It was a half-truth.

Lou had never been introduced to her and certainly never since she'd been Mia Simms. She hadn't been important enough to warrant an introduction, she'd simply been the gangly kid in the background not worth noticing.

No. Don't even think about those times.

She picked up her fork and started eating her dessert in a pretence of calm normality. 'As you said, everyone is supposed to have a double somewhere.' She licked her fork. 'Mm. This tiramisu is superb.' She may as well have been eating cardboard.

Connor reached across the table and touched his finger to the corner of her mouth where she must've left traces of cream. Slowly, he placed his finger to his mouth. 'You're right. I hope you weren't saving the coffee cream for later.' Mia didn't have time to enjoy the intimacy of the moment as he continued, 'I got the distinct impression you didn't want Correlli to recognise you.'

She supposed Connor's tenacity and his refusal to take anything at face value was what had made him so successful in the business world, but he had to let this go.

'How on earth could he recognise me? He's American and I'm nobody famous.'

He let out an audible, impatient breath. 'I don't know how he knows you but he does, doesn't he?'

'Really, Connor! That's absurd. I don't know why you'd think it.'

'You told me a few nights ago it was important not to oversell your product. You were way overselling. You think I didn't notice your accent? Bloody hell! It sounded as though you were trying to hobnob it at a Buckingham Palace garden party.'

When she remained silent he mimicked, *'Thank you ever so much. I'm so awfully glad.'*

Unable to think of a sassy reply, or even a denial, she spooned some more of the dessert into her mouth making certain this time that none of it ended up on her lip. 'Please don't make fun of me. I get a bit nervous when I meet strangers. I guess my accent becomes more pronounced because I'm tense.'

'Oh, come on.' He sat back and made a dismissive gesture with one hand. 'Even if I did believe that, it wasn't necessary to go into such detail about your necklace. It was as though you were trying to throw him off. And then there was the mistake you made on his surname. Please. He said Correlli with a distinctive American roll on the 'r'. There's no way it sounded like Comelli.' He leaned forward again and pinned her with his gaze. 'Who is he, Mia, and why don't you want him to recognise you?'

Connor was way too smart.

'Hey, I don't get out much, remember?' She matched his low volume. 'I'm the twenty-six-year-old who spends her Saturday evenings playing mahjong, so you've got to expect me to be a bit socially awkward.' His grim expression told her he wasn't convinced. 'You paled *before* you made your mad dash under the table. I thought I'd made you panic by talking about us being together for longer than another two days.'

'Panic?' She tilted her head back and laughed. 'I wasn't panicking about anything. I don't know how you come to that conclusion.'

Shut up! You're overselling again and if you keep talking he's going to hear the tremor in your voice.

She steeled herself to say what had to be said. 'As for us staying together, if you're going to be jumping to ridiculous conclusions like this—mistrusting me and turning what was a pleasant evening into an argument—then maybe we should end this here and now.'

'Oh, for God's sake!' He bunched up his serviette and threw it down on the table.

Calm down, Connor. Don't draw any attention to us.

'Please, Connor. Can we simply enjoy our dessert before we head to the airport?'

There wasn't a chance she'd enjoy her dessert, but it might raise suspicion if they rushed out too quickly. Hopefully Lou would simply pass the whole incident off. But if he didn't ... if he went digging...

Damn that he knew Connor's name.

Thank God they were flying out of Venice tonight. Even if Lou connected the dots and phoned every hotel in the city looking for Connor, they'd be long gone. But, a simple internet search would tell Lou exactly who Connor was and where to find him. And that would lead Lou to her.

She had to call Stanley about this.

Stanley! Of course.

Stanley was in Paris.

The weight pressing down on her shoulders eased a little.

She'd phone Stanley from the airport and arrange to meet with him—provided she could slip away from Connor.

Guilt pressed on her again. She'd have to phone her liaison agent at the FBI and tell him what'd happened. He'd be furious when he learned that she'd been wearing her mother's necklace.

'I'll let this go for now, Mia, but I don't believe you're telling me the truth and I want to know why.'

Reaching up to push her glasses up the bridge of her nose she realised she wasn't wearing them. 'My glasses!'

'I wondered how long it'd take you to miss them,' Connor said as he reached into his jacket pocket. 'I picked them up from the floor when you were under the table.'

Oh hell.

As if seeing Lou hadn't been bad enough, he'd seen her whole face, unobstructed.

'Why didn't you give them to me straight away?'

'I was enjoying looking at you without them.'

She held her hand out for them.

'I'm surprised you didn't miss them sooner.' He took his linen napkin and began to clean the lenses. 'You should get contact lenses, or at least buy a different frame.'

Her gut knotted. 'Please give them back. They're clean enough.'

A law unto himself, he held them up to the light to make certain they were clean. Her stomach hollowed out as she watched his eyes widen.

Lord! The evening was going from catastrophic to ... whatever it was that was worse than catastrophic.

'Spill,' he demanded.

There was no use pretending she didn't know what he was talking about but what could she say?

'Why are you wearing these God-awful glasses if you don't need them?' 'You're an optometrist now, are you?'

'I don't have to be an optometrist to know these are only ordinary glass!' To illustrate the point, he perched them on the bridge of his nose. 'That's it. We're leaving and going somewhere we can talk without having to keep whispering.'

'No!' She reached out and grabbed his arm to stay him. 'We can't leave yet.'

'Why not?'

'Because...' She cast around for a plausible excuse. 'I want to finish my dessert.' 'You're just pushing it around your plate.'

'Connor, we promised Violet we'd have dinner here. I'm not leaving until I'm finished.' She held out her hand. 'Please give me my glasses back, I feel naked without them.'

With obvious reluctance, he offered her the spectacles. 'Mia, are you in some sort of trouble?'

That was an understatement.

She was in trouble on a whole lot of levels.

Any other time she would've dwelt more on the little shock of electricity that arced through her body when her hand brushed against

Connor's as he handed the glasses back. Now, all she could think about was whether or not Lou Correlli would identify her and if so, how long it would take him to reach out to Giovanni and act on the instructions Giovanni was certain to give him.

Kill her.

She tried to put a cork in the hysteria that made nausea rise in her stomach.

Connor sat perfectly still and waited for her to answer his question.

'No, Connor. I'm not in trouble.' *Not for the moment.* Her voice was steady, but her hands shook as she spooned some more dessert into her mouth willed her stomach to keep it down.

'I don't believe you. There's something going on here that you're not telling me about.'

Oh, how she wanted to tell him.

In a gentler tone he said, 'You've shared your body with me in the most intimate ways possible. I believed what we shared was real and honest. Was I wrong?'

His words were like knives to her heart. 'Of course not.' The last thing she wanted to do was taint the memory of what they'd shared.

His lips twisted into a parody of a smile. 'So what's this?'

Self-loathing weighed her down as she perpetuated the lie that was her life.

It was unfair for her, but it was even more unfair to Connor because he had absolutely no idea what was going on. No idea of the stakes. No idea she'd selfishly dragged him into this. He'd told her she was playing a dangerous game, but he was the one here who'd unwittingly stepped into a world of evil.

'Don't shut me out, Mia.'

She tilted her head as she looked at him. If she came across as cold and unfeeling it would be easier for him to walk away. 'Connor, when I went to bed with you, you warned me not to get too close. We agreed this would be temporary.'

'And not half an hour ago you agreed to let it reach a natural conclusion.'

Hardening her heart, she said, 'I did. And it has.'

'Just like that?'

Of all the lies she'd had to tell to keep her past a secret, this was the most difficult. She clenched her jaw and used every bit of sheer bloody determination she had to keep her tears at bay. Spine rigid, she swallowed down on the words she really wanted to say.

Ending it now is the last thing I want but it's the only thing I can do to keep you safe.

It had to be a clean break.

But it had to be a brutal break.

'Taking me to bed didn't earn you the right to know everything that goes on in my life.'

His head jerked back and his lips thinned. For a split second, she imagined she saw a wounded look in his eyes, then it was gone, replaced with fury.

Everything in her longed to tell him she adored him.

Oh, God. What she felt for him was stronger than adoration.

The truth almost knocked her sideways.

She was in love with Connor.

Deeply in love.

Totally, madly, head over heels in love.

Of course it had happened.

Part of her had loved him even before they'd become lovers—loved the strong, smart, fair man she knew him to be. Now, as she looked across at him and saw the raw emotions playing over his features, she accepted the truth.

Hell.

What a mess!

How could she have been so stupid?

Hysteria swamped her and she was uncertain whether to laugh or cry at the cruelty of it all. She'd finally fallen in love and fate had intervened to cut short her happiness.

Danger bit at her heels and, loving Connor, she *had* to protect him. She had to swallow down on all she wanted to say—all she wanted to reveal—and walk away.

'Mia,' he tried again, 'regardless of how short a time we've been lovers, if you're in trouble I may be able to help.'

Yes, she was deeply in love with this wonderful, generous man who was offering to share her troubles even though she'd wounded him. But short of hiring a hit man to take out Giovanni and end this nightmare, nobody could help her. She shook her head. 'Thank you, but I don't need your help.'

His teeth must've gritted together because she could see the muscles in his cheek tensing.

As her heart splintered, she changed the subject. 'You know I tried to make this dish once.' She launched into a story about the Italian cooking class she'd attended with two of the ladies from the Saturday evening mahjong group. But all the while, tension made her shoulders ache.

She feared that at any moment she'd hear Lou Correlli's New York accent behind her shoulder, rasping, 'We've been searching for you, Callie.'

Chapter Fourteen

In a secluded corner of the first-class lounge at Marco Polo Airport, Connor's patience finally snapped.

Damn it all! Not only had Mia called a halt to their affair, she'd retreated behind a wall, chatting dizzily about anything and everything ever since the New Yorker had spoken to them. It was obvious she was jittery and unsettled—hyper aware of everything around them and possibly running on adrenalin.

That she was ending their relationship and denying she was in trouble when they'd shared such a deep and intimate connection sent him into a tailspin. He was still losing altitude—as though he'd lost his stomach at thirty thousand feet and was rapidly plummeting towards the earth without a parachute.

It was time to be honest with himself.

This had not been an ordinary affair. His desire for Mia had hit hard and fast but, even before he'd taken her to bed, he'd made an emotional connection with her. He genuinely cared about her.

But how can you believe that when you know so little about her?

Emotion battled logic. The taunting voice in his head was right. What did he know about Mia?

All the initial misgivings he'd had about her flooded back and he turned to her. 'I want to know what's going on with you.' When she remained silent he said, 'Those glasses you don't need to wear, the figure you hide, the hair you dye—are you trying to disguise yourself, Mia?'

Her short laugh was forced. 'Don't be silly. Why would I do that?' 'I don't know. That's why I'm asking.'

'Given the women you've dated, I realise it may seem strange to you, but I really don't like drawing attention to myself.'

'You certainly didn't like the American noticing you.'

Her whole body jerked. 'Leave it, Connor.'

'I can't leave it. I genuinely care about you, Mia. Deeply.'

'I didn't ask you to care about me.' She looked away from him, but not before he noticed the slight trembling of her lips and the sudden sheen of moisture in her eyes.

His gut wrenched.

'Having sex with you was obviously a mistake, Connor. I'm starting to feel uncomfortable and ... crushed by you trying to force your way closer.'

Her words rendered him speechless, his brain reeling at how quickly she'd erected barriers between them. Only a few short hours ago he'd been the most relaxed he'd ever been with a woman and everything had seemed so right.

Now she was calling it a mistake and felt crushed by him?

'We've got two more days to go to honour our promise to Violet and make certain she has the operation. But, as of now, we end this and go back to sleeping separately.' She stood. 'Excuse me. I need to use the bathroom.'

Bloody hell.

No. This wasn't right. None of this was right.

Every instinct told him she was in trouble and warned him not to take her words at face value. He needed to dig deeper if he was going to help her through whatever it was she faced.

He needed to find out more about Mia.

He needed to find out about Lou Correlli.

Considering Mia wouldn't provide him with answers, Connor was left with only one option. Watching as Mia wound her way through the lounge and reached the ladies' bathroom, he got out his phone and made the call.

'Hey, Connor! I was only thinking of you today.'

'Really?' He wasn't in the mood for small talk and it was a strain to respond casually. 'You want to be thrashed in another game of tennis?'

Tony chuckled. 'Actually, I'm arranging a reunion from our Eton class. I sent you an invitation.'

'Sounds good.' Tony had always been the lynch-pin that kept the group in contact.

'What's up?'

'This is actually a business call.'

'Shoot.'

Connor looked again at the women's bathroom. He suspected Mia would hide there until they were called for their flight. 'I employ a young woman, Mia Simms, in my London marketing department. I have her file from HR and will email it to you shortly, but I want a background check on her.'

'No sweat. Anything in particular you're looking for?'

That was part of the frustration. He had no idea. 'A general search to make certain she's above board. Educational qualifications, finances, criminal record, where she lives and...' he tapped his fingers against the armrest of his chair as he tried to sift through all the questions he'd asked that she'd skirted around, 'her family. Her parents died in a plane crash.'

'No problem. All that's easy enough and the parents' names should be on the passenger manifest. Just send me the flight number or, if you don't have that, the airline and year of the crash.'

'All I know is that it was around eleven years ago and they were on their way to Australia.'

'That'll do. Air crashes aren't common.'

He slid one hand around the back of his neck and rubbed a spot to ease the tension there. 'I want to know whether she's in any major debt or receiving any regular payments apart from her salary.'

Even though he'd dismissed his earlier suspicions, he couldn't be sure about anything now. He needed to know that Mia wasn't about to squeeze wealthy elderly ladies for money or give them a sob story and have them come to her rescue.

Now the most pressing question; the one he wasn't even certain he wanted answered. 'I also want you to do a background check on an American. The name is Lou Correlli.'

'Lou Correlli. Okay. Is he connected to Mia Simms?'

'I suspect he is and, if he is, I want to know how.'

'Sounds intriguing.'

'I'm sure you'll come up with some answers.'

'I'll do my best.'

The dye was cast. 'Thanks Tony. I know I can count on you.'

'Is there anything else you can tell me about her? Friends, social activities, political affiliations?'

Despite having spent the last couple of days with her, he knew very little about Mia. 'She helps out at the Saturday soup kitchen in London with my grandmother and plays mahjong with Gran's group of ladies on a Saturday evening.'

'Okay.' It sounded as though Tony was writing everything down. 'If you think of anything else, text me.'

'If you can, please make this a priority.'

'Absolutely. I'll get on it straight away.'

'Great. And, I'll look forward to the party invitation.' He knew a small sense of relief when he disconnected the call and forwarded the email with Mia's personnel file on to Tony.

He glanced at his watch. Twenty minutes until boarding and Mia still hadn't come out of the bathroom. Clearly, she was going to stay where she was until the last minute.

Was he being brutish?

Possibly. But in this situation he believed it was necessary.

Waiting out the time, he sent Dawson a text to check in on his grandmother. So much for

Gran refusing to take calls because she wanted him to enjoy his time with Mia.

It's backfired big time, Gran!

He looked at the ladies' bathroom and there was still no sign of Mia.

Hopefully Tony would have some answers quickly. Meanwhile, Connor needed to get through the next forty-eight hours with Mia in Paris.

Wonderful.

Being in the city of lovers would emphasise the chasm that'd opened between them.

Only five minutes before they'd be called to their gate to board.

Ping!

Expecting the incoming text to be Dawson's reply, Connor was surprised it was from Tony.

That was quick.

Opening up the message, he saw a photo of Lou Correlli. Tony had written, 'This isn't the Lou Correlli you're talking about, is it?'

Connor had no sooner typed back an affirmative than Tony rang him. Without any greeting, Connor's friend launched, 'Are you absolutely certain this is him?'

He looked again towards the bathrooms to make certain Mia wasn't returning. 'No mistake.' Nobody could miss the ugly scar on the right side of his face.

'Holy shit!'

Connor's stress level spiked. His friend was not prone to dramatics. 'Who is he?'

'One very bad dude. He's connected to a New York Mafia family.'

Mafia.

The word made Connor's blood run cold.

'A simple internet search turned up a heap of articles about him and I hope to hell your employee doesn't have any connection with him.'

'Tell me.'

'He's a hitman known as "The Reaper".'

'Shit.' A heavy boulder settled in his chest and it was a struggle to get enough breath to speak. 'What the bloody hell is Mia mixed up in?'

'I don't know. She has no internet profile at all. No social media. Nothing.'

'She knows him, Tony. And he was fairly certain he recognised her.' Dread clamped around his vocal tract and made each word strained.

'I'll keep digging tonight.'

Panic flared inside Connor. It was probably baseless, but he'd never forgive himself if he didn't follow through on his instinct. 'Do me another favour, will you?'

'Name it.'

'Send a security detail to my grandmother's home. Make it covert.'

'What makes you think she's at risk?'

'I doubt she is, but as I told you, Mia's a friend of hers.'

Tony let out a low whistle. 'Is she home now?'

He looked at his watch again. 'Yes, she'll be home.'

'I'll have a detail at her place within the hour.'

'Thanks Tony.' He closed his eyes for a moment. 'I owe you big time.'

'Anywhere your gran goes, we'll follow, but it'd be easier to protect her if we had bodyguards by her side.'

'No way she'd agree.'

'Do you need a security detail too?'

'I'm headed for Paris from Venice. The flight will board any minute. I think I'll be good for now.' But Lou Correlli did know who he was. 'Let's see what you find out and we'll make a decision then.'

'Stay safe, Connor. Even if there's a link between your employee and the Mafia guy, I wouldn't expect you'd be in any danger ... unless she's doing something illegal at work and you catch her out. Could she be trying to get something on you for them to use as blackmail? Some type of hold on your business empire?'

Holy hell.

'I don't know. I need answers as quickly as possible.'

'You need them. I want them. It's a long time since I've had a case like this to get my teeth into. I'll call a couple of my people and put them on it immediately. Don't worry buddy, we'll work all night if we have to.'

'Impressive.' Especially given it was late on a Sunday evening.

A boarding announcement for the British Airways flight to Paris came through the public address system.

'I've got to board now.'

'I'll phone you in the next couple of hours when we have something more.'

Seconds later, Mia emerged from the bathroom.

Connor wanted to tell her what he'd learned and demand an explanation. He suppressed the instinct. It was better to hold his cards close to his chest and wait for more information.

'Let's go,' was all he said as she joined him and picked up her carry-on luggage.

Mia liked to blend into the background. Was she hiding from this Mafia guy?

Why had she cultivated a friendship with his grandmother?

Questions circled around in his head like a revolving door.

She'd demanded they sleep separately from now on, and that was fine with him. Until he worked out Mia's game, common sense told him to keep his distance from her.

When had it ever been so bloody difficult to listen to common sense?

Chapter Fifteen

'Goodnight, Connor.'

They were booked into the two-bedroom Suite Impériale at the Ritz Hotel, but once she had her room key, Mia stalked off to the lifts without bothering to wait for him.

Their entire trip to Paris had been one of stony silence.

Connor would've preferred an argument. Anything would be better than this awkwardness.

Remember you need to keep your distance.

Uncertainty pressed in on him. A man used to having all the answers, he was way out of his comfort zone. Fighting the urge to follow her and demand answers, he made his way to the Hemmingway Bar. Once he was nursing a scotch, he used his phone to search the internet for Lou Correlli.

Bloody hell.

There were a staggering number of references to the mobster known as 'The Reaper'. The first article claimed that Correlli worked as a hit man for Giovanni Lucetti—the son of one of the five Mafia dons in New York. Although Correlli was suspected of having orchestrated over eighty murders for the Lucetti family, he'd never been convicted of any crime other than failure to pay parking fines.

How could Mia possibly be mixed up with Correlli?

Connor typed in a search for Giovanni Lucetti. Looking up from his phone as the articles loaded, he saw Mia walking through the lobby towards the exit.

Where the hell was she going at this time of night?

Even from this distance, there was a strong pull. A need to be by her side.

Ruthlessly, he crushed his feelings of desire.

Putting the scotch down without taking another sip, he reached the hotel entrance as Mia got into the back seat of a taxi.

In a scene reminiscent of every old-fashioned spy movie he'd ever seen, Connor jumped into the next waiting taxi and said, 'Bonsoir, monsieur. Follow that taxi!'

The driver obviously saw the funny side and chuckled before adding, 'I saw the lady. I can understand why you are following her.'

The guy had no idea.

Tension worked its way up across Connor's shoulders and tightened the muscles at the back of his neck as they followed the taxi along the Place Vendôme and into Rue de la Paix. When it pulled up ahead of them at the Westminster Hotel, Connor said, 'Pull over here, will you?'

Without a concrete plan, he waited until Mia entered the hotel before he paid the driver.

Each breath shallower than the last, he got out of the taxi slowly—almost afraid of what he'd discover if he kept following her.

From the footpath, he could see her inside speaking to a staff member at the concierge desk. There was a lot of nodding going on. Then the staff member picked up a phone and spoke for a moment before passing something to Mia and pointing her in the direction of the lifts.

'Excusez-moi, monsieur.' The doorman approached Connor. 'Avez-vous besoin d'aide?'

'I'm fine. Thank you.' He took out his phone and pretended to scroll through the screen. 'Just checking I'm in the right place.'

'You need the Westminster Hotel?' the doorman asked.

'Yes.' Connor looked beyond the man, making sure Mia had disappeared. 'I see I'm in the right place. Thank you.'

The door man nodded and went back to his post to open the door.

Surely Mia wouldn't have booked in here when she had her own room at the Ritz?

No. She carried nothing more than her handbag.

She had to be meeting with someone but who was it and how the devil was he going to find out?

While he took a discreet seat in the corner of the lobby bar where he could see Mia if she emerged from the lifts, his phone rang.

'Hi Tony. You have answers already?'

'Some answers and a whole lot more questions.'

Tell me about it. 'So have I. I've just followed Mia to the Westminster Hotel.'

Tony made a disgruntled sound. 'I'm not certain following her is the wisest course of action.'

The ominous words and hesitation in Tony's tone ramped up Connor's unease. 'Tell me what you've found.'

'Firstly, I checked the electoral roll and found only one Mia Simms listed in London.'

'There'd be an address listed on the roll, right?'

'Yes and you're not going to believe where she lives.'

Connor closed his eyes briefly as he leaned back in the chair. 'Tell me.'

'Just around the corner from your grandmother.'

A frown pulled at his forehead. 'That's one of the most expensive suburbs of London.'

'She lives in the Nova Apartments.'

He knew the apartments. They were a fairly new development right on the corner of Palace Street and directly across the road from Buckingham Palace Shop.

'They're absolute luxury living,' Tony said. 'Views of Belgravia and Buckingham Palace Gardens mean they rent for thousands of pounds per month.'

'Way over what she could afford on her income from Stewart Corporation,' he confirmed. 'How is she affording it?'

'The apartment she lives in is owned by the Harcher Trust.'

Harcher Trust. 'I know that name.' He frowned as he tried to remember in what context he'd heard of it.

'That's interesting, because it's a private discretionary trust fund set up in the Cayman Islands.'

The mystery around Mia became murkier.

'Do you have any idea who the trustees are?'

'No and I'm not likely to find out. These trusts are created with a private document to which the settler, the trustees and any protector are the only parties. Information relating to this type of trust is not accessible by the general public. We've pulled every string and have drawn a blank.'

Connor swore.

'Also, it looks like she's living at the apartment rent-free.'

'How do you know that?'

'I've looked at her bank account. Those are strings I *can* pull ... off the record,' he explained. 'Her account's been building steadily since she started working for your company. The income goes in every week and very few deductions are made. From the transactions listed, she's spending her money on weekly groceries and that's about it.'

Well, she certainly hadn't been spending her income on fashion or at the salon. 'I suppose she would've had an inheritance when her parents died.'

'Possibly.' The scepticism in Tony's voice was unsettling. 'It could be she comes from a wealthy family but her background is a real blank.'

'What do you mean?' Unease beat harder through his blood.

Tony released an audible breath. 'The records from the boarding school she attended when she was sixteen check out, but it's a very exclusive school and the cyber security is so advanced we haven't been able to find out who was paying the fees.'

'The money must have come from an inheritance, she would've had a guardian by then.

What else did you find?' He was growing increasingly impatient to uncover every jigsaw piece he could to complete the puzzle that was Mia Simms.

'The first school listed in her resume burned down and all student records were lost. Tomorrow I'll send a couple of people to the township to interview anyone who was at the school at the time Mia Simms was supposed to have been there. They'll be asking if people can remember her or her parents.'

'You sound sceptical.'

'I am.' 'Why?'

Tony cleared his throat. 'I left the most alarming thing until last.'

Connor had to consciously relax his fingers as they tensed around the phone.

'By sheer coincidence I had to investigate an insurance claim and had a passenger manifest on file for the very flight Mia Simms' parents were supposed to have been on when they died.'

Supposed to have been on. Connor's stomach hollowed out. 'They weren't listed?'

'Get this!' Tony made a sound of disbelief. 'They weren't listed on the *original* manifest I had on file. But, when I got an updated manifest, their names were there.'

'There was a mistake on the first list?'

'Unlikely.' He paused. 'Listen Connor, I don't know what your interest is in your employee but it may be you've got me digging into something I'm not supposed to unearth.'

'What the hell does that mean?'

'Someone doctored the passenger list. It's the only explanation.'

Adrenalin raced through Connor's bloodstream kicking up his heartbeat. 'Why would someone do that? How is it even possible?'

'It shouldn't be possible, so I double checked. I went back through a news source that named all the crash victims. The configuration of the aircraft meant it could carry 215 passengers. It was reported to be a full flight.'

'Go on.'

'Well, the names on the original manifest I had on file matched those listed by the news source and added up to 215 but on the manifest I pulled up for this investigation—which listed Mr and Mrs Simms—there were 217 passengers which was—'

'Impossible.' Connor finished for him.

'Yep.'

'Holy shit.'

'You got that right. Who is this woman, Connor, and why am I investigating her?'

Tony's question struck right through his heart.

Who was Mia Simms?

'She's my employee and a friend of my grandmother's.' *She's the woman I've made love to. The woman who's consumed my every waking thought since I met her properly only days ago.* That was as much as he knew. 'What I want to know is, what's she mixed up in?'

'It has to be a government agency, Connor.'

'I'm not following you.'

'If my suspicions are correct, Mia Simms wasn't born Mia Simms and we're looking at a falsified identity.'

His blood ran cold. 'You're telling me she's someone else?'

'I suspect so. Attending a school that burned down is a convenient way of explaining that all student records have been erased. Add in the doctored passenger manifest and there being no emergency contact person listed in her personnel file and she strikes me very much as a person who has no concrete links to the past. A secretive person who doesn't want to be identified.'

It rang true yet Connor speared his fingers through his hair as he tried to make sense of it. 'I forgot to mention that she dresses herself right down and says it's because she's more comfortable in the shadows. She wears glasses that only have plain glass and dyes her hair.'

'As though she's trying to disguise her appearance?'

'Yes.' He didn't want to accept it, but all the facts were staring him in the face.

'We've got far more we can look into, but from what we've unearthed in this couple of hours, I'm leaning towards the conclusion that the government's issued her with a new identity.'

'Why would they do that?'

Why? Why? Why?

'She's either a spy—'

Could that be it? His mind raced. If Mia was a spy, was she using her friendship with Violet ... not to get to Connor as he'd first thought, but to get to Violet's lifelong friend, Stanley?

Hell!

When he'd been head of MI5, Stanley had top security clearance and even now was acting for MI5 on some information sharing arrangement with the French. Who knew how many secrets he was carrying around in his head that could still be damaging if they fell into the wrong hands.

But how was Mia tied to Correlli?

Tony was speaking and Connor had missed some of what he'd said—something about it being unlikely Mia was a spy because of her age?

Tuning in again, he heard his friend say, 'My most likely guess—and a guess is all it is—is that she's in some kind of witness protection program.'

Witness protection.

Connor swore. He didn't know what to think or which was most likely. Either possibility could be the reason for Mia's evasiveness, but witness protection would make sense of her response to Correlli.

If he lived in New York, though, how would she have ever come into contact with him?

Memory of her bunged on upper crust British accent made his eyes widen. 'Tony, is it possible she's not British?'

'That's impossible to find out unless we had another name to investigate. There's nothing we've located on Deed Poll about a change in name, but if she is in the witness protection program—'

'When will you know for certain?'

'I *won't* know, I'm afraid. I don't have any contacts with that type of clearance or access to those security systems.'

That wasn't good enough. 'I have to know.' There had to be a way.

'Yeah, I get it. You're worried about your grandmother.'

His grandmother and Stanley.

Stanley!

Of course.

The former MI5 Director would definitely be able to unravel the mystery surrounding Mia Simms—or whoever the bloody hell she was—and Stanley should be warned about the possibility that Mia could be a spy who was targeting him.

Hell. A spy.

Connor felt sick to the gut. No. She couldn't be a spy.

Despite the way she'd acted since her encounter with Correlli, Mia wasn't naturally a cold woman any more than he was a bully. She was warm, enchanting...

'You still there, Connor?'

'Sorry. Thanks for doing this, Tony.'

'No problem. It's exactly the sort of puzzle I like to solve.' Tony cleared his throat. 'I'll update you with anything else as soon as I learn more.'

'Thanks. Talk soon.'

'Be careful, my friend.'

Did he need to be?

'I will.'

Connor looked across at the lifts. It was hardly surprising there was no sign of Mia yet.

His stomach clenched as he wondered again who she was meeting.

Tony had provided a lot of answers but unearthed more questions.

Harcher Trust.

The words teased at the corner of his brain. He knew he'd heard of it...

Slam.

No! He hadn't heard of it, he'd *seen* it. Closing his eyes, he summoned the image. Yes. He'd seen the words Harcher Trust on a bank statement—a bank statement on the desk in Gran's study years ago. He'd quizzed her about it but she'd brushed aside his questions and he'd let it go.

It was another shadowy link between his grandmother and Mia.

Multiple questions beat at his brain, demanding answers.

Why was Mia living rent-free in a very expensive piece of London real estate owned by the Harcher Trust?

What was this trust? Where did the money come from? And how the bloody hell was his grandmother involved?

His fingers raked through his hair. None of the jigsaw pieces fitted together. The whole thing was shrouded in mystery.

Stanley. He had the connections to access this sort of information.

Connor dialled Stanley's number. The call went straight through to message bank, but he left a message asking Stanley to call him back regardless of the time. Connor needed to meet with him as soon as possible.

Now, Connor's most immediate problem was how he should behave with Mia. If he let on he had questions about her past and her very identity and it turned out she *was* a spy, it could be dangerous.

The woman he'd made love to could be a complete fraud.

It wasn't the first time he'd been duped by a woman but, bloody hell, it'd be the last!

Chapter Sixteen

Five minutes later, Connor's phone rang again.

'Stanley.' Connor didn't waste time on pleasantries. 'I'm in Paris and if you're still here, it's important I see you tonight.'

'Is Violet well?' The older man's voice was heavy with concern.

'She's fine. Where are you staying? I'll come and explain.'

There was a long pause and for a moment Connor thought the call had been disconnected.

'I can't meet you tonight, but I could possibly make breakfast tomorrow before my meetings?'

Connor looked at his watch. He didn't want to wait until morning but it was already late, and Stanley wasn't a young man. Besides, he had no idea how long he'd be waiting for Mia to reappear and he wanted to see if he could learn who she'd met with. 'Breakfast sounds good. Tell me where and when and I'll be there.'

'I'm at the Westminster Hotel on Rue de la Paix.'

Connor's jaw slackened.

'Are you still there Connor?'

'I'm here. I'm right here, Stanley. At your hotel.'

'But I thought you were staying at the Ritz?'

'I'm ... How did you know that?'

There was a slight pause before Stanley said, 'Violet must've mentioned it.'

Connor was unconvinced. 'Stanley, do you know my grandmother's friend, Mia Simms?'

'Er ... Yes. I've met Mia.' He sounded guarded.

'How well do you know her?'

'Connor, what's this about?'

'I've just followed her to your hotel.' There was another pregnant pause and Connor's thoughts raced. *Bloody hell! Could it be Mia actually was an MI5 agent?* 'Is Mia with you now, Stanley?'

The silence dragged.

'Stanley?' Tension stiffened his spine. 'Tell me.'

'Yes, Mia's here.' Stanley's sigh was one of resignation. 'You'd better come up too. Pass your phone to the concierge and I'll authorise him to give you a pass for the lift.'

Tension set like concrete across the muscles of Connor's shoulders. After doing as Stanley directed, he entered the lift, slid the security pass through the scanner and waited to arrive at the fifth floor. This intrigue might be part of a normal day for Stanley, but it was too cloak and dagger for Connor's liking.

Despite being desperate for answers, dread clasped around Connor's ribcage as he made his way up to the room and knocked on the door.

'Come in.' Stanley ushered him in, then peered out into the hallway before closing the door behind them both.

Force of habit or a sign he was expecting danger?

Connor was barely two steps into the room when Mia launched at him. 'Stanley said you followed me here!'

'Hello to you too, Mia, and yes, I did.'

'How dare you!' Her eyes flashed fire and she pointed an accusing finger at him. 'You had absolutely no right!'

'You're in Paris with me. You're my responsibility.'

'Your responsibility? Listen to me, Connor. I—'

'Calm down both of you,' Stanley insisted.

Whatever Mia had been about to say, she stopped at Stanley's command. Now the muscles of her cheeks were tight, as though she gritted her teeth.

'I have no intention of adjudicating a slanging match,' the older man warned.

Connor ignored Stanley. 'What the bloody hell is going on?'

He was ready to brace against more of her outraged indignation, but it didn't happen. Instead Connor's throat tightened as Mia covered her face with her hands and sank into a chair by the window. Her shoulders slumped and all the fight seemed to drain right out of her.

When she lowered her hands, she looked vulnerable. 'You shouldn't have followed me.'

It was far from the sassy comeback he'd expected and now she sent Stanley a pleading look.

Connor fought against the urge to go to her side and draw her into his arms. 'I want answers, Mia. Are you mixed up with the Mafia?' Mia gaped at him.

Stanley clicked his tongue against the roof of his mouth. 'How did you reach that conclusion, young man?'

'Lou Correlli.' Although he answered Stanley, Connor didn't take his eyes off Mia. 'He's a hit man for a New York Mafia don and his son. He saw Mia tonight at a restaurant in Venice, thought he knew who she was but couldn't place her. He recognised her pendant, too.'

'Now Connor—' Stanley began.

'You knew him,' Connor told Mia tightly. 'That's why you dived under the table. You were hoping he wouldn't see you and recognise you.'

'Stanley?' Mia's voice was shaky.

Connor saw she was very pale, but he couldn't let this go. He had to know what kind of trouble Mia was facing so he could help her. 'What are you hiding?'

'Sit down, Connor.' The words were an order, yet there was an almost defeated note in Stanley's voice. 'This could take a while.'

'No!' Mia gasped.

'You know what's going on?' Connor cut over her protest.

'Yes.'

'It's none of your business, Connor.' Mia's words were panicked now. 'Please go back to the Ritz and forget all of this.'

Connor sat. 'What's your connection to Correlli, Mia?'

She nibbled at her lower lip. 'You have no right to ask and I won't tell you.' Her gaze flicked back to Stanley. 'Neither of us can tell you.'

'Surely you know you can trust me, Mia.'

'It's better that you don't know,' she insisted.

'Better for whom?'

'For you!' Her voice was full of despair and she jumped to her feet and crossed her arms over her chest in a self-comforting gesture. 'Damn it all, Connor! Keep out of it.'

He stood too. 'It's definitely my business when the woman I care about is obviously mixed up in something dangerous.'

Her eyes widened for a moment before she hugged herself tighter and looked as though he'd wounded her. 'Why can't you accept that our affair is over?' There was a tremor in her voice and the sheen of tears in her eyes. He barely heard her as she whispered, 'It's safer this way.'

There was that word again.

Safety was all-important to Mia. Connor realised now that it governed her every action.

Stanley placed a hand on Mia's shoulder. 'I think we're past the point of playing this safe, dear. From what you told me, Correlli knows Connor's name. If he joins the dots, Connor is Giovanni's link to you. Connor may need protection too, but at the very least he should know what's going on.'

Giovanni.

Protection.

Connor's gut twisted.

'Giovanni Lucetti—the Mafia don's son?' Whatever Mia was involved in really was serious.

'How do you know that?' Mia's words were a whispered thread of sound.

'I see you've been doing your homework,' Stanley said, 'and you're correct. Giovanni's been looking for Mia for the past ten years.'

'Stanley!' Mia protested. 'Connor can't be involved.'

'He's already involved,' Stanley insisted.

'You're part of a witness protection program,' Connor guessed and although Mia neither confirmed nor denied his statement, Stanley gave a small nod of his head.

'You've stumbled across the truth,' Stanley said as Mia bit her lip and maintained her silence. 'There are very few of us who know her identity and whereabouts. It's safer for her this way.'

Connor's heart cramped. Mia was obviously in danger.

Deadly danger.

'It was wrong of me to become involved with you.' Every word held a note of anguish and the sheen of moisture he'd noticed in her eyes now turned to tears. 'For the first time in my life I lived for the moment and snatched happiness. It was only meant to be for four days.' She shifted restlessly from one foot to the other as she wiped at her tears. 'The chance of Lou being in Venice let alone running into us at that restaurant—it's unbelievable.' She shook her head. 'If I'd believed it was possible, I'd never have left London. Never have put you in danger.'

He believed her. 'Am I in danger?'

'There's no reason to assume that,' Stanley said swiftly. 'At most you might be followed to see if you lead them to Mia; that's if Correlli works out who she is.'

Connor ran one hand through his hair as he battled his need to hold Mia close. 'Why are you in a witness protection program?'

'I think you should tell him, Mia,' Stanley prompted gently. 'He knows some of it. He may as well know it all.'

Mia sat and rubbed her hands up and down her arms.

'Better that you do it before Carlisle arrives,' Stanley said when Mia remained silent.

'Who's Carlisle?' Connor asked.

'Mia's FBI liaison agent.' Stanley glanced at his watch. 'Agent Carlisle Roberts is taking the tunnel from London and should be here soon.' Looking at Mia, he asked, 'Would you prefer me to stay while you fill Connor in, or shall I go and wait for Carlisle in the lobby bar?'

'I want to speak to Mia alone,' Connor said.

Stanley looked to Mia for confirmation. 'Mia?'

She gave a reluctant nod of assent.

'Call me when you're finished explaining things. If Carlisle arrives in the interim, I'll buy him a drink and bring him up to speed on what you've told me.' Stanley switched his attention to Connor. 'I presume you've hired an investigator to figure out as much as you have?'

'Tony Jones, my friend from Eton.'

Mia swore.

Stanley's lips thinned. He raised his index finger and pointed at Connor. 'Ring Jones right now and tell him to stop his investigation.' He paused for breath then said sternly, 'Mia will tell you all there is to know. The last thing she needs is for people to be asking questions about her.'

'I'll make the call.'

Damn! Tony had warned him this might be something he shouldn't be digging into. Connor hoped to hell the investigation he'd ordered hadn't put Mia in any greater danger.

Chapter Seventeen

The muscles in Mia's shoulders were like knotted ropes.

Damn Connor!

Damn him for hiring an investigator and damn him for telling her he cared.

Everything was complicated enough and she struggled to stay afloat in the sea of anxiety that kept sucking her under.

As Connor moved to the far side of the room and phoned his friend, Stanley said quietly, 'All the years I've known you, you've never shown any interest in a man. You and Connor ... I can see he cares about you, Mia, and it's too late now to close the floodgates on this whole mess. You should be open with him.'

Clearly, Stanley had decided Connor wouldn't be placed at any risk by knowing.

Part of Mia longed to tell Connor the truth, but she'd guarded her secrets for so long she wasn't even sure where to begin.

Then, there was the conflicted part of her that resented being pushed into this position and left with no choice but to admit the truth. That part of her still wanted to rant at him.

And finally, to make the whole thing messier, there was the part of her that loved him and wanted to seize the chance to be with him.

'I'll be downstairs if you need me.' Stanley leaned down to give her a quick hug before he left.

Disconnecting the call, Connor thrust the phone back into his pocket and walked back to sit opposite Mia.

She bit down on her lip as she looked at him, trying to figure out where to start.

This has to be done.

Resentment wouldn't achieve anything and a confession might ease the tension thrumming between them.

'I never intended for you to get caught up in this,' she reinforced quietly.

'I'm still waiting to understand what "this" is, Mia.'

'It's a long story.'

'I'm not going anywhere.'

She lifted one hand to her temple and her fingertips worked against the tightness there. 'My mother was English. Against the wishes of her parents she went off to Hollywood to pursue her dream of stardom.' She ran her palm down her face and her heart cramped as she thought of her mother's broken dream.

Keep it detached, Mia.

'Instead, she struggled to make ends meet, fell in with the wrong crowd and got pregnant. She moved from Hollywood and I was born and raised in New York.'

'You have no trace of an accent. How old were you when you moved to England?'

'Almost sixteen, but I had elocution lessons when I arrived.'

'Your father?'

'I don't know who he is.' Standing up, she walked restlessly to the window and looked out onto the street below, still busy despite the lateness of the hour. 'My mother was a destitute, illegal immigrant, long outstaying her visitor's visa. With no job and no money, she became Giovanni Lucetti's mistress.'

Connor straightened. 'Is she still his mistress?'

'No.' Sitting again, she started to correct all the lies. 'My mother *is* dead, but she didn't die in a plane crash. That was the story the FBI invented—the story I was trained to trot out.'

Oh God, she had to get this out.

'Mum was killed before I came to England. I...' She swallowed down on the emotion clogging her throat. 'I witnessed her murder.'

'Oh, sweetheart. That's why you're in witness protection?'

The endearment was nearly her undoing. 'Yes.'

'What happened?'

It was too hard to look at him as she forced herself to recount the gut-wrenching memories as matter-of-factly as she could. 'I'd been at a friend's slumber party, and ... well a lot of stuff was said about my mother and I raced home to confront her. But when I came into the house, I could hear her fighting with Giovanni.'

Closing her eyes for a moment, she heard Connor shift his chair forward. Then, her hands were clasped in the protective strength of his giving her the courage to continue.

'My friends had been talking about Giovanni being in the Mafia, but all I knew was that he was my mother's boyfriend.' She shuddered.

'Did your mother know about his connections?'

Shame washed over her and she pulled her hands out of his hold and hung her head. 'Absolutely. He paid for our house—for everything. I feel dirty thinking about it.'

'It wasn't your decision.'

No. It hadn't been.

Mia had always worried her mother had been forced into making bad choices to support her. Then Violet told her that her grandparents had reached out to her mother before she'd left

Hollywood and offered their support. Her mother had been too stubborn, and maybe too ashamed, to return home. She'd gone to New York without telling her parents where to find her.

Her mum hadn't been happy, but every time Mia urged her to leave Giovanni, she'd said, 'We need him, Callie. Where else would we go? What would we eat? Without him, we're on the street.'

Shutting down the memories of the fights she'd had with her mother she looked up at Connor. There was no distaste on his face. No judgement. Only patience and support. Her breath hitched because she loved him even more for it.

'Giovanni was livid that afternoon and Mum sounded scared. She said she wanted to return to the UK.' Mia's pleading with her mother must've finally swayed her. But it had also got her killed and that was a burden of guilt Mia would carry forever.

The sharp sting of tears pricked her eyes and she dug her fingernails into her palms to keep them at bay.

'Giovanni killed your mother?' There was steadfast support in Connor's voice as he encouraged her to continue.

'Yes.' The memories of what happened next hovered on the edges of her mind. Like blades scraping against a sharpening stone, they were honed into clarity and equally as cutting even after all these years. 'I was at the bottom of the stairs and I saw Giovanni pick Mum up by the neck and push her against the wall.' She shook as she remembered the horrible choking sound.

Connor stood and pulled her to her feet and into his embrace.

Even though she knew she should be putting distance between them, she couldn't resist the comfort of his arms.

'I get the picture,' he murmured against her temple as one hand shifted from her waist to smooth down her hair. 'You don't need to go into the details.'

But now she'd started, she needed to tell him everything. Resting her head against the exposed flesh at the vee of his shirt, she closed her eyes. 'I was so frightened, I froze. Finally, Giovanni let her go and she slumped down the wall, coughing hard.' Without conscious thought, Mia raised her own hand to her throat and rubbed it. 'I was about to back away to call the police when Mum spoke. Her voice was so hoarse, I could barely make out what she said.'

Connor's lips pressed against the top of her head and he hugged Mia tighter.

'She said something about incriminating files she'd copied onto a USB. Then she demanded he buy us plane tickets back to the UK or she'd go to the police.'

'Shit! What was she thinking threatening him?'

'I had no idea she was that desperate to leave.' Mia sniffled.

'Giovanni wouldn't let her go?'

'No. He demanded to know where the USB was and she told him he'd never find it.' With a shudder she forced herself to continue. 'Giovanni pushed her down the stairs and I watched her tumble.' She shook her head trying to dispel the vision. 'I saw it happen and I couldn't do anything to save her.' Lifting one hand to her face, she felt dampness on her cheeks and wiped away the silent tears.

'Let it out, sweetheart. I'm here for you.'

'Her head was ... bleeding and her neck was ... It was at an awkward angle. I ... I saw her eyes. Lifeless. It was too late to call for help.' Mia's breaths grew shallow as she relived her panic and could only sob out the rest. 'I shrank back further into the hallway as I heard Giovanni coming down the stairs. I hid in the laundry before he could see me.'

'He didn't find you?'

Mia didn't look up at him. 'No.' Another sob escaped from her throat. She'd been so scared of discovery, so terrified he'd kill her too. Every breath she'd taken had sounded horrendously loud to her own ears. 'He would've assumed I was at the party.'

Connor rubbed her back in reassuring, circular movements. 'It was a damned good thing you had the presence of mind to hide instead of screaming.'

Mia closed her mind against the last images she had of her mother. 'Survival instincts are powerful things and screaming wouldn't have helped. The coroner said Mum died instantly from a broken neck.'

'Giovanni would've killed you if he'd known you were there.'

'Yes.' She finally looked up at him as she confessed, 'But by staying out of sight, I allowed Giovanni to set up his alibi.' Bitter anger rose up and supplanted her grief. 'While I was hiding, he sent a text to his own phone from hers and that text helped him avoid prosecution.'

One of his dark eyebrows rose in question and his hand stilled against her back.

'The text said she was feeling giddy and off-colour and would he please come over straight away.'

'So, the coroner thought your Mum had just fallen down the stairs.'

She nodded and swallowed down on the bitterness that filled her mouth. 'All the coroner could say was that the fall had killed her.

Giovanni was clever, texting her phone to say he was on his way. He made sure his thugs backed up his alibi that he'd been at a card game when Mum texted. He had one of them send a text to another guy to ask if he could come and take Giovanni's place at the game.'

'It's not hard to figure the rest out,' Connor said. 'He waited a decent amount of time—the time it would've taken for him to travel from the card game to your home—before calling for emergency services, backing up that he'd arrived after the fall.'

'Yes, and he played the devastated lover.' She sniffled again and pulled away from him. 'Sorry, I need a tissue.'

'When did you come out of hiding?'

Sniffles taken care of she said, 'When the police and ambulance officers arrived, I told the police what I'd seen.'

'Which Giovanni denied, of course.'

'He said I was in shock, but Giovanni was a known criminal. The police charged him with murder based on my testimony.'

'But he avoided prosecution?'

'Yes.' She scorned the so-called justice system. 'Giovanni had a solid alibi. The coroner found bruising around Mum's neck consistent with my testimony, but Giovanni said they'd used a choker during sex earlier in the day and that Mum ... Mum liked it rough.'

'But you gave eyewitness testimony.'

'His lawyer told the DA that if it proceeded to court he'd paint me as a disturbed teenager who was jealous of her mum's boyfriend.' Nausea churned in her stomach. 'Giovanni told the police I'd been flirting with him.'

'Bastard!'

'Yes, he is.' Every cell brimmed over with her hatred of the man. 'He said I'd arrived home minutes after he did and made up the whole story about him pushing Mum.

'I told the police about the USB Mum had threatened Giovanni with but I had no idea where it was. Giovanni said I'd made that up too.' She shrugged helplessly. 'The FBI turned our home upside down but found nothing. There was no evidence she'd put it in a bank safety deposit box either so I don't think it exists. I think she was bluffing.'

'Damn.'

Another wave of anger crested within her. Giovanni was free while her mother lay dead and Mia's life had been upended. 'In the end, the District Attorney decided they didn't have enough evidence to prosecute.'

Connor seemed to be turning everything over in his head. 'Why is Giovanni still after you?'

'There's no statute of limitations on first-degree murder.' Mia sat back down, picked up a cushion and held it tightly in front of her. 'If new evidence came to light, the cold case would be reopened and Giovanni may have to face trial.'

'Is it likely after all these years?'

'No. The agent I dealt with said that *if* the USB could be located and there was incriminating evidence for any of the guys who'd provided the alibi for Giovanni, they might be persuaded to turn State's witness. Then the DA could charge Giovanni with Mum's murder and any other crimes they could tie him with from the USB evidence. I was told I still might have to provide eyewitness testimony in the future if anybody else came forward to corroborate my story.'

'That's an awful lot of ifs.'

She nodded. Despite the sordidness of her past, it was a relief to have honesty between them. To be able to confide in him pulled the connection between them tighter. She knew she should be severing it, but for now it was comforting.

'Giovanni was worried. Even after he was told the DA was dropping the charges, I was a loose end. He must've given the order for someone to kill me. I was released from protective custody and fired at as I left the police station.'

Connor swore.

'I can thank my clumsiness that they missed.' Although she tried to make a joke of it, the incident still scared her.

'What happened?'

'I dropped my phone and bent over to get it as the shot was taken, so the bullet missed.' She didn't add that it had been such a narrow miss she'd felt the air current as it'd passed. 'An officer leaving the building pushed me behind cover before a second shot could be fired.'

'Hell, Mia.' He closed his eyes for a split second as he let out a pent-up breath. 'Did they catch the shooter?'

'No. But realising I was at risk, they entered me in the witness protection program.'

'I can't even begin to imagine how tough it must've been to go through all you did—especially after losing your mother.'

'I wish Mum and I had both been able to return to England.'

'You're strong Mia.' His admiration warmed her. 'I can't imagine how you coped with leaving behind all you knew.'

'Violet and Stanley were my saviours.'

His whole body drew back. 'My grandmother knows about all this?' 'She does.'

'When did you tell her?'

'She was there right from the start. She met me when I was a scared teenager who'd lost my mother, dodged a Mafia bullet and been shipped off to a brand-new country.' Tears blurred Mia's vision. 'I love Violet so much, Connor. She and Stanley have been like my grandparents. They were my guardian angels when I most needed light in a world that'd been blackened by fear and death.'

A thoughtful frown marred his forehead. 'If you've known Gran since you were a teenager, how is it that you and I never met?' Before she could answer, he said, 'I guess I would've been about twenty-five and I'd moved out. Did she become involved with you through Stanley?'

'Your grandmother was my grandmother's closest friend.'

His eyes widened with comprehension. 'Your grandmother was Ivy—the duchess? You're Elizabeth Buckley's daughter?' She nodded. 'Yes.'

He raised his hands and smoothed his fingers against his brow and she realised it was a lot to take in. 'I was told Ivy had a daughter who'd left home without her blessing. I knew her name was Elizabeth, but I didn't know any more.' He looked at her in wonder. 'My God! You're a duchess. You inherited the title and...'

'No. I changed my identity. I'm not a duchess.'

'Did you inherit your grandmother's estate?'

'Yes. The inheritance was put into a trust and the trustees set up an off-shore account so none of the money could be traced back to me.' Despite being extraordinarily ill, her grandmother had taken steps to protect Mia when she'd learned the circumstances of her mother's death. 'Stanley and Violet were the trustees until I turned twenty-five and then I took control as sole beneficiary.'

'The Harcher Trust.'

She sucked in a shocked breath and alarm raced along every nerve. 'How can you know about it? It's supposed to be untraceable.'

'There's no direct link. My investigator said you were living rent-free in an apartment owned by the Harcher Trust. The name teased my memory because I'd seen correspondence on Gran's desk years ago. I'd asked her about it, but she wasn't forthcoming and I respected that.' Connor looked as though his mind raced to try to absorb everything he was learning about her. 'Stanley's connections to MI5 facilitated your new life in the UK?'

'Yes.' She smiled with gratitude. 'Because I was born in the US, I wasn't even a British citizen. Stanley pulled all sorts of strings and worked closely with the FBI to create my new identity.'

'You were lucky he was able to help you.'

'Very lucky. When my grandmother knew she was dying, she asked Stanley to track Mum and me down. By the time he did, Mum had been murdered. Ivy died a few days after he told her the news. I didn't get to meet her, but it meant a lot to me that she'd tried to find us and asked her two closest friends to protect me.'

'I'm glad you had them, Mia. I know how supportive Gran was of me when I needed her and I know you mean a lot to her.'

'Now you know the whole story.' Mia leaned back in the chair, bone weary.

It'd been a long and emotional day and what she wanted most was to curl up in bed, but she doubted she'd be able to sleep. There was still Agent Roberts to talk to and plans to be made.

Looking at Connor, regret pierced her heart. Any plans that were to be made wouldn't include him.

'I feel like an idiot for thinking you were trying to swindle a group of old ladies out of their fortunes when you're an heiress.'

Mia couldn't resist smiling. She might have suspected the same thing had their positions been reversed. 'Well, fifteen million pounds doesn't come anywhere close to your fortune, but I don't think I'll ever have to resort to preying on old ladies to make ends meet.'

'All this time and I had no idea.' Connor let out an audible breath. 'So, you're really Mia Buckley.'

'Not Mia. I ... I've been drilled never to share my birth name with anyone.'

He shrugged. 'It doesn't make any difference one way or the other. To me you *are* Mia.'

'But I'm not.' An unexpected tidal wave of emotion hit her and her words emerged as a half sob. All the trauma had caught up with her and she couldn't keep herself in check. Burying her face in her hands she tried to pull herself back together and was horrified when she couldn't stem the fresh tears.

If she'd been Mia, she and Connor might've had a chance.

Connor's arms were around her. He lifted her out of the chair, held her against his broad chest and carried her to Stanley's bed where he sat, cradling her to him and planting kisses on her forehead. 'You've endured so much sweetheart, but we'll find a way through this.'

His voice was so steady and confident she almost believed him. Connor was very powerful in the business world, but he played by the rules and had no idea of the power Giovanni wielded. Dark, insidious power that encompassed everything that was heinous and corrupt.

She pulled away from him, eased herself from his lap and stood as she should: alone and on her own two feet. 'This isn't your fight, Connor.'

'I've made it my fight, Mia.'

'Mia?' she said the name he knew her by scornfully. 'Mia was born and raised in England. Mia had two loving parents who tragically died in a plane crash.' She bit down on her lip as tears threatened again. 'I wish I was Mia—that I didn't have to keep my secrets by telling lies. I wish I didn't have to keep looking over my shoulder in fear of discovery, but that's not my reality.'

'Come back here.' Connor held out his arms, but she shook her head.

'This isn't something a hug can fix.'

'I'm offering you more than a hug, Mia. I'm going to stand by you, whether you like it or not.'

'Why?' She angled her head as she regarded him. 'Why would you do that and potentially place yourself in the firing line?'

'Because I care,' he said impatiently before he used a hand to gesture back and forth between them. 'There's a tangible thread linking us together. It's real and it's strong and I have no inclination to cut it and walk away. I won't do it, so don't ask me to.'

His support meant everything to her, but there was only one thing that would give him the right to support her. Not an obligation because she was his lover, employee or his even his grandmother's friend.

No.

The one thing that would earn him the right to offer his support wasn't on offer.

Connor might desire her.

He might admire and respect her.

But Connor didn't love her.

Keeping that fact front and foremost in her thoughts was the only way she prevented herself from running back into the supportive warmth of his embrace.

She didn't belong there.

Chapter Eighteen

Rejecting Connor's support, Mia walked to the opposite side of the room on legs that were suddenly too heavy. It was as though she fought a traction beam that pulled her back to him.

Then, against all good sense—compelled by a force she didn't understand—she found herself turning back.

She loved and trusted this man.

'I was born Callie Buckley.' The words were instantly accompanied by a huge sense of relief.

'Callie.' He turned the name over on his tongue. 'It suits you.'

'It's not who I am anymore.' She shook her head vigorously, desperate for him to understand her identity crisis. 'I left Callie behind when I was driven from the police station to the safety compound. When I got into the bulletproof vehicle, it had darkened windows to stop outsiders seeing in. Ever since, I've had to stop everyone from seeing the real me—everyone except Violet and Stanley.'

He got up from the bed and closed the distance between them. 'You were completely uprooted.'

Mia resisted the urge to lean into him as his hand stroked over her hair. 'I had to be. The most important rule for those in protective custody is never to contact former friends, associates or family members.' She willed herself to keep the emotion from her voice. 'I was told I must never return to my home town. Apart from the agent you'll meet shortly, I left everyone else from New York behind.'

A tender kiss landed on her temple. 'It must've been unsettling, particularly as you were so young.'

Don't lean into him.

You must keep standing alone.

'It was a leap into the unknown, but I had no choice.' She took a deep breath and willed her voice to be steady. 'Even with the completely new identity and life story, I kept looking over my shoulder. I was afraid to make friends in case I slipped up and revealed too much of myself. Since the day my mother was murdered, I've wanted to keep to the shadows.' She pulled herself up as the truth hit her. 'No. It was even before then.' God, she'd been doing it all her life. 'I made myself scarce whenever Giovanni or one of his men were at our house.' A distressed sound emerged from the back of her throat. 'I was hiding myself away even before Mum was killed.'

'I'm not surprised.' Connor's arms wrapped around her. 'Now I understand why you didn't want to attract media attention.' He shook his head. 'Gran knew about your background and yet she persisted with her plan. I can't believe she'd put you at such risk.'

'Violet convinced herself I'd never be recognised.' Her voice was hoarse. 'I need some water.' She pulled out of Connor's arms to get a glass of water.

Don't let him comfort you. It's only bringing you closer together and you have to keep your distance.

'Surely you went a bit overboard with the disguise?' he asked as he looked her over.

'Those clothes made me feel unnoticed.'

'Which made you feel safe.'

She nodded, sat down and enjoyed the water moistening her dry throat as she swallowed.

'Do you think Correlli will realise who you are?'

'I'm afraid he won't give up until he's figured it out.'

'Let's hope he's got more pressing issues to think about.'

'I'm not certain my appearance alone would make him link me to Mum. The necklace caught his attention. Mum didn't have much in the way of valuable possessions, but she almost always wore this necklace given to her by her father. The jewellery box was her favourite gift from her mother. I took those two things and they're the only physical things I have that belonged to Mum.'

Mia touched the pendant. 'I rarely take this off, but it's normally hidden beneath my clothing. If I'd thought about it being a distinctive piece, I would never have worn it.'

Connor sent her a gentle smile. 'Thank you for telling me the truth, Mia. It stops wild conjecture running through my mind.'

'What did you think was going on?'

He moved one hand dismissively. 'Honestly, I didn't know what to think. But, when Tony told me there was no trace of a school record from your younger years and that the passenger list on the flight over India had been tampered with, I knew you were involved in something serious.'

'You found all that out tonight?'

'Yes.' His fingers scratched along the stubble of his jaw. 'Tony suggested you were either in witness protection or possibly a spy.'

Her eyes widened. 'A spy?' She gave a small laugh. 'Oh, Stanley would laugh at that one!'

He knelt before her, taking her hands in his. 'Sweetheart, you might've thought these last few days were only about sex but you're wrong.'

What was he saying?

'We agreed on a short-term affair for a reason, Connor. It suited both of us.' He couldn't know how much she'd love it to be more. His hold on her hands was very distracting. She needed to sever this link between them—both physically and socially—so she eased her hands out of his.

'Connor, I can't have anything more when my life is based on a lie.' She willed him to understand. 'I can't build on that sort of foundation. Nobody can ever know who I really am.'

He sent her a puzzled look. 'But I know who you are. You're Mia Simms and although Callie has been left behind, she's still very much part of you.'

'A part I can't talk about.'

'Sweetheart, you're so tied up in knots about this, the obvious has escaped you.'

She sent him a questioning look.

'You've talked about it now. I know about your past so we go forward on a *solid* foundation.'

'Forward? No. We have no future.' She shook her head. 'Are you saying you still want to keep this going until it reaches an "organic" ending as you term it, even though you know your life could be at risk?' She couldn't expect it of him. She wouldn't ask it of him.

'My life won't be at risk. If Stanley thinks it's necessary, I'll hire a team of bodyguards to keep us both safe. You may as well accept that I won't take no for an answer.' There was no way she could let him do it. 'We may not have known each other long, but you've shaken my priorities up, Mia Simms. Every time we've made love, my world's been rocked off its axis.'

She was dumbstruck. She wanted to rejoice, but she couldn't. He was talking about great sex, but he didn't love her. If they kept this going she'd never survive when they eventually broke up.

'You'll find I'm not so easy to get rid of when my mind is set on a particular course of action, Mia.'

'You and Violet both!' The pair of them were like steamrollers, smoothing over any bump in their path.

This may be what you want most of all, but you know you can't have it.

'My answer's still no, Connor.'

He raised both eyebrows in an expression of bemused disbelief.

'I know it's not a word you're used to, but it's my final word and you need to accept it.' When he would've objected, she put up her hand. 'I appreciate what you're prepared to do for me, but this...' *Find a word that doesn't reveal how much this has meant to you.* 'This ... fling over the last couple of days is at an end. It's all I ever wanted and you need to accept it.'

'We'll see.' Completely unperturbed, he reached out and tucked a loose strand of her hair back behind her ear.

'Connor! Have you heard a thing I've—?'

He placed a finger up to her lips, cutting off her stern words. 'How about you call Stanley. I'd like to hear what he and this agent have to say about what should happen next.'

He was exasperating!

Damn it all. She knew Connor would pursue her relentlessly. For now, she bottled up her frustration, dug out her phone and called Stanley.

He and Agent Roberts would be straight up.

She was so mentally, emotionally and physically spent she looked longingly at Connor's broad chest, yearning to be wrapped against it.

He's offered, Mia. All you need to do is agree.

No. No. A thousand times, no.

I have to stand firm.

Chapter Nineteen

'As far as we know Correlli doesn't know who you are,' Agent Carlisle Roberts said ten minutes later when they were all sitting around Stanley's hotel room. 'He simply thinks you remind him of someone.'

The FBI man was tall and athletic looking and Mia had always found him intimidating. Tonight was no exception. 'Lou hasn't joined the dots yet, but I think he'll keep turning it over in his mind until he makes the connection,' she said.

'You shouldn't have been wearing your mother's necklace.' Carlisle shot her a fierce look. 'Are you holding on to any other pieces of your past?'

'There's no need for that tone, Agent Roberts.' Connor's words were laced with warning and he placed a protective arm along the back of Mia's chair. While she appreciated Connor's support, she knew she deserved the agent's wrath. She'd broken the rules when she'd taken the two items belonging to her mum.

'Mia was a teenager,' Connor continued. 'You think it was easy for her to see her mother killed and then walk away from everything that'd ever been familiar to her?'

'We don't make rules up lightly,' Carlisle shot back. 'Every rule, every condition, is for the safety of the witness we're trying to protect.'

'Let's move along, gentlemen.' Stanley's quiet authority went a little way to easing the atmosphere of antagonism that had sprung up between Connor and Carlisle. 'What's done is done.'

From the moment he'd entered the room it'd been obvious to Mia that the FBI agent resented Connor being here and knowing her background. Now Connor's defence of her was making things worse.

'I'm sorry.' Mia was eaten up with anxiety layered in guilt. 'I knew I was breaking the rules, but I didn't think it would do any harm.' She held her hand up in entreaty when Agent Roberts looked like he was about to give her another rebuke. 'I brought my mum's necklace and her jewellery box with me. Nothing else.'

'Was there any other jewellery inside the box?' the agent asked.

'No.'

'Alright.' Carlisle stood and paced the room with one hand on his hip and the other rubbing back and forth across his forehead. 'There are two main options.'

'We discussed this downstairs, Mia,' Stanley put in. 'Each has merit, so tell us which you'd prefer.'

Her tension coiled tighter.

'The first is the most drastic, but definitely the safer,' Carlisle said. 'We assume you've been made, give you a different identity and relocate you—possibly back to the States.'

The bottom dropped out of her world.

'No,' Connor said at the same time Mia shook her head vehemently. 'Mia can't be expected to uproot her life again.'

'I don't want to become someone else.' Desperation surged through her and she shot to her feet. 'I *won't* be someone else and I don't want to go back to the States.'

'It's okay, sweetheart. Nobody's going to force you to do that,' Connor said before he asked, 'What's the other choice?'

Carlisle's posture was stiff. Ignoring Connor, he told Mia, 'The second option is that you go on living as you've been doing, but with increased security. You stick to your normal routines unless we get evidence you've been made.'

'And what if it looks like Giovanni's found me?'

'Then there are another two options,' Stanley said.

'How the hell are you going to know she's been identified?' Connor demanded before Stanley could continue.

'Before I left London I put a team in place to monitor the situation,' Carlisle said. 'If anyone starts searching for Mia Simms online, we can relocate you immediately while we assess the risk.'

'Relocate me temporarily?'

'Yes. Until we determine the risk has passed.'

'But what if you miss something?' Connor argued. 'What if they hire an investigator who has a more sophisticated way of tracking Mia down than online searches?'

'You have no idea how these things work,' Carlisle growled at Connor. 'That risk is minimal, but it's why Mia will have bodyguards.'

Mia had questions of her own. 'What exactly are the team in London doing?'

'They're tracking the IP addresses of anyone who searches the internet for Connor Stewart or Mia Simms. They've already found recent activity on you, Mia,' the agent paused to shoot Connor a narrow-eyed glare. 'Stanley informed me that the private detective and security agency responsible for the searches were enlisted by you, Stewart.'

'They've been called off the case now,' Connor assured him.

Carlisle's look said they'd better be off the case. 'If we get any leads—particularly where both searches are generated from the same address—that'll tell us someone has linked you two together.'

'I have no internet presence,' Mia put in quickly. That was one of the other rules that'd been set out in the witness protection program and it'd been easy to follow as she had no social network to speak of on or offline.

The agent nodded. 'Provided you have no new social acquaintances in common, and you don't get a promotion and therefore a higher profile at the Stewart Corporation, we can assume anyone searching both names from this point is associated with Giovanni.'

'Unless the media gets a hint we've been away together,' she said.

Connor looked at her. 'The reason you hide in the shadows.'

'Yes.' Was he beginning to understand?

He was a global businessman. Billionaire. Philanthropist. Eye candy of the most delicious sort. All these factors combined to make him newsworthy and underlined why Mia could never be at his side publicly.

'Have you been photographed by the paparazzi?' Carlisle asked.

'Not as far as I'm aware,' Connor said.

God but she hoped not. 'Stanley, you said I have options if I'm identified. What are they?'

'If you refuse to be relocated and assume a new identity, you have only one option,' the FBI agent answered before Stanley got a chance. 'You keep living exactly as you are with your security team in place and we hope to draw out whoever Giovanni sends after you.'

Connor exploded. 'You want to use her as bait?'

'We know what we're doing, Stewart,' the agent said.

'Connor, I'll have security. I want you to have bodyguards too,' Mia told him.

'I've been telling you and Violet for years that you should have security,' Stanley agreed. 'I seriously doubt you're at risk from Giovanni, but anyone of your worth could be a target at the best of times.'

'They know Connor's name,' Mia pointed out. 'They could use him to get to me.'

'And all he has to do is tell them he knows nothing about you except that you're an employee who assisted on his business trip,' Carlisle said firmly before looking at Connor. 'You should be photographed out with other women this week so no one suspects you're personally involved.'

'I'm not going to—'

Stanley raised a hand. 'Connor, get security and make sure you have other dates this week. It could help keep Mia safe.'

'Please do as they ask,' Mia said.

He looked as though he'd like to protest but, in the end, he released a pent-up breath. 'If that's what it'll take to keep you safe.' He turned to Stanley. 'Do I need to organise extra security at work?'

'Apart from your own security, leave everything else to us,' Stanley replied. 'The last thing we want is everyone on top of one another.'

'Remember, this is the Mafia, not a terrorist cell,' Agent Roberts added. 'When they strike, it's with a hit man. Individual and direct, all loose ends taken care of. They won't be bombing Mia at work or home. It'll be a straightforward, single bullet.'

Shit! Mia knew the score, but his clinical statement still shocked her.

'Oh, for God's sake,' Connor muttered as he squeezed one of Mia's shoulders in reassurance.

'You'll have MI5's finest, Mia,' Stanley assured her.

'If there's nothing else, gentlemen, I think Mia and I should get back to our hotel. It's been a hell of a day and we have a busy day planned tomorrow.'

'No more sightseeing,' Stanley said. 'Mia needs to be back in London where we can put everything into place for her protection.'

'But Violet—' Mia started.

'She can't be told about this threat,' Connor said. 'Her heart mightn't stand the worry.'

'Of course,' Stanley agreed and offered a plausible explanation for their early return.

'I'm going to hire a car in my name, Connor,' Stanley said. 'I want you to go to your hotel, get your things and then drive to London. *Tonight.*'

Connor's displeasure was obvious by the tightening of his mouth and the stiffening of his broad shoulders. 'Why in your name?'

'If Giovanni has some way of tracing your flight to Paris from Venice, it's better to let them think you're both still here. That'll give us more time to set things up in London. Mia will go separately with Agent Roberts.'

Sensing Connor was about to protest, Mia said, 'It's better this way, Connor.' It might be unnecessary secret service smoke and mirrors, but Mia had learned her lesson tonight. She was determined to follow every future instruction to the letter. 'When we get back to London and I see you at the office, we're back to Miss Simms and Mr Stewart. The only time I'll see you is during our marketing presentations.'

She couldn't make it any clearer to him.

It was over.

For both their sakes, she hoped he'd accept it.

Chapter Twenty

Back in their hotel suite at the Ritz, Connor sat on the sumptuously comfortable lounge while Mia gathered her things together. She'd hardly had time to unpack anything before she'd hared off to see Stanley, so it wouldn't take her long. Connor's bag was still in the corner where the bell hop must've left it.

Leaning forward, Connor rested his elbows on his knees.

Miss Simms and Mr Stewart.

It wasn't possible for him to go back to their employer-employee relationship. He hoped Mia wouldn't be able to turn away as easily as she imagined from all they'd shared.

His hands clenched. Although he understood why Mia was intent on cutting him out of her life, it was difficult to accept her decision.

It's only temporary, he told himself.

When all this mess sorted itself out, he and Mia would resume their relationship. How could they not when it'd been so good between them?

'Goodbye Connor.'

He hadn't heard her come into the lounge area, but she stood in front of him with her glasses firmly in place and her hair wound up in its signature bun.

Mia placed an item and a piece of paper on the coffee table. 'I'm leaving my necklace and jewellery box behind. I've written a note so the housekeeping person who comes to clean can keep them and won't be in trouble for theft.'

Hearing the slight wobble of her voice, he stood and urged, 'Don't. You've carried those things with you for a decade. You said yourself they're the only link you have to your mother.'

'Wearing Mum's necklace put me in danger. Agent Roberts is right. I have memories. I don't need material possessions as well.'

'Mia, you can't let go of the meaningful things in your life just because you get into a tight spot.' He wasn't only referring to the necklace and jewellery box, even though he gestured to them.

Holy hell.

For a moment, his heart stalled.

'That jewellery box was your grandmother's.'

'Yes.'

'My grandmother has one exactly the same.' He walked forward and picked it up, smoothing his fingertips over it as he did. 'I remember Gran told me that she and your grandmother had identical ones. When they were teenagers, they had them custom made copying a design that'd been in the duchess's family for centuries.'

'I didn't know that. All I knew was that my grandmother gave it to Mum.'

Did Mia know? 'As a youngster, I was always fascinated with the secret compartment and the precise mechanics needed to open it.'

Her lips parted and her eyes widened. 'Are you sure it's the same box? Mum didn't mention a secret compartment and I've never found one.'

'Watch.' He picked up the box. 'I tip the box upside down and at the same time I push the clasp in. I can then put my fingernail into a barely noticeable groove on the foot of the box right here and—' He performed each action as he spoke. 'See! I can slide the false bottom along.'

Mia gasped as the bottom panel moved.

'Voila!'

Her gasp turned into 'Oh my God! Connor!' as a USB clattered onto the table surface.

Connor stared at the USB.

'This must be it,' Mia whispered as she picked it up. 'It has to be the one the FBI searched for.'

Connor's heart felt like it took great leaps around his chest. 'We need to get this to Agent Roberts straight away.'

'No!' She spoke rapidly, 'I need to see what's on it first. He's already upset that I wore Mum's necklace. I don't want to waste his time if all it contains is recipes or something else completely innocent. I need to know this is what we think it is.'

Connor was convinced the thumb drive held the key to dispelling the menacing shadow Giovanni cast over Mia's life, but he understood she wanted to be certain. 'Let me get my laptop and we can take a look.'

'Yes please.' Mia passed it to him.

He couldn't set his laptop up fast enough.

'I can hardly breathe right now,' Mia said a few minutes later as he inserted the USB, opened the folder and scrolled through the files.

It was like winning the lottery. Every file had something to do with Lucetti.

'I don't know what all this means, but it must be evidence of criminal activity,' Connor said. Elation fizzed through him knowing it could be the key to Mia's safety.

'Thank you, Connor!' She hugged him tight. 'This is all thanks to you.'

Before he could kiss her, she was pulling away and reaching for her phone.

'I'm going to call Stanley and tell him what we've found. Then I'll call Agent Roberts up.'

Connor was surprised the FBI agent wasn't upstairs already, pounding on the door and demanding Mia hurry up. 'How about we secure these files by downloading a copy onto my laptop?'

'Great idea.' Her smile was radiant. 'Thank you, Connor. You know how important it is for me to feel safe.'

'Your safety's important to me, Mia.' He willed her to understand that he'd do whatever it took to keep her safe.

'Stanley will be so excited!' She shook her head as she punched in his number. 'All these years I thought Mum must've been bluffing. You know, if I'd left the jewellery box and the FBI had found it, they'd never have guessed it had a secret compartment. It would probably have ended up in a dumpster bin or antique store. Thank God you knew about the compartment.'

As Connor downloaded the files he listened to Mia share the news with Stanley and then call Carlisle. 'Agent Roberts is on his way up,' she told Connor. 'I hope there's enough incriminating evidence on here to turn some of Giovanni's associates against him. I want him in prison for the rest of his life.'

It was torture to be so close to Mia and not touch her.

'Do you think I could at least get another hug for my role in finding this?'

Mia threw herself against him, her arms reaching up over his shoulders and behind his head. 'I think you deserve more than a hug.' She raised herself up on her tiptoes, but didn't need to use her hands to draw his head closer as Connor took control and plundered her mouth with his own.

It was sweet heaven to taste her mouth again and he kissed her like a dying man who knew that only her kisses could save him. Mia returned his kisses with equal fervour, affirming his belief that she didn't want to end their relationship. These files were the chance for their relationship to move forward.

Only the knock at the door announcing Carlisle's arrival made them break apart.

For a moment, they held each other's gaze as they caught their breath. Need pulsed between them. Regret stamped itself on her features as she took a step back from him. Her lips parted, words seeming to hover upon them, longing to be said—or was she waiting for him to speak?

A seething mass of something unidentifiable tangled in Connor's chest. He should speak. He tried to find the words...

The moment passed.

Whatever it was she'd wanted to say—whatever it was he'd been trying to put into words—remained unsaid.

'I'll answer the door.'

As she turned away abruptly to let the FBI agent into the suite, Connor felt every step she took toward the door like a blow to the heart. The gap between them was widening and he didn't know how to close it.

Soon, Mia would leave Paris with the agent and it could be days before Connor saw her again.

Chapter Twenty-one

'Good morning, Dawson.'

'Mr Stewart! What are you doing here?' 'I'm here to see Gran, of course.'

'But ... It's only Monday!'

'I'm well aware of what day of the week it is, Dawson.' It'd been well past midnight when Connor had left Paris but he'd been unable to sleep when he reached home. Instead, he'd showered, attempted to answer some emails and ended up trying to work off his restlessness in his home gym. Failing, he'd got ready for work, but decided to call in on his grandmother on the way to the office.

The butler recovered. 'Sir, you weren't expected. Mrs Stewart said you'd be overseas until tomorrow night.'

'As you can see, I'm back.' It was unusual for Dawson to be in such a flap. 'Now, are you going to let me in so I can surprise Gran?'

'Er ... Mrs Stewart isn't at home for visitors, sir.'

What the hell? 'I'm hardly a visitor, Dawson. For God's sake, why aren't you letting me in?' Anxiety crept up his spine. 'Is Gran okay?'

Last night, Dawson had said she was doing fabulously and there'd been no call through the night to say otherwise.

'She's perfectly well, Mr Stewart.' He stepped aside and Connor walked past him.

'Is she in the breakfast room?'

'When I said she's not at home for visitors, sir, I meant she's not at home.'

Connor glanced at his watch. 'It's only seven-thirty! Where the devil is she at this time of the day?'

She had to be at home. Gran always enjoyed lingering over breakfast no matter what else she had planned for the day.

Besides, Tony had linked Connor into an app that tracked Gran's new bodyguards. The app showed all four were still guarding the house.

Irritation needled the nape of his neck.

He couldn't believe his friend's security team had failed in their duty and let Gran slip past them early this morning.

The butler let out a long breath. 'Mr Stewart, please don't be alarmed. Mrs Stewart is fine, but she's at London Bridge Hospital.'

'What?'

'I was under strict instructions not to tell you unless something went wrong but she decided to have her *scheduled* surgical procedure.'

What the devil?

'When did this happen?'

'Nell and I drove her to the hospital on Friday afternoon while you were on your way to Venice, and your grandmother was the last patient on Dr Forrester's surgical list for Friday evening.'

Connor swore savagely, and Dawson flinched. 'I should've been told.' What if something had gone wrong?

Gran had manipulated him. Again.

Huh! The bodyguards had been deployed late last night and had no doubt assumed Gran was already in bed. They weren't to know they were guarding an empty house.

'Dr Forrester says that Mrs Stewart is as good as new,' Dawson rushed to placate him. 'It seems likely she'll be home later today or early tomorrow morning. She was hoping to be out of hospital by the time you arrived home *tomorrow night.*'

Damping down on his shock and aggravation, he tried to keep uppermost in his mind that the surgery had gone well. How bloody typical of Gran to go off and do things her way. Honestly, she was the most steely-minded, stubborn ... 'Does Miss Simms know about this?'

'No, sir. Mrs Stewart made it clear nobody was to be told.'

'Thank you, Dawson. I'll make my way there directly.' As frustrated as Connor was, he wouldn't vent his annoyance on Dawson. 'Is there anything I need to take to her this morning?'

'No, sir. As far as I'm aware, she has everything she needs.'

'Right.'

He turned to go, but stopped when Dawson said, 'Sir, I know you're upset, but this is the way your grandmother wanted it. I truly would've called you if she had needed you to come home.'

'I know you were following her instructions, Dawson.' The older man's first loyalty lay with Gran. 'I'm glad she's had the surgery and everything's going well. That's the most important thing.' It was the whole reason he'd agreed to the five dates with Mia in the first place. 'I'll see you later.'

As he got into his car, he phoned Tony. Stanley had assured him that Violet didn't need any protection, but Connor wasn't taking any chances. Some of Tony's men needed to be redeployed to the hospital.

Carlisle had been very specific that Connor wasn't to visit, phone or even text Mia, so he sent a text to the FBI agent instead and asked him to update both Mia and Stanley that Gran's surgery had already taken place.

***

'Dash it all, Connor, what in God's name are you doing back so early?'

'Fancy seeing you here, Gran!'

'Sarcasm doesn't sit well with you and Dawson's already phoned to say you were on your way.' She sat up straighter against the pillows. 'Why aren't you still enjoying one of the most romantic cities in the world with Mia? You didn't leave her in France by herself, did you?'

'I'll tell you, but you need to explain yourself first.' And there was no way he was going to let her back out.

She raised her eyebrows in a somewhat haughty expression that reminded him very much of Mia's grandmother. Duchess Ivy had been the epitome of intimidating whenever he'd encountered her as a child.

'I needed the procedure and I had it. You didn't really think I was so foolish I was going to sit around with a "ticking bomb" in my chest for any longer than I needed to, did you?' She smiled. 'Besides, I would never put either of you in the position of blaming yourselves if I'd delayed and had a heart attack or a stroke.'

'So all that emotional blackmail was a bluff?'

'If one is going to have a heart problem, one should at least make the most of it to achieve one's goals!'

Connor gritted his teeth together, but through his annoyance he had to work to stop the grin that tugged at his mouth. He and Mia had been well and truly played—by an expert. 'You're a thoroughly wicked old woman and you should be ashamed of yourself.'

He wasn't going to tell her he was grateful for her machinations.

'Desperate times call for desperate measures.' Violet allowed herself a very brief chuckle before she sent him an admonishing look. 'For all my manipulation, you're home early. What went wrong, Connor?'

He ignored the note of disappointment in her voice. 'I'll get to that. This is still about you.' Given her level of manipulation, she could damned well wait. 'Dawson said Dr Forrester was pleased with how the operation went.'

'He's very pleased. You've only just missed him on morning rounds. He's approved for me to go home later this afternoon with my nurse, Giselle. Truly, there's no need for any of us to be concerned. I'm going to be back to normal and sparking on all cylinders so to speak.'

'Heaven help us all.' He made light of her words, but she had no idea that there was every need to be concerned. Except now his worries were mostly about Mia.

He and Mia had decided the best course of action would be to tell Violet that while they'd declared a truce and enjoyed each other's company, there was simply no spark between them.

Stanley had concocted an excellent cover story to keep Mia away from Violet in case Lucetti found her and followed her. While they didn't seriously believe he would be interested in harming anyone close to Mia, they were playing it safe.

'Now, that's my news done and dusted. Tell me about your trip. Did you and Mia fight?'

Connor looked Gran straight in the eye and hoped he'd be able to pull off the lie. He wasn't used to lying and when he'd tried to be a little liberal with the truth during his teenage years, she'd always pinned him with her steely blue gaze and seen right through him. The consequences of his bending of the truth had been swift and stern.

'Actually, we both enjoyed our time together in Venice. You were right that we'd get along well together. She's a very bright, spirited lady.' *Careful. Don't oversell.* He'd learned that much from Mia.

'But?'

'There's no spark, Gran.'

She sent him a puzzled look. 'I was certain I picked up on some sizzling vibes when she walked down the stairs in that stunning red dress. And it definitely went both ways.'

'I was shocked at her transformation. Nothing more.'

'I see.' Connor saw her disappointment. 'I really thought ... You're sure there was no spark?'

'Believe me, Gran, I know a spark when I feel one.'

'Hm.' Her lips pursed. 'What about Mia? I guess I shouldn't say anything—especially when she's never confirmed it in so many words—but I could've sworn she was keen on you. Is she happy, or is she feeling totally devastated because you don't return her feelings?'

Huh! If only Gran knew.

Connor was the one feeling hollow and devastated after Mia's rejection. And, while he was absolutely certain Mia was only trying to protect him, it didn't make it any easier to accept.

What man wanted to be pushed away and not allowed to support the woman he loved when she was going through a crisis?

Oh God.

Bloody hell.

The room spun around him and he felt light-headed as realisation dawned.

There it was.

There were the words he'd been trying to find back in the hotel suite in Paris right before Carlisle had knocked on the door.

Connor had fallen in love with Mia.

Were they the sentiments Mia had wanted him to express?

If he'd been able to qualify the depth of his feelings then by using those three small words, would he still be at Mia's side?

But, he couldn't love Mia, could he? He'd only started getting to know her in the last couple of days.

Careful, Connor.

He'd imagined himself in love with Rachel, too, and look how that'd ended up.

Confusion swamped him. He knew he felt a much stronger connection with Mia than he had with Rachel. But he needed to rein his thoughts in and not rush into anything. He needed more time to sift through and understand his feelings.

'...hope so. I suppose I'll be able to judge for myself tonight. I'll phone her and ask her to come and visit me at home this evening.'

'No.' He hadn't heard the first part of what Gran had been saying, but he'd tuned into the last part. 'The reason we came home early from Paris was because Mia's come down with a cold.'

'A cold in the middle of summer?'

'Yes. She's feeling all sorts of miserable with a fever, a blocked nose and a cough.'

'That came on quickly.' There was a definite note of suspicion in Gran's voice.

'Well ... er ... she wouldn't want me to tell you, but I believe you already know how clumsy she is?'

Violet raised the tips of her fingers to her temples. 'Oh no! Don't tell me! I'll bet she—'

'—fell into the Grand Canal,' he supplied.

Violet groaned. 'Oh dear. I guessed it! No wonder she got sick.' She shook her head. 'Anyway, she sends her love and will give you a call when she's recovered, but the last thing she wanted to do was expose you to her bug *before you had your procedure*.' He sent her a disgruntled look. 'Of course, we didn't know you'd had it. Still, you can't afford to get sick while you're recovering either.'

'That's true. I'll ask Nell to make her some chicken soup and get Lucy to take it to her.'

Uh-oh. The last thing they needed was for Gran to find out Mia wasn't sick at all.

'I'm sure she'll appreciate it.' He'd have to get Carlisle to warn Mia she was going to have a visitor.

She was spending the day at home while the security on her apartment was upgraded and the MI5 bodyguards were assigned. Tomorrow, she'd be back at work.

'Probably should get Nell to make a big batch so Lucy can drop it around and then leave Mia in peace. Nothing worse than being sick and having to keep getting out of bed to answer the door.'

'That's true.'

Connor felt a small degree of satisfaction at having out-manipulated the expert manipulator.

'Did you at least manage to get through most of my plan for Venice before Mia became sick?'

'Yes, and Mia will show you the photos to prove it as soon as she's well.' All the photos except the ones Peppi took.

Connor closed his eyes and remembered the heaven of his first taste of Mia's lips.

Had it only been a couple of days ago?

'I don't think I ever told you the tale, but your grandfather realised he loved me when we were sitting at the cafe on St Mark's Square. I was hoping history would repeat itself and you'd both fall in love with each other in Venice.' She sighed. 'I'm so disappointed I was wrong, but at least you each found you enjoyed the other's company. Will you see her again?'

He fought to keep from revealing his disappointment. 'Only at the office.'

If Gran was still holding out hope their friendship would deepen, she'd be disappointed when she read tomorrow's paper.

Carlisle had insisted Connor take someone out tonight and ensure the photos were splashed across the social pages tomorrow. To protect Mia, Connor would play the role he'd been assigned and make certain he looked appropriately interested in his date.

He already knew which gorgeous woman he'd be photographed with. Skye was a model and would-be actress who'd be more than willing to go out with him. No doubt the media would speculate that because they were dating again after a few months break, there might be something more serious between them.

A nurse came into Gran's private room. 'Time to take your blood pressure again, Mrs Stewart.'

Perfect timing!

Connor stood and gave Gran a kiss on the cheek. 'Don't give the nurses any trouble, Gran.'

'As if!'

He rolled his eyes at her indignation. 'I'll call in to see you tonight before I go out.'

'You're going out?'

'A man has to eat.'

Before she could invite him to have dinner with her, Connor made his escape. With one quick phone call to Skye he arranged his date for the evening. Knowing he was going to spend the evening with one of the hottest models in London did nothing to stir his pulse—or any other part of his body.

Skye simply wasn't Mia.

Chapter Twenty-two

The following day, Connor's executive assistant popped her head around the door of his office. 'You're due at the marketing presentation in five minutes.'

'Thanks, Grace.' Time had dragged—especially since lunch when he'd started looking at his watch every few minutes, impatient to see Mia.

'Will Mia Simms be there?' Grace asked.

For a second he thought he must've spoken his thoughts aloud.

'I expect so.' Hoping he'd injected the right degree of casual indifference into his voice he looked back at his assistant. 'Why?'

'I was going to phone her, but I got caught up with a few things and she's probably already on her way to the meeting. Would you pass on a message for me?'

'Of course.' His curiosity was piqued.

'Tell her not to worry about her watch. I got a call from a man who's found it and he's going to forward it here to the office for her.' Grace smiled. 'Nice to know there are still some honest people in the world.'

'Her watch?' Apprehension pricked along his shoulders. Mia hadn't been wearing a watch when they were away. Was it because she'd already lost it? Hang on ... 'Grace, why did the man call *you?*'

'Oh, he said the woman who'd had dinner with you in Venice had dropped her watch on the floor and that he'd only noticed it after you'd both left the restaurant. He said the name "Mia" was engraved on the back of it and he was hoping I'd know of the lady and have her address so he could get the watch to her.'

Shit. 'What did you tell him?'

She frowned and Connor realised he hadn't been able to keep the urgency from his voice. 'I said it would be Mia Simms from our marketing department, and he could send the watch here.'

Connor bit down on the curse that threatened to burst from his lips. 'Did he give his name?'

'No. He wasn't ringing regarding anything to do with our office, so I didn't think to ask.' She shrugged. 'He sounded American.'

His heart booted his ribcage. 'When did the call come through?'

'About half an hour ago. He asked me for her home address, but I said I couldn't give out that information.'

'Anything else?'

When she spoke, every word was thoughtful. 'I asked if he wanted me to put him through to

Mia but he said no, that he didn't want to disturb her—he'd just pop it in the mail.'

The caller had to have been Lucetti or one of his men.

'Did I do the wrong thing, Connor?' Worry laced every syllable.

'Not at all.' He schooled his expression to show none of his inner alarm, but he could see Grace was turning it all over in her mind. 'I'll let Mia know. I'm sure she'll be pleased it's been found.' He gestured to the paperwork spread out in front of him on his desk. 'I've got a few more documents to review, then I'll be along to the meeting. Please call Mike, apologise for my delay, and tell him I'll be there shortly.'

'Sure.'

'Close the door behind you on your way out.'

She sent him a puzzled look as the door between their offices was almost always left open.

The second the door closed, Connor swore under his breath.

The caller had struck the jackpot. Now he not only knew Mia's surname but that she worked for Stewart Corporation.

The first call he made was to Mia's mobile, just to be certain he wasn't jumping to conclusions.

'You're not supposed to be ringing me! Is Violet okay?' she asked in hushed tones.

'She's fine. Have you lost a watch?'

'No.' He heard the surprise in her voice. 'I don't own one.'

'Right. I'll see you soon.'

'Connor, why—?'

He didn't bother to explain. Adrenalin shot through him as he disconnected and dialled Carlisle.

The FBI agent answered after the first ring. Connor gave a quick explanation and Carlisle reached the same conclusion.

'It makes sense,' Carlisle said. 'Correlli must've realised Mia's true identity this morning because there were two internet searches from the same IP address for your name and Mia's name just after we left Paris. We traced the searches to Venice.'

Shit. 'Did you tell Mia?'

'No point in worrying her, but I have worse news than that.'

Connor's hand tightened around the phone. 'Go on.'

'You told me your bodyguard was sure you were being followed to the restaurant last night.'

'Yes.' Connor had called Carlisle as soon as Tony's man had revealed they'd been tailed to the restaurant where Connor had met Skye. The bodyguard hadn't seen a tail on the way home—suggesting the tail was looking for Mia and had left when another woman had turned up.

'Your guard would've been spot on the money. One of Lucetti's hit men landed in London yesterday morning.'

Connor's skin crawled. 'Correlli?'

'No. Correlli and Lucetti have left Venice and flown back to New York.'

'Lucetti was in Venice then?'

'He was, so it was damned lucky he didn't see Mia.'

Shit.

'The guy who flew into London is Hank Sullivan, known as Sully. Mia mentioned on the drive to London that she'd seen him in Venice right before you met Correlli.'

'Jesus.'

'Sully's an expert sniper. Keep Mia away from any windows and don't let her leave the building. We've already got people in place, but I'll alert the whole team that he now knows Mia's surname and place of work.'

Connor swore again and fear, stronger than any he'd ever known, coursed through his veins. He listened as Carlisle gave him a brief outline of the steps he intended to put into place to ensure Mia's safety. When the call ended, Connor barely resisted the urge to call Mia again. He didn't want to spook her.

His mind flew to the configuration of the boardroom with its large glass windows. Grabbing his paperwork, he jumped up and raced out of his office, barely stopping to look at Grace as he ordered, 'Call Mike back and tell him I want everyone in meeting room six pronto.'

'Room six?' Grace's disbelief was in every syllable of her high-pitched question. 'You do know staff refer to that meeting room as the closet?'

'That's the one.'

'Oh-kay.'

Yes, it was a strange request—especially when the team was already assembled in the boardroom waiting for him—but the small meeting room had no external windows so there was no chance Sully could take a shot at Mia.

Mia walked into the room behind the rest of the marketing team, adopting the mousy wallflower persona Connor now detested.

To him, she'd never be Miss Mouse from marketing again. It didn't matter how she dressed herself, she'd no longer fade into the background. As the presentation dragged, he could hardly take his eyes off her. Even though her figure was concealed by her clothes, Connor had to stop himself from playing out the scenes of their amazing lovemaking in his memory. When his body reminded him how much he craved her, he thought of the sniper threat to cool his desire.

After an hour of sitting feigning interest in the marketing slides, tension had worked its way from his shoulders right up his neck and now there was tightness at his temples.

'Thanks, Mike. Thanks, everyone. I like your ideas and can see how appealing those advertisements will be to the retiree age group.' He hoped he could rely on the team's past performance because he'd barely caught any of the key concepts they'd presented.

'They're the ones with the disposable income who can afford to take a Stewart Luxe Cruise,' one of the team members said.

Connor nodded. 'Mike, I want to go over a couple of things from my trip with Miss Simms.'

'Okay. I'm looking forward to hearing more about it when you're ready to fill me in.'

'All in due course.'

While the rest of the team filed out, Mia stood stiffly opposite Connor. 'This isn't a good idea.'

'Mia, you need to listen.' There was no point sugar-coating it. 'A man made a phone call to

Grace earlier, claiming to have found a watch you say you've never owned.'

'Oh my God!' She visibly paled. 'Have you told Agent Roberts?'

'I called him as soon as I found out.'

'What did he say?'

'One of Lucetti's men has flown into London. This man, Sully, is—'

'Oh my God! Sully.' Her hands flew to her face. 'It's all happening then,' she whispered. 'Everything I've always feared.' She dropped down quickly into a chair and he went and sat on his haunches in front of her.

Taking hold of her hands and stopping their wringing action, he said quietly, 'Carlisle has organised agents to stake out the building and there's a team devoted to monitoring every public security camera in the area for facial recognition. If Sully gets anywhere close to this building, someone at MI5 is going to pick up on it and there's a very real chance he'll be caught.'

'Is that why we moved rooms?'

'Yes.'

She took a deep breath. 'I see.'

'They're throwing every resource they have into this.'

'Now we sit and wait?'

He heard the helplessness in her voice.

'Yes.' His thumb rubbed over the back of her hand. 'We're in this together, sweetheart.'

The silence dragged between them, broken only when Mia disengaged her hands from his and blurted, 'No. We're not in this together. You're not with me at all.'

'Of course I am.'

'It sure didn't look like it this morning when I opened the newspaper. You made the social columns today in headline grabbing fashion.'

Her words were distressed and he saw the flash of hurt accusation in her eyes.

'You know I was *told* to be photographed with a woman.'

'It looked like it was a real chore for you, too.'

'Hey!' She was jealous. He'd be a liar if he didn't admit that a small part of him was pleased, but a larger part of him wanted to reassure her—to make her understand she could trust him. 'I played the part and achieved what Carlisle and Stanley asked me to achieve. That's all I was doing, but I needn't have bothered because this Sully's found you anyway.'

She covered her mouth with the palm of one hand and her cheeks went from pale to bright red. 'I'm sorry. I ... I'm just shocked and scared and ... I lashed out at you. I had no right to comment.'

'You have a right, Mia. I gave you that right when I told you I wanted our relationship to continue.'

'No.' She shook her head and stood up. Every movement was stiff as she walked around the table, seeming to want to put a physical barrier between them. 'Our affair is over. You're entitled to do whatever you like with whomever you choose.'

'Were you jealous when you looked at the newspaper photos, Mia?'

'Jealous?' Her laughter sounded forced. 'More like amazed at the ease with which you can go from one lover to another, but then I guess you've done it so many times since your divorce. I'm truly envious, but I guess I'll be able to do it too, with practice.'

No bloody way! 'I haven't moved on and nor will you. I'm the only lover you're going to have.'

'Damn you, Connor. Don't say things like that to me!'

'I don't want another woman by my side or in my bed, Mia.'

'You had me and the rest of London fooled!' As he rounded the table, so did she, keeping the distance between them.

'That was the idea, but all I shared with Skye was dinner.' He had to make her believe him. 'The only woman I want in my bed is you.'

A hiss of self-loathing escaped from her lips. 'Yeah, right. You gave last night's date such a scorching hot look of sexual desire, I'm surprised her clothes didn't melt off!'

This was the same Mia who'd faced him down in her office. The one who barely paused for breath while she ranted at him, except now he knew she cared.

'And the looks she sent you. My God, I'm surprised there's anything left of you because it looked like she had every intention of taking you home and eating you up!'

He'd closed the distance as she'd railed at him, and now he stood directly in front of her. 'I'm sorry you've been turning yourself inside out about those photos—'

'I have not!'

'—but if you didn't care you wouldn't be jealous.'

'I don't care. You can date all the models in the world.'

'Don't say what you don't mean, Mia.'

Her jaw dropped open and he made the most of her speechless outrage. He slipped her glasses off her nose, placed them on the table and took her in his arms.

'What do you think you're—?'

Like a man driven to the brink, he kissed her with all the pent-up passion that had been building up within him since the last time he'd kissed her.

God, but it'd been too long.

Mia didn't resist. After a few moments she took control, unleashed all her sensuality and kissed him hungrily. Ravenously. She nipped at his lower lip and her body plastered against his. Each kiss sent his pulse rocketing and every nerve ending sang in a sweet symphony of bliss.

Mia was everything to him and he longed to mean as much to her.

'I could report you for sexual harassment, Connor,' she panted when they finally paused for breath. But his forehead rested against hers and she made no move to pull away. Instead she used her fingers to knead the muscles of his shoulders. 'We're both at work. You're my boss and you promised to leave our affair in Europe.'

'That presentation was sheer bloody torture,' he groaned. 'All I want to do is to take you to bed and show you how much I love you, Mia.'

Her head jerked back and she looked at him wide-eyed. *'What did you say?'*

'I love you, Mia.' He hoped his love shone from his eyes. 'I should've told you when we were in Paris—hell, I probably should've told you when we first made love in Venice, but I didn't realise I loved you back then. I didn't recognise my feelings for you until I was back in England without you. Worrying about you. Aching for you. Wanting the right to do everything in my power to protect you, and wanting the world to know how I feel about you.'

He watched as her shock morphed to concern, then to anger. 'You can't love me.' She wrung her hands together. 'Damn it all, Connor. I don't want this.'

No. She didn't mean it. She couldn't have kissed him so uninhibitedly if she didn't love him back.

'Be honest, Mia.' His words were urgent. 'You've said you can't build a future based on lies, but now you're lying to me and to yourself. There's no reason we can't be together.'

She paced away from him then spun on her heel and held out her hands in a gesture of entreaty. 'Connor, if I leave the building and walk down the street, there's every chance I could be dead within a couple of blocks.'

'Sully will be found before he does you any harm.'

He hadn't planned on doing it in this setting. Hell, he hadn't really planned it out properly at all. And, although there were a million more romantic ways of doing this, he had to do it now because he wasn't going to let her walk away again. So, he took a couple of steps towards her, took one of her hands in his and dropped down on one knee. 'Mia, will you do me the very great honour of becoming my wife?'

Her response wasn't the one he'd hoped for, but it was probably the one he should've expected.

She reefed her hand out of his and hugged her arms over her chest.

'No.' The word seemed to force its way out of a throat that sounded thick with tears.

'No. No. No.'

He got back onto his feet. 'Mia—'

'Damn you, Connor!' The anguish in her eyes made his heart heavy. 'Damn you for loving me when I'm not someone who can ever be loved!'

Oh hell!

Connor reached out and drew Mia against him as her whole body racked with sobs.

'Mia, sweetheart. I'm sorry. The last thing I want is for you to be upset.' He ran one hand over her hair and barely resisted unpinning the wound-up bun. 'I love you, darling. I can't help it. It sounds crazy to say it when we've known each other for such a short time but you're in my heart—in my very blood—and more important to me now than my next breath.'

'Why?' she sobbed. 'You can't possibly know how hard it is for me to be shown a glimpse of heaven knowing it can never truly be mine.'

'I'm yours. I want you to be my wife, Mia. We'll figure the rest out along the way and get through this together.'

She lifted her tear-stained face away from his now damp shirt and looked up at him. 'You don't even want to get married. You told Violet—you told me—you'd never marry again. Why would you change your mind?'

He wanted to make her happy and instead her eyes were awash with grief. 'Come and sit down,' he urged gently. 'Let me explain a few things.'

The fight must've drained out of her because she allowed him to lead her to the couch along the back of the room and was unresisting when he sat so close to her that their thighs touched.

He steeled himself to speak of his marriage failure because Mia needed to understand what had happened. 'Everyone assumes I was heartbroken when I was divorced.'

'Weren't you?' She reached for a tissue from the box that was on the coffee table and wiped her nose.

'I didn't even have a chance to feel hurt before I discovered that the woman I thought I'd loved had been an illusion.' His lips twisted as he relived Rachel's betrayal.

Mia sat perfectly still.

'I was a gullible fool. Right from the start, she'd set out to marry me. She'd done her research to find out what I liked, what I didn't like, who I'd dated and why it hadn't lasted. She was like a chameleon, moulding herself into the exact sort of woman she thought would interest me.'

'Obviously she was successful.'

'Oh, yeah. She caught me hook, line and sinker. And then I came home early one day and found her with her bags packed, ready to walk out on me.' He laughed bitterly. 'The guy she was with was supposed to have been her cousin, but she'd lied about that too. He was her lover even when we first met.'

'You must've felt so betrayed.'

'I believe in fidelity, Mia. It was a blow to know that Rachel had never been faithful.' He gritted his teeth together and launched into recounting the embarrassing tale. 'Her lover was infertile and they couldn't afford a fertility clinic. They'd decided Rachel would marry me, get pregnant then divorce me. They thought they'd bleed me through the divorce settlement and child support.'

'That's unconscionable.' She shook her head. 'They confessed their plans?'

'Yes. Very smugly. They thought their plan had worked. Rachel had found out she was pregnant and packed her bags the same day.'

Leaning closer to him, she asked in a shocked tone, 'You have a child?'

'No. Rachel miscarried.' His words were flat, his shoulders slumped. 'I was a heel because all I felt was relief when I learned she'd miscarried the week after she'd walked out on me.'

Mia reached out and placed her hand on his arm. 'I'd say yours was a fairly human reaction. It wouldn't have been pleasant having to keep seeing her and her partner as you shared custody of your child. And children sense hostility between their parents. That would've been an unhealthy environment to grow up in.'

He made a sound of disgust. 'Once I understood the extent of the lies and deceit she'd practised against me, I knew Rachel was toxic.'

'I had no idea.' She clicked her tongue against her palate. 'Violet told me you were divorced, but she didn't go into any details.'

'All she knew was that Rachel had cheated on me. I didn't tell her anything else. Apart from my lawyer, I've never told anyone any of the details. And I made Rachel sign a non-disclosure as part of the divorce proceedings.'

'After all you've been through, I can't blame you for having me investigated.'

'Actually, I called Tony to find out what you were involved in so I could help you.'

'Thank you.'

'Mia, I've laid my heart bare. I do love you, far more than I ever thought it would be possible to love someone. Please, tell me you'll—'

She reached up and placed a finger against his lips. 'I don't know whether I can ever marry you, Connor, but that doesn't mean I don't want to. I love you with my whole heart.'

Connor felt tears pricking at his eyes and he struggled to keep himself together.

She reached up and traced her fingertips over his cheeks. 'I swear I've never told Violet, but I've been in love with you for years. Every time I heard about something wonderful you'd done for her or for the charities you support...' She shook her head. 'I can't tell you all the little—and enormous—things you've done over the years that have made me notice you, admire you and grow to love you.'

He blinked against the moisture in his eyes, but when Mia's eyes also filled with tears and she sent him a watery smile, he didn't care about baring his emotion to this woman he loved.

Lowering his head, his lips sought hers. No words were necessary. Their mutual love was in every kiss.

'I can't believe you love me,' she said breathlessly.

'I hope you'll see it in everything I—' Connor broke off as his phone rang. Checking quickly, he saw the caller ID and had to answer it.

'Is Mia somewhere safe?'

'Yes. She's with me.'

'Carlisle?' Mia mouthed and Connor nodded.

'Good. I'm going to send you my photo. I want you to forward it to your head of building security and make sure he escorts me up to you. Just me. Nobody else. Got it?'

'Got it.'

'Stay where you are and keep her away from windows. I'll be there soon.' The second he hung up, Mia asked, 'What's happening?'

'Carlisle's coming up. We have to stay put and wait for him.'

Every nerve in his body stretched tight. If Carlisle was here telling Mia to keep away from windows, there was a very good chance Sully was getting into position to take a shot at his target.

Chapter Twenty-three

Agent Roberts was ushered into the meeting room by the head of security and wasted no time getting straight to the point.

'Sully is in London, Mia.'

'Connor's filled me in.' Mia's stomach churned like a washing machine on a permanent deep rinse cycle but with Connor sitting next to her, holding her hand, she could cope.

The FBI agent pulled out a folder and started drawing on a piece of paper. 'This is the Stewart Corporation building. We have agents here, here, here and here.' He drew little crosses to indicate the positions. 'Fifteen minutes ago, Sully entered this building.' He drew a box to indicate the building directly opposite Connor's office block. 'We've confirmed he's set up on the rooftop and he's not there for surveillance. He has his weapon and a good view of the entrance to this building.'

Nausea swirled in Mia's stomach. 'Can't you arrest him?'

'We can arrest him for possession of a firearm in a public place but it's not enough,' the agent said. 'We need to catch him in the act.'

Breathing became impossible.

Connor's arm tightened around her shoulders as panic seized her. They both knew what was coming next.

'Very soon I'll have our own sniper in position in this building over here.' He drew another square on the paper.

'That's a fair distance away,' Connor said.

'It's the closest building that's taller than the one Sully's on.' The agent cleared his throat. 'It's well within range, there's no wind, and our man will have a clear shot.'

'Your plan?' Connor demanded.

'Mia, you're going to be fitted with a bulletproof vest.'

Dread leeched through her.

Connor jumped to his feet. 'You're *not* going to use her as bait. No way!'

'It's the only way,' Carlisle argued. 'The whole thing will be filmed. The evidence will be irrefutable.'

'It's too bloody risky!' Connor yelled. 'For Christ's sake, Carlisle! A bulletproof vest is all well and good, but what if he goes for a headshot?'

'He's never made a headshot before. He always hits the heart.'

Mia sat in silence, unable to stop the tremors that shook her from head to toe.

'Listen to me,' Carlisle continued. 'Sully won't even get to squeeze the trigger. The second Mia comes out of the building and Sully is filmed taking aim, our sniper will fire. He'll be taken out—not killed. Operatives are in place inside the building even now and they'll swarm and grab him the second he's hit.'

Mia finally found her voice. 'You expect Sully to turn on Giovanni?'

'There's evidence on that USB you located that will send him to trial in some states that still have the death penalty. I think he'll give up Lucetti.'

'If you've got the evidence, move in and arrest him now!' Connor demanded.

'If we can't get anyone else to turn on Lucetti and implicate him in the murder of your mother, an attempt on your life should convince a jury that Lucetti wants you dead because you were an eyewitness. We follow my plan. We get video evidence of the crime. This way we're not relying on computer records or a witness statement. The jury will see the attempt on Mia's life themselves and there'll be no reasonable doubt in any of their minds about his intention.'

It made sense. She didn't want it to, but it did. 'I hope it goes without saying that your sniper is the best there is?'

'Mia, all I can tell you is that if you were my sister, I'd still be sending you out there at close of business today.'

'Do you even have a sister?' Connor asked angrily.

'Connor, please.' Mia tried to calm him. 'Agent Roberts is on our side.'

'Everything will be in place shortly,' Carlisle said. 'At five pm, we let the main rush of employees exit the building. Then—'

'Provided they can't possibly be mistaken for me,' she cut in.

Carlisle agreed. 'I spoke to the head of building security and have briefed him. He will stall the lifts for two and a half minutes to make certain there are no other employees exiting the building. During that time, you leave.'

Mia took a deep breath. 'Okay.'

'Darling, don't. Please don't do it.' Connor dropped to the couch next to her.

'I want a future with you, Connor. A future where we don't have to keep looking over our shoulders every second of every day. I'm willing to do this for a chance to seize our future.'

'We can hire more security.' 'No. That's no way to live.'

'Then we could both disappear,' he said. 'We could both join a witness protection program and be relocated.'

He had no idea what that meant. 'You'd have to give up everything.'

'You've fast become my world and I'm not prepared to give you up.'

Tears threatened to overwhelm her again. What he suggested was beyond her wildest dreams, but it was also impractical. She'd lived through the witness protection program and didn't want to make him live that lie. Even if Connor loved her now, she didn't want him to sacrifice all he knew—all he'd worked for and built up—for her. Especially when there was a chance that, if the plan worked, this entire nightmare that had been her life for the last ten years might finally come to an end.

'I love you,' she told him. 'Please understand. This is something I've got to do for me, as well as for us.'

May God protect me.

Chapter Twenty-four

Time had never passed so slowly for Mia.

Every second stretched interminably as she sat with Connor waiting until ten to five. That's when she'd make her way down to the foyer.

Tick. Tick.

She couldn't possibly need to use the restroom again, it was simply her nerves stretched tight and that damned clock sounding like a dripping tap.

There was so much she wanted to say to Connor and time was running out.

She planned the sentence before she said it. She practised it over in her head in the hope that she wouldn't cry, then began, 'The days we spent in Venice were the happiest days of my life.'

He kissed her temple. 'I'm glad. But we missed sightseeing in Paris. When this is over I'll take you back to Paris and we can walk along the banks of the Seine and watch as the Eiffel Tower lights up at night.'

It sounded wonderful, but all she could do was nod as a huge lump of anguish clogged her throat. God but she prayed they'd have a chance to share those experiences.

Tick. Tick.

'Violet...' Hell. She should've practised this sentence in her head first, too. She swallowed hard. 'I love Violet and Stanley as though they're my grandparents. I'm so grateful for ev-everything they've...'

'Shh.' He pulled her more firmly against him, but she didn't enjoy it as much through the bulk of the bulletproof vest that was safely concealed underneath her oversized shirt.

'But ... But, make sure they know.'

'They know, Mia.' His hands held her cheeks and he pulled back to look at her. 'You don't have to do this, darling. I don't want you to do this.'

Biting down on her lip, she looked away and willed herself to find strength.

She knew this terror.

She'd felt it when her mother had died and she'd hidden in the laundry scarcely daring to breathe in case Giovanni found her.

Connor's hands trembled and she looked back up at him. 'You're shaking.'

'I'm not good at dealing with situations I can't control,' he told her.

His words gave her fortitude. She wanted to be strong for him—to ease the anxiety etched in the lines bracketing his mouth and the furrow between his brows. 'I'm looking forward to Paris.'

'And returning to Venice. Next time we'll go and see the glass factory,' he added. *Tick. Tick.*

Mia looked back up at the clock. 'It's time.'

'Don't go.'

'You know I have to.'

He closed his eyes and let his forehead lean against hers. 'You're the bravest person I know.'

'And you're the most handsome, caring man I've ever met.' She could no longer dam up the tears in her eyes, nor keep the waver from her voice.

Just as she'd tried to pull herself together for him, Connor summoned up a smile for her. 'I'm glad arrogant, conceited and egotistical aren't the words you use to describe me now.'

He was so pale it was difficult to credit he'd only enjoyed some time in the sun in Barbados a little over a week ago.

She leaned forward and brushed her lips over his. 'I love you.'

He swallowed hard. 'I love you too.'

'Walk me down to the lobby?'

'Try to stop me.'

Uncaring of the attention they attracted as they made their way down to the entrance of the building, they held each other's hands like they never wanted to let go.

'Right,' Carlisle said when they reached him in the lobby. 'Now you're here we'll stop the lifts.' He waved his hand at somebody. 'Whatever you do, Mia, don't look up. Walk out of here like you do every other day. One glance up and you could blow the whole thing.'

Her breath out was unsteady.

I can do this.

Walk out. Don't look up.

Walk out like I'll be walking back in tomorrow—same as any other day.

Oh shit! What am I doing?

But one look at the man beside her shored up her resolve. She was doing this for her future with Connor.

She was also doing it so her mother's killer would finally face justice.

'Are you certain it's necessary for her to stop a few yards from the exit and dig her phone out of her handbag?' Connor demanded.

'It's necessary.'

'I'll be fine, Connor.' Despite his tan, he looked ashen and she had to be strong for him. 'Britain's finest operatives are out there for me.'

He drew her to him and kissed her. 'There has to be another way.'

'I'll be fine.'

'Got to move now,' Carlisle ordered.

Mia pulled out of Connor's arms and walked away from him before she lost her nerve.

I'm doing this for us.

This is the only way to move forward—the only way to have a future with Connor.

Almost at the door, she slowed. Another couple of steps and she'd be outside in full sight of Sully. In the sight of his gun.

'Go Mia. Go now while there's nobody else around,' Carlisle urged.

A couple more steps. Mia stopped.

She turned back to face Connor and gave him a tremulous smile. 'I will, Connor. When all this is over, I will marry you.'

Before he could reply, she turned around and walked out of the building. Heart hammering, she only just remembered to count her steps.

Three. Four. Five.

These steps away from Connor would ultimately allow them to have a beautiful future together.

Seven. Eight. Nine.

They would have the love and happiness that had eluded her poor mother.

Eleven. Twelve. Thirteen.

History wasn't going to repeat itself. Mia was going to live a long and happy life.

When she got to fifteen, she stopped and rummaged through her handbag for her phone. *Shit.* Where was it? It didn't help that she'd started to shake from head to toe and her hands were sweaty. Any moment now she'd dissolve in a pool of perspiration as her nerves took over.

Finally. Her hand connected with her phone case. She took it out and looked at the screen while Sully was likely to be looking at her through the sight of his weapon.

Please protect me.

Her whole body tensed and she closed her eyes as she raised the phone to her ear and prayed there'd be no gunshot.

'It's over!' She heard Connor shout from behind her. 'Sully's down!' Carlisle confirmed.

Oh, thank you God.

Mia couldn't help herself. The relief coursed through her and tears rolled down her cheeks as she let out a loud sob.

Then she was swept up in Connor's arms and kissed like there was no tomorrow. Their kisses tasted of salt and she wasn't sure whether it was her tears or Connor's.

'You want to take this inside?' Carlisle had a hint of laughter in his voice.

Not particularly, Mia thought. She was alive and she was with the man of her dreams and she didn't care who knew it.

On second thoughts, somewhere private would be good. Somewhere she could take off the blasted bulletproof vest. And she had no intention of stopping there.

Chapter Twenty-five

Later that evening, Mia stretched contentedly as she lay beside Connor in his bed. Her limbs felt boneless now the adrenaline had passed. Or maybe it was a result of physical satiation. Whatever the cause, she loved this feeling. 'It's so good to be here with you.'

'It's better than good to have you here. You're the only woman who has ever shared this bed with me.'

That had her attention. 'Really?'

'Yep.' He smiled. 'I moved out of the home I'd shared with Rachel and got rid of the bed after our divorce. Moving was such a pain in the arse, I decided if I never had a lover in my home again I'd never have to bother moving to free myself of bad memories.' He tapped the end of her nose. 'You, my darling, are the exception. You're here forever.'

She'd heard people describe melting from sheer happiness, but now she could relate to the feeling. 'I love knowing that.'

Mia's stomach rumbled and spoiled the romantic moment.

'Time for food. Sorry, sweetheart. It's so long since lunch, you must be starving.' Connor got out of bed and walked into his closet before throwing one of his shirts to her. 'You can put this on.'

'I thought you didn't like me in oversized clothing?'

'Hm. Another thought I have to revise. It'll be sexy to have you pad around downstairs in nothing but my shirt.' His phone rang and he groaned. 'I'd love to be able to turn that off.'

'It might be Agent Roberts.' The agent had promised he'd phone them if he had any news.

'It is.' Connor confirmed as he picked up his phone. 'Hello Carlisle. Mia's with me, I'll put you on speaker phone.'

'How are you, Mia?' the agent asked.

She grinned at Connor. 'Exhausted,' she said, with a wink.

'Naughty girl!' Connor mouthed.

'That's to be expected,' the agent said. 'You went through more stress this afternoon than a lot of people face in their lifetime.'

And after the stress, more ecstasy than a lot of people know in their lifetime.

Mia cleared her throat. 'Have you got any good news for us?'

'I sure do. Sully started singing like a canary as soon as we showed him the evidence your mother armed us with, Mia.'

Thank you, Mum.

'Do you think you'll get enough on Giovanni to lock him up?' Connor asked.

'Enough for five lifetime sentences, I'd guess. Sully's agreed to testify that Giovanni ordered today's hit. He also admitted it was Correlli who took the shot at you outside the police station in New York, and he named two guys he thought would be prepared to recant their statements providing Giovanni's alibi at the card game.'

'So that, along with my testimony, should mean he'll finally be convicted of Mum's murder?'

'I'm certain of it.'

Tears pricked at her eyes. It was going to be damned hard to go back to the States and rehash the details of her mother's murder in a courtroom, but her mother deserved justice.

'Hey, Mia.' Carlisle's voice was gruff. 'I'm sorry I came down on you so hard about the necklace. While it did lead Giovanni to you, the jewellery box led to his downfall.'

'Thanks to my mum and to Connor.'

'Did Sully say that Correlli made the connection between the necklace and Mia?' Connor asked.

'Correlli mentioned he'd encountered a British woman and was certain he'd met her before but couldn't think where. When he started talking about the Georgian necklace that also looked familiar, Giovanni asked him to describe it. It was Giovanni who made the connection. He asked Lou to describe you, and whether it was possible you could've been Elizabeth Buckley's daughter. It was pure chance they worked it out.'

'How safe is Mia now?' Connor asked.

'I believe Giovanni will go to prison even without her testimony. But I won't be relaxing her bodyguards until Giovanni is safely behind bars.'

'I still can't believe he was in Venice,' Mia said.

'His old man is very ill and not expected to last out the next six months. Sully said they were in Italy to shore up some connections. Once old Don Lucetti is dead and Giovanni is behind bars, there'll be an inevitable turf war. Giovanni will have so much trouble battling that war, Mia will be the last person he's worried about.'

'But you said he'd be in prison?' Mia asked as she shot Connor a worried frown.

'Yes,' Carlisle said, 'but the prison system is rife with corruption. He'll bribe guards here and there and end up running the damned joint.'

Her stomach took a dive. 'Are you telling me I won't be safe unless I change my identity again?'

Connor put his arm around her as the agent said, 'We've kept you safe this long, Mia. We're not going to drop the ball now when we're so close to scoring the home run. You don't need to change your identity, but I do want you to disappear until the trial for—'

'Oh no.' She fought back tears.

'—six months or so, tops. Hopefully sooner as it's so high profile. We have a cabin up in the Canadian Rockies. We'd like to send you there.'

'Can't I—?'

'I'm going too.' Connor spoke right over her protest.

'*What?*' Mia's jaw dropped.

'I thought you'd say that,' Carlisle said.

Was she the only one doing a double-take?

'I'll set things in motion and get back to you, but be ready,' the agent continued. 'We'll probably move you both first thing tomorrow morning.'

Tomorrow? Mia shook her head. 'But how can you possibly...? You can't just disappear for six months, Connor.'

'I'm way overdue a lengthy break.'

'But—'

He placed his index finger gently against her lips. 'Thanks, Carlisle. We'll both be ready tomorrow.'

When Connor disconnected the call, Mia frowned at him. 'I don't know what to say. Can you truly walk away from the company for so long?' Although each word was laden with uncertainty, she couldn't keep the hopeful note out of her voice.

'I can't bear the thought of being separated from you for a week let alone half a year.'

Her happiness soared but ... 'What about the company?'

'I have a plan. Let's eat, and I'll tell you about it.'

***

Two hours later, Mia was sitting with Connor in Violet's small parlour having confessed all that'd happened in Venice and since their return. Both she and Connor were mindful to tell Violet the shocking news as gently as they could so as not to overwhelm her.

'I don't think I'll ever forgive myself for placing you in such danger,' Violet said, shakily.

'But it's all turned out for the best.' Mia hastened to reassure her. 'Giovanni is finally going to be arrested and I should be able to get on with my life.'

Connor smiled and put his arm around Mia. 'We should be able to get on with *our* lives.'

Violet's eyes lit up. 'Really?' She looked from one of them to the other. 'Are you together?'

'Yes!' Mia got up and went to give Violet a gentle hug. 'Thank you, Violet. You were right. You've led me right to my soul mate.'

'Oh, wait until I tell Stanley! He gave me a real serve for interfering.' Violet laughed then started to mist up. 'Nothing else could possibly make me happier.'

'I'm glad to hear it,' Connor said. 'But Stanley is right. You've got to stop meddling because things might not always work out so well.'

'Well maybe there's one thing that could make me happier, but I'm presuming that will take at least another nine months?'

'Gran!' Connor admonished.

'Hopefully one day, Violet,' Mia said.

'Not so fast my darling,' Connor warned before he turned his steel-blue gaze to Violet. 'There's one thing we need from you before we add to the Stewart family.'

Mia sat back and hid a smile. Violet was about to get a taste of her own medicine. 'Anything, my darlings,' Violet vowed.

'The doctor has said you're doing brilliantly.'

'Because I am. You should know I can do anything when I set my mind to it, Connor, and hearing your news, I feel as though I can take on the world again and win.' 'What about the reins of the company?' he asked.

'Pardon?'

'I wouldn't ask it of you if it wasn't absolutely necessary, but the FBI wants Mia to disappear until Giovanni's trial and I'm not letting her out of my sight. So, I need to take a leave of absence from the company for the duration.'

'Oh.' Violet tilted her head. 'How long will you be away?'

'Maybe eight months or maybe not quite as long. It depends on how the trial goes.' Connor shrugged. 'I could hand over to someone else, but do you think you'd be able to step back in as CEO during my absence? I could do the bulk of the work from afar and I may be able to make it back to London for any urgent issues—'

'No, Connor,' Mia said firmly. 'You couldn't come back. You could work on your computer—they can set up all sorts of encryption codes and re-routing so nobody can trace you—but you can't physically come back to London in those months we have to be away. That's not how witness protection works.'

'Okay. Well, the point is, I can still guide the company, Gran. You wouldn't have to carry a massive load, or work long days, but I'd need you to represent me at any important meetings.'

'I can do that, no problem.' Violet nodded. 'In fact, I'd enjoy stepping back into the seat again for a short time.'

'Thanks, Gran.'

'I mightn't be quite what I used to be, but—'

'But nothing,' Connor interrupted. 'In the last week you've proven you still have formidable insight and can drive a bargain that's impossible to refuse. I think you'll do just fine and I did phone Dr Forrester on the drive over here.'

'He gave it the seal of approval,' Violet said, confidently.

'He did. He called you an extraordinary patient, but you have to keep the office hours to a maximum of four a day.'

Violet beamed at them both. 'I'm so glad I was right about you two. To think Mia was under your nose the entire time, young man, and you never bothered to look past her woeful exterior to the gem that lay beneath.'

'Woeful exterior?' Mia threw her hands up in the air. 'Thanks very much.'

'Don't pay any attention to her, my darling,' Connor said. 'I love you and that's all that matters!'

Mia laughed.

'This definitely calls for a small sip of champagne!' Violet pronounced, then whispered, 'We won't tell Dr Forrester.'

'Gran, you're incorrigible.'

'And aren't you glad I am? And you, Mia—your five dates turned out for the best, didn't they?'

'I haven't had five dates with him yet,' she answered. 'But that's okay. Now I have a lifetime of dates to look forward to.'

Epilogue

As soon as he heard the helicopter, Connor straightened up from his wood chopping and buried the blade of the axe in the chopping stump. Reaching for a towel, he wiped the sweat from his torso and put on his shirt.

Mia emerged from the log cabin wearing a cute pair of cut-off denim shorts. 'They're early. We're not expecting a supply drop for another two days.'

Connor looked at the gorgeous pair of legs on display and smiled. 'They must've guessed we'd be running low on condoms.'

'Connor!'

She still blushed prettily and he loved seeing the extra colour in her cheeks. As gorgeous as she was, he thought she'd be even more beautiful when her tummy rounded with their child. That would be a year or two away. They'd agreed to put a family on hold so they could focus on each other.

Their isolation from the rest of the world had been a blessing in disguise. Deep in the Canadian wilderness, these last six weeks had been the best of Connor's life. It'd been precious time spend together and reinforced what he'd already known instinctively—that they were thoroughly compatible both in and out of bed.

Connor was in no doubt that Mia was the love of his life and he knew she loved him just as much in return.

He looked up again at the helicopter, expecting to see the crew preparing to hoist a parcel out, but there was none.

His tension ramped up.

Had Giovanni found them?

His blood chilled. 'Mia. Go inside.'

'But—'

'Now.'

The chopper got closer.

Still no sign of a parcel of provisions.

Connor pulled the axe back out of the stump and moved into the shadow of the cabin.

Closer.

His grip was tight around the axe handle and only relaxed when he confirmed the markings on the chopper were the same as the FBI helicopter that'd dropped them off here. Still...

He looked around the corner and saw Mia just inside the doorway of the cabin. 'They're not dropping supplies. It looks like they're going to land.'

Perhaps the trial had been moved forward?

'Isn't that Agent Roberts?' Mia asked.

Connor looked closer. So it was.

This danger Mia was in was making him see possible threats in every situation. He had no idea how she'd lived like this for so long and he couldn't wait for Giovanni's court case to be over.

Placing the axe back on the stump, he motioned for Mia to join him. They stood together, buffeted by the wind from the rotor blades, waiting for the chopper to land in the cleared area.

'Hi there!' Carlisle said as the chopper's engine shut down. He ran towards them with his body lowered to clear the still-slowing blades.

'Hi yourself,' Connor responded. 'What brings you here?' 'Great news!'

Connor looked at Mia and saw the sudden tension in her shoulders at odds with the light of hope in her eyes. 'Let's have it, Carlisle.'

'Giovanni's father died, but not of natural causes. It was poison and the Lucetti family has fallen apart.'

'What?' Connor hardly dared to believe their troubles were over. 'What happened?'

'There was a huge shoot out with one side of the family blaming the other side, and most of them—including Giovanni and Correlli—were killed in the gun fight.'

'But wasn't Giovanni in custody awaiting trial?'

'No.' The agent shook his head. 'He was granted bail—which we were vehemently opposed to, but it's actually worked out in the end.'

'Oh my God!' Mia exclaimed as Connor hugged her to his side. 'Is it true?'

'You're free, Mia,' Carlisle told her with a broad grin. 'No more looking over your shoulder. You're free as a bird.'

'Thank God.' Connor felt Mia sway against him and guessed she was giddy with sheer relief because he felt the same light-headedness as he processed the news.

'I don't need any more protection?' Mia asked breathlessly.

'No,' was Carlisle's firm response. 'You're free to live your life wherever you want and however you want.'

'I ... I never thought I'd...' Tears streamed down Mia's cheeks and Connor lifted a finger to wipe them away. 'I ... can't imagine it.'

'Nobody will spare you a thought,' Carlisle assured her. 'Those who weren't killed are in hiding—fearful they'll be picked off by one of the other New York Mafia families who are trying to gain control of the Lucetti turf. Sully's still alive, but he'll spend the rest of his life as a guest of Her Majesty's prison system after the attempt on your life.'

'That's such good news!' Mia exclaimed again and threw herself into Connor's arms as tears of relief rolled down her face.

It was an outcome even better than they could've hoped for but, as far as Connor was concerned, Mia would still have security.

Tony's security people were watching over Gran already and would start acting as bodyguards for both Mia and him as soon as they got back to London. Stanley was right that Connor and Violet probably should've had security long ago and, not only was Mia a millionaire in her own right, but soon she'd be his wife.

'You'll be fine, sweetheart,' Connor told her.

'I'll be better than fine because I'll be with you,' she said.

'If you'll excuse me, I'm going inside to visit the bathroom,' the agent said. 'It's been a long trip.'

Mia looked up at Connor and he saw the wonder and sheer happiness in her expression. 'Can you believe it?'

'It's incredible news.'

'We can go home and plan our wedding!'

Mia drew his head down to hers and Connor was only barely aware of someone walking towards them, so consumed he was by his fiancée's kisses.

'Er...' The clearing of a masculine throat broke them apart. 'You folks got any coffee?'

'Sure,' Mia told the pilot. 'Inside. Help yourself.'

'I can't wait to make you my wife,' Connor murmured near her ear.

No sooner had the pilot left them than Carlisle came back outside. 'How soon can you two be packed?'

'It won't take too long,' Connor assured him.

'Great. We thought we'd have a quick coffee break and something to eat, then head back to Vancouver. We've got you booked on a flight back to London later tonight.'

'Okay.'

Mia sighed as the agent went back into the cabin. 'Back to London.'

Back to the hustle and bustle.

Connor looked over at the wood pile, the log cabin and the beautiful woods around them. All these weeks they'd been surrounded by the picturesque, snow-peaked caps of the Rocky Mountains. At night, they'd been lulled to sleep by the sound of running water from the pristine glacial stream at the back of the cabin.

'You don't want to leave?' Mia asked, sensing his mood.

'Only to marry you. I've got to say I'm going to miss it here,' he admitted. He wouldn't mind staying here with Mia forever if it wasn't for Gran.

She planted a kiss against his lips. 'You're too dynamic to be holed up in the Canadian wilderness forever, my darling. London calls and Stewart Corporation needs you at the helm. But,' Mia pulled a sad face, 'I'm going to miss having you all to myself.'

Connor shook off his reluctance to return to the pace of life in London. 'It's been great, but it's time to return and I promise we'll still make time for each other.'

'Hm.' Mia tilted her head at him and smiled. 'I'll go back to London, but only on one condition.'

He arched an eyebrow at her. 'You have a condition? You're starting to sound like Gran.'

'Funny you should mention Violet. This all started with her insisting I have five dates with a certain gorgeous billionaire.' She lifted her hands to his head, urging him closer so she could kiss him. When she drew back she said, 'I want you to promise me that every year we'll escape to the wilderness together and I can have five weeks alone with my hot lumberjack.'

Connor laughed. 'Done!' It was an easy decision and one he never regretted.

Thanks for reading *Five Dates with the Billionaire*. I hope you enjoyed it.

If you liked this book, you might like to read my **The Billionaire's Baby** series – *Seduced by the Enemy, Seduced by the Stranger,* and *Seduced by the Billionaire.* You don't want to miss out on *The Magic of Christmas* and you might also love my **Royal Affairs Series** – *The Defiant Princess, The Irredeemable Prince, The Formidable King* and *The Irresistible Royal* collected together in a new four-book collection A Royal Affair. My other books are *Roses for Sophie, Echoes of the Heart,* and *Mistaken Identity,* collected together as *The Billionaire Meets His Match.*

Sign up to our newsletter romance.com.au/newsletter/and find out about new releases, must-read series and ebook deals at romance.com.au.

Reviews can help readers find books, and I am grateful for all honest reviews. Thank you for taking the time to let others know what you've read, and what you thought.

Share your reading experience on:
Facebook
Instagram
romance.com.au

ROMANCE
.COM.AU

ESCAPE
publishing
A novel approach

Bestselling Titles by Escape Publishing...

Discover another great read from Escape Publishing...

Seduced by the Billionaire
Alyssa J. Montgomery

An enemies-to-lovers story about second chances and risking it all for love.

Of all the people to be here, why does it have to be him? As if this isn't hard enough for me already.

Sarah Bryant hasn't let her traumatic past stop her from achieving number one status in the modelling world. She will do whatever necessary to fight for opportunities for her wheelchair-bound brother—even if it means facing her fears. When a scandal threatens to destroy everything she has worked for, Sarah must play ball with a man she detests. But everything is not as it seems. Could she have been wrong about Nick Henderson? And what does that mean for the undeniable chemistry between them?

She might make my heart race, but there's something about Sarah Bryant that I just can't trust. She's hiding something, and I'm going to uncover the truth.

Nick might not like Sarah, but he needs her. She is the perfect choice for the documentary that will raise the profile of his ocean conservations charity. Nick's urge to unwrap her secrets—and her clothes—gets stronger every time he sees her. But Sarah is holding onto a bombshell that has the potential to hurt his family, ruin his reputation ... and destroy any growing feelings he might have for her.

Seduced by the Enemy
Alyssa J. Montgomery

Olivia

I have every reason to know the Borghettis are pure evil...

So why won't my heart listen to my head?

Luca Borghetti might be pure Italian sex appeal, and powerful, and a damn billionaire, but he and his family are responsible for EVERYTHING I've lost. My sister. The baby. My father. All gone because of him.

Luca

I may have made mistakes, with tragic results, but one thing I know: I will protect what I love. No matter what.

And this woman will give me what I want. No matter how self-interested she is.

Hatred. That's all these sparks between us are. But it doesn't matter. This heartless woman has what Christiana needs and whatever that little girl needs, I will get.

But if what Olivia is telling me is true ... someone has lied to both of us.

From hotshot contemporary author Alyssa J. Montgomery comes a passionate enemies-to-lovers story of an Italian billionaire and an Australian primary school teacher as they fight for the life of a child they both love—and fight the flames of attraction burning between them.

Seduced by the Stranger
Alyssa J Montgomery

No matter what is thrown their way, true love will endure...

I can't do this. I can't go through with it.

Moments from the altar, dressed in an ugly wedding dress that is the least of her problems, Jenna Sinclair has a moment of clarity. For weeks she's been living in a fog, trying to piece together her life after the accident that almost killed her. Believing, all the while, that she has no other option but to proceed with a marriage to a man she doesn't love. Now she finds herself torn between her trust in family and the attraction she feels for a man who's a complete stranger. But if she doesn't even know who she really is, how can she know if she can trust the stranger who is claiming her as his?

'Stop! This wedding is not taking place!'

Max Bennett has only ever loved one woman—Jenna. Time after time her family has ripped them apart but now, when Jenna's life is in danger and she needs him the most, there's not a chance in hell he'll let her go. All he needs to do is reignite the love she once had for him ... which means keeping a secret that could destroy her trust.

With danger stalking them, can Jenna and Max find their way back to each other before it's too late?

The Magic of Christmas
Alyssa J. Montgomery

'This year, you'll have to help create your own Christmas magic.'

Billionaire Jack Mancini has pulled himself up out of the worst circumstances to become a self-made CEO. The one thing Jack can't face is Christmas. Carols, Christmas trees and cheer only remind him of his dark past. But when he's asked to stay in London for Christmas by the only person who understands his pain, Jack's fierce loyalty demands that he agree.

Ever since tragedy struck, Grace Robertson has done everything she can to give her younger brother the life he deserves, ignoring her own passions to focus on her housecleaning business. The two things Grace lets herself indulge in? Fantasising about her handsome employer Jack and playing his beautiful grand piano when she's finished cleaning his house. When Grace is caught playing the piano, the last thing she expects is for the man of her fantasies to offer her everything she's ever wanted.

But even as the line between fiction and reality blurs, it seems that the darkness that haunts Jack is inescapable. If only Jack would let in just a little bit of Christmas magic...

The Billionaire Meets His Match
Alyssa J Montgomery

Mistaken Identity

Greek tycoon Alex Kristidis will do anything it takes to prevent his brother marrying pop star Susie Hamlin, and Susie's twin sister Leah will do whatever it takes to stop him. But, posing as Susie to throw Alex off the trail as she and her lover rush away to get married has unexpected consequences: Leah is attacked by a drug dealer's henchmen, whisked off to Alex's private island, and becomes entangled in a web of lies.

Something is different about Susie, and Alex can't put his finger on it. No longer the self–absorbed, selfish celebrity, she is warm and innocent and inspires feelings in him that he thought impossible. But the last thing he will do is indulge in an affair with his brother's manipulative cast–off. He just has to find the strength to stay away...

Echoes Of The Heart

Australian media tycoon Jake Formosa does not believe in forgiving ... or forgetting. So when he discovers that Amanda — the woman who once broke his heart — is newly widowed, he immediately enacts his revenge. Jake is intent on making Amanda remember him, and making her suffer for what she did. He will leave her broken and alone, and finally have his closure.

But Amanda is not the sweet girl that Jake remembers, and her life is far from perfect. As the web of lies surrounding her begins to unravel, Jake finds himself once again ensnared. Can he learn to overlook the past and risk his heart again?

Roses For Sophie

To convince the court that his playboy days are over and to keep a desperate promise, Australian billionaire Logan Jackson needs a wife ... fast.

To make her grandfather happy and sway him into making her managing director of the family company, mining heiress Sophie Hamilton needs a husband ... fast.

With common goals, similar values, and a very definite end date, there is no reason why Logan and Sophie shouldn't be able to strike a deal to satisfy them both. No reason except that the sizzling attraction arcing between them is too hot to trust.

A Royal Affair
Alyssa J. Montgomery

Four royal affair romances from Australian author Alyssa J. Montgomery.

The Defiant Princess

When choosing between the life she's built and the duty she's left behind-what's a reluctant princess to do?

Australian-raised Sabrina has had nothing to do with the conflicted desert region of Rhajia, the land of her birth. But now her life is in danger, and the only way to save her country is through a temporary marriage to Khalid, the Crown Prince of Turastan.

Khalid has already chosen a wife-a woman who understands the rules for a good consort. He just needs to deal with Sabrina and her ridiculous plan. After all, the defiant princess may be beautiful, but she's the last woman he would ever want to marry.

The Irredeemable Prince

The ultimate royal bad boy is about to meet his match.

If one ever needs to find Prince Devereaux of Santaliana, one needs only look for the nearest newspaper: His Royal Highness is sure to be splashed across the scandal pages.

But enough is enough. No more night clubs, no more drinking, absolutely no more one-night-stands. Devereaux will step into his responsibilities, or he will be cut off. But the recalcitrant prince is about to find out that self-improvement can be surprisingly seductive...

The Formidable King

A chance meeting, a misunderstanding, and a second chance for a royal love affair.

Once, King Gabriel was bewitched by a violet-eyed beauty at a masquerade ball who disappeared without a trace. Now, Cinderella has a name and Gabriel is determined to expose India Hamilton as the gold-digger he knows her to be.

But as Gabriel gets to know India, his attempt at revenge loses its appeal. It's becoming clear that this is not a Cinderella story at all: India is a beauty, and Gabriel has been behaving like a beast.

The Irresistible Royal

He's everything a bad boy royal should be. He's everything she doesn't want. But he might be just what she needs.

Prince Marco of Ralvinia is lethally handsome, incredibly rich and irresistibly sexy. But after tragically losing the one woman he's ever loved, Marco indulges only in casual affairs, never risking his heart.

Thrown into Prince Marco's path by her social-climbing mother, Chloe Salvatore isn't interested in his glamorous life. But just one night of hot, no-strings-attached sex can't hurt. Until their explosive interlude has unexpected consequences...